Room Service

W9-BRF-068

By best-selling author Rochelle Alers

The Innkeepers series

The Inheritance

Breakfast in Bed

Room Service

The Bridal Suite

The Book Club series

The Seaside Café

The Beach House

The Perfect Present
Christmas Anthology:

A Christmas Layover

Room Service

ROCHELLE
ALERS

Fountaindale Public Library District
300 W. Briarcliff Rd.
Bolingbrook, IL 60440

www.kensingtonbooks.com

This book is a work of fiction. Names, characters, businesses, organizations, places, events, and incidents either are the product of the author's imagination or are used fictitiously. Any resemblance to actual persons, living or dead, events, or locales is entirely coincidental.

To the extent that the image or images on the cover of this book depict a person or persons, such person or persons are merely models, and are not intended to portray any character or characters featured in the book.

DAFINA BOOKS are published by

Kensington Publishing Corp.
119 West 40th Street
New York, NY 10018

Copyright © 2018 by Rochelle Alers

All rights reserved. No part of this book may be reproduced in any form or by any means without the prior written consent of the Publisher, excepting brief quotes used in reviews.

If you purchased this book without a cover, you should be aware that this book is stolen property. It was reported as "unsold and destroyed" to the Publisher and neither the Author nor the Publisher has received any payment for this "stripped book."

All Kensington Titles, Imprints, and Distributed Lines are available at special quantity discounts for bulk purchases for sales promotions, premiums, fund-raising, and educational or institutional use. Special book excerpts or customized printings can also be created to fit specific needs. For details, write or phone the office of the Kensington Special Sales Manager: Kensington Publishing Corp., 119 West 40th Street, New York, NY 10018, attn.: Special Sales Department, Phone: 1-800-221-2647.

The DAFINA logo is a trademark of Kensington Publishing Corp.

ISBN-13: 978-1-4967-2574-5
ISBN-10: 1-4967-2574-3
First Kensington Trade Edition: August 2018
First Kensington Mass Market Edition: April 2021

ISBN-13: 978-1-4967-0735-2 (ebook)
ISBN-10: 1-4967-0735-4 (ebook)

10 9 8 7 6 5 4 3 2 1

Printed in the United States of America

A woman giving birth to a child has pain because her time has come; but when her baby is born she forgets the anguish because of her joy that a child is born into the world.
—John 16:21

Chapter 1

"You're a genius when it comes to selecting restaurants."

Jasmine Washington's head popped up and she stared across the table at her friend. The mass of black curls framing Nydia Santiago's round face made the thirty-two-year-old appear no older than a college coed.

"Why would you say that?"

Nydia's hazel eyes sparkled like semi-precious jewels in a complexion that always reminded Jasmine of frothy mocha icing. "Whenever you ask me what I want to eat, somehow you're able to select the most incredible restaurants. When I told you I wanted Brazilian, I thought you would've suggested Green Field in Corona."

Jasmine smiled. It was Nydia's turn to select the cuisine for their now bimonthly early-dinner get-togethers, and when the accountant mentioned she wanted Brazilian food, Jasmine told Nydia to meet her at Delícia, a quiet little hideaway in the West Village. "I probably know most restaurants in at least four of the five boroughs and Long Island because it's a holdover from my former life as an interior decorator. Whenever I was referred to a potential client I'd take them out to eat and after a couple of hours I'd know whether or not I'd want to work with them."

"What would they have to do for you to turn them down?" Nydia asked.

"I'd suggest meeting at a restaurant because for me that was the litmus test. If they ordered the most expensive bottle of wine or item on the menu I knew instinctively they would attempt to nickel and dime me when it came to my commission. They usually would go on incessantly about how I was charging them too much, and I'd smile and tell them it was obvious they couldn't afford me."

Nydia cocked her head at an angle. "Do you miss decorating?"

It took Jasmine, interior decorator-turned human resource specialist, a full minute to think about her friend's question. "Yes and no. Yes, because I was my own boss and I loved the process of transforming a space into something that reflected a client's taste or lifestyle. And no, because I'd occasionally tire of trying to placate someone I knew I could never satisfy. The end result was they really didn't know what they wanted. I couldn't understand whether it was a gender thing, but once I married Raymond and we went into business together things changed when it came to complaints. Some clients would question every decision I'd make or suggest, while they would go along with anything he said."

There was a pause before Nydia said, "Do you know that this is the first time in a very long time that I've heard you refer to your ex by name?"

A hint of a smile tilted the corners of Jasmine's mouth. "That's because I've reached the point in my life where I can say his name without adding an expletive. I usually don't make New Year's resolutions, but this year I decided not to give him any energy because he's definitely not worth it. I've forgiven him, although I know it's going to take time for me to forget what he did to me."

Nydia picked up her glass of sangria in a toast, touching it to Jasmine's. "Good for you, *mija*. It's the same with me and Danny. Subletting Tonya's apartment was one of the best decisions I've made in my life thus far. I don't have a landlady clocking my every move, and now that I'm not seeing anyone I've gotten to appreciate my own company."

Jasmine nodded. "I'm with you because now I really like being single. I remember when there was a time I said I wanted to be married by thirty, and that's probably the reason I accepted Raymond's proposal." She and her ex-husband had had a yearlong relationship spanning more than eight thousand miles, and when they exchanged vows she did not realize she had married a stranger.

"We women do a lot of things we shouldn't do because we truly believe in love," Nydia said. "Speaking of single, I still can't believe that Tonya's going to marry St. John's cousin."

Jasmine swallowed a spoonful of *vatapá*, an Afro-Brazilian fish stew. She agreed with her friend. During their first trip to New Orleans, their former coworker Hannah DuPont-Lowell took them to a jazz club where they saw Gage Toussaint playing trumpet with a local band. It was apparent that after Tonya Martin moved from New York to the Big Easy that she had fallen under the spell of the drop-dead gorgeous musician, and now she planned to marry him.

Jasmine and Nydia had bonded with Tonya and Hannah one day the year before, after half the staff at Wakefield Hamilton was suddenly downsized when the private investment bank merged with another company in New Jersey. They'd spent the morning and early afternoon at Hannah's apartment talking about their futures. A generous severance package allowed them to delay seeking immediate employment, which had given them the option to take the summer off. They'd promised Hannah, the bank's former corporate attorney, they would come to New Orleans to spend time in the city where she owned a historic plantation-style home in the stunning Garden District.

Hannah's plan to convert the eighteen-room mansion and two guesthouses into an inn with a café and supper club was now underway. She had convinced Tonya, a professional chef, to invest in her new venture, and was still inviting Jasmine and Nydia to join them.

Jasmine had thought about taking Hannah up on her offer but it meant leaving her parents and possibly selling her condo—two things she wasn't ready to do. And if she did become an innkeeper, then she would be responsible for overseeing employee benefits design, recruitment, training, and development.

"Wasn't Tonya the one who claimed once is enough when it came to marriage?" Jasmine asked.

Nydia's eyes held Jasmine's dark-brown ones. "No. *You* are the one who has sworn off marriage."

"Do you blame me after my ex tried to screw me out of everything I'd worked for?"

"No, I don't, but that still doesn't mean you should swear off men for the rest of your life."

Jasmine ran a finger down the stem of her wineglass. "I haven't sworn off men. I just don't trust them."

Nydia grunted under her breath. "I think if I had discovered that Danny had cheated on me I would've broken it off with him sooner rather than later."

"Please don't tell me you're still seeing him?"

"No! The last time I saw him was in November and that was before I gave my landlady notice that I was giving up the apartment. But once I moved from the Bronx to East Harlem without telling him, I was finally able to get rid of the bum. And I took Tonya's advice and blocked his number. My former landlady called me last week and said he'd come by asking for me. I suppose he didn't believe her when she told him I'd moved and left no forwarding address. A couple of days ago he had the audacity to visit my parents' place to inquire about my whereabouts. Unfortunately for him he picked the wrong day and time because my brother had stopped by before his shift and he told Danny in no uncertain terms to stay the hell away from his sister."

Jasmine knew Nydia's police officer brother was very protective of her. "Maybe Danny is still in love with you."

Nydia rolled her eyes upward. "That's a load of shit. He never loved me. What he loved was the fact that I'd earned enough that he didn't have to get a full-time job. He used to brag to his boys that his girl was an accountant and she made a lot of money working for a bank."

"Why should he get a real job if his girlfriend can take care of him?"

"Well, that was never going to happen, because the only male I intend to support is my son until he's emancipated, and we both know I don't have any children."

Jasmine gave Nydia a long, penetrating stare. She understood exactly what her friend was talking about because she'd trusted her ex-husband to oversee their decorating firm after she returned to college to earn a degree in human resource management. However, once she'd been hired by Wakefield Hamilton, she'd handed Raymond full control of the business to which she had given her blood and sweat, and occasionally a few tears, while she was content to remain a silent partner.

A wry smile twisted her mouth. "What's the expression? You can't cry over spilt milk. I'm giving myself until the end of the year to plan what I want to do with the rest of my life. Working part-time for that social services agency definitely kept me from going stir-crazy."

Nydia waved away the waiter who had approached the table with a sword crammed with sirloin, lamb, pork tenderloin, and chicken. "I'm glad I took your advice to go into business for myself. I don't expect to earn half of what I made at the bank, but I'm not bothered by that because now I make my own hours. This will be the first year that I'm doing tax returns at a discount for my employers' workers, so hopefully I'll be able to count on them to become regular customers come next year."

"Good for you," Jasmine said without a hint of guile.

It was apparent Jasmine's former coworkers were getting their lives together while she was still uncertain how to proceed with her own. Last October Hannah married her former high-school classmate, and now Tonya was scheduled to marry his cousin the second Saturday in June. Although currently solvent, Jasmine still had another twenty years before she could even consider retirement, while she had Hannah McNair née DuPont-Lowell to thank for giving her the legal advice she needed to get her share of the business she had established before marrying Raymond Rios.

The distinctive ringtone on her cellphone indicated someone had sent her a message. "Excuse me. I need to check my messages." Jasmine was expecting her cousin to confirm whether she was coming down from Buffalo to spend a week with her.

She tapped in her passcode and then the Messages icon. She went completely still when she read the message:

I'm in town and would like to take you out to dinner.

"What's wrong?" Nydia asked when Jasmine stared at the screen.

"It's Cameron Singleton. He's in New York and he wants to take me out to dinner."

Nydia leaned closer. "Isn't he Hannah's investment banker?"

Jasmine nodded. "He'd asked me out at her wedding reception, but when I told him I lived in New York he said he comes to New York every May to hang out with his college frat buddies."

Nydia smiled. "It's now May fifth, so are you going out with him?"

A slight frown furrowed Jasmine's smooth forehead. "I don't know. It's been almost seven months and I thought he would've forgotten about me."

Nydia gave her a *'you've got to be kidding me look.'*

"Don't you have a mirror, Jazz? There's not much about you a man would forget. And, you have nothing to lose if you go out with him. After all, it's only dinner."

Jasmine wanted to tell her friend she was more than aware of her looks, and she'd lost count of the number of times people referred to her as *exotic*. She wanted to tell them that she wasn't a plant but mixed race—African-American and Filipina. "You're right. It's only dinner." She tapped the keys on her phone.

Jasmine: When and where?

Cameron: What night are you free?

Jasmine: I'm free every night this week.

Now that she was unemployed again, she had nothing but time on her hands.

Cameron: How's tomorrow night?

Jasmine: Tomorrow's good

Cameron: I'll pick you up at your place at 6:30. I'll make reservations at a restaurant in the Financial District

Jasmine: What if I meet you there?

Cameron: No problem. Cipriani Club 55

Jasmine: See you tomorrow at 7

Cameron: Thank you.

"What are you smiling about?" Nydia asked.

Jasmine handed Nydia the phone. "Take a look."

"Hey now. That's what I call a real gentleman. He's thanking you for going out with him. I'd like to think of him as a keeper."

"You're getting ahead of yourself, Nydia. As you said, *it's only dinner.*"

"Isn't that how a lot of relationships begin?"

Jasmine retrieved the phone "Forget it. Remember, Raymond and I had a long-distance relationship when he lived in the Philippines, and you know how that turned out. Even though I'd go back there several times a year I never really got to know him that well."

"Well, Ms. Washington, Cameron is only a couple of hours away. I think it's time to let a man wine and dine you, especially after what that horse's ass of an ex did to you."

Jasmine took a sip of wine. "You're right."

It had been more than two years since her divorce and over time she had turned down a number of requests from men who appeared interested in her. There were a few in the building where she owned a one-bedroom unit, and once the single men at the social services agency where she had worked three days a week uncovered her marital status they zeroed in on her like bees to a flower. She had a hard-and-fast rule not to go out with anyone whom she lived close to or worked with because she did not want to run into them if things did not work out. It had taken her a while to learn to enjoy coming home and being alone where she didn't have to encounter hostile stares or exchange acerbic words with the man she had come to despise as much as she had loved.

"Were you working for the bank when we had the holiday party at Cipriani?" Jasmine asked Nydia.

"How can I forget it," Nydia said, grinning. "I'd been hired a couple of months before and Wakefield Hamilton was my first serious job after passing the CPA exam. I couldn't believe it when the so-called buttoned-up white-collar executives showed their natural asses after they'd had a few too many drinks."

Jasmine nodded in agreement. "What really shocked me was Victoria Samuels accusing Harry Trillin of being a liar because he'd promised her he was going to leave his wife, but that was before Harry had gotten his wife pregnant for the third time."

Nydia appeared deep in thought. "I vaguely remember her."

"She worked in the securities division. The next day one of the senior vice-presidents came to HR and asked for her file. Regrettably for her several of her evaluations were less than favorable. That gave them the excuse they needed to let her go, plus she had broken the rule against personal fraternizing on the premises."

"That's some bullshit!" Nydia drawled. "They fire her and keep the cheating SOB because the proverbial old boys' club requirement is that you must have a particular appendage between your legs."

Jasmine tried to suppress a giggle, but couldn't control her outburst of laughter. She could always count on Nydia to make her laugh. There was something so carefree about the brilliant accountant she found infectious. Even that awful day when they'd been standing on the sidewalk before ten in the morning with their banker boxes, Nydia had been the one to talk about needing a drink. That was when Hannah invited them to come to her apartment for omelets, mimosas, and Bellinis. What began as an impromptu gathering at their coworker's apartment had segued into an unlikely friendship among four women from very different backgrounds, which led to new beginnings where their futures were inexorably linked.

She had talked to her parents about relocating to New Orleans to start over, and they had encouraged her to follow her dream to become an innkeeper, but Jasmine, an only child, had expressed her concern at living more than thirteen hundred miles away from her retired parents. Her mother was recently diagnosed with hypertension and had to carefully monitor her diet and exercise to avoid taking medication.

Their conversation moved from relationships and workplace antics to her temporary position at one of the city's social services agencies focusing on transitioning women and children from homeless shelters to permanent housing—a position that had ended last Friday. She had been hired for six months, and was paid from a discretionary budget to alleviate the backlog of cases caused by a shortage of caseworkers. It had taken Jasmine less than a month to grasp the frustration caused by the roadblocks and bureaucratic red tape involved in securing permanent housing for mothers and their children.

"What is it with the month of May?" she asked Nydia.

"What's wrong with May?"

Jasmine touched the napkin to the corners of her mouth before placing it beside her plate. "Last May we were let go by the bank, and now I'm unemployed again."

Nydia lifted her shoulders under a tee stamped with a NEW YORK YANKEES logo. "I don't know. Maybe it's just a coincidence."

Resting her elbow on the table, Jasmine cupped her chin in the heel of her hand. "If my cousin hadn't talked about coming down to visit for a week, I would seriously consider flying down to New Orleans to hang out before Tonya's wedding."

"Why go now when we've made plans to go down together for her wedding?"

Jasmine exhaled an audible sigh. "I said that because I'm feeling restless and useless, and that's the reason I signed on with the social services agency as a per-diem worker. I had watched so many HGTV, DIY, and house flip episodes that I could repeat them verbatim."

"That's why you should take Hannah up on her offer to assist her managing the inn."

"I would in a heartbeat, but I don't want to leave my parents."

Nydia waved her hand. "Your parents aren't so old they need someone to look in on them every day."

Jasmine nodded. "Daddy's sixty-eight and Mom is sixty-five so they're really not elderly. Nowadays people are working well into their seventies."

"Come on, *mija*. They're Baby Boomers who're probably still knocking boots like my folks. Papi is sixty-one and Mami fifty-six and they've warned me and my brother never to come over before calling because they may be indisposed. And when I asked my father what he meant by *indisposed,* he said now that his kids are out of the house he and wife enjoy walking around butt naked and what he likes most is that he doesn't have to put his hand over his wife's mouth whenever they make love. Mami is a screamer," she added, smiling.

Jasmine's jaw dropped. "He really said that?"

"Yeah." Nydia's eyes were sparkling with amusement. "My mother was sixteen when she met my father who'd just graduated the police academy. Her father said he was too old for her, so he promised *abuelo* that he wouldn't date her until she graduated high school."

"Did he keep his promise?"

"He did, even though he'd come around whenever the family had celebrations for birthdays, baptisms, or weddings. He became a role model for the boys in the family who wanted to grow up and be cops, and the girls always whispered how handsome he looked in his uniform. Mami graduated high school in June and the next month they were married. Papi took her to Puerto Rico for their honeymoon where she met his family, many of whom still live on the island. My mother had just celebrated her nineteenth birthday when she gave birth to Joaquin. Nelson came along two years later, and then me when she was twenty-four. My father wanted four kids, but my mother said he had his sons and she had her daughter, so that was it. And once I turned six she enrolled in cosmetology school and became a hairstylist. She worked in a lot of beauty shops before she saved enough money to open her own full-service unisex salon."

"I was always under the impression that you only had one brother."

"I usually don't talk about Joaquin because by the time he was twelve he realized he was gay, and I didn't want to go ape-shit if someone came out with a homophobic slur. Joaquin managed to hide his alternative lifestyle until he was eighteen. That's when he came out. He told my parents that he had met an older man who was an architect and that he was moving to Nebraska to live with him."

Jasmine was thoroughly intrigued by this disclosure. "Do you ever hear from him?"

Nydia smiled. "Yes. He sends my parents presents for their birthdays, wedding anniversary, and every Christmas they receive wonderful gift baskets. His benefactor paid for him to attend college and they're now partners in an architectural and design firm. A few of their clients are on the Fortune 500 list."

"Good for him. So, your family never rejected him because of his alternative lifestyle?"

"No. Papi was very angry because Joaquin didn't trust him enough to come to him and open up about his wanting to be in a same-sex relationship. They didn't speak for years until I told my brother he was wrong because no matter whom he would've chosen as a life partner, Papi would've accepted them. Two years ago Joaquin invited us to come to Omaha to attend his wedding. My parents flew out a week early, but I couldn't get out of New York because of the snowstorm that buried the city in more than two feet of snow. I finally got to see my brother for the first time in years last April. He lives in a six-bedroom ranch-style house he designed himself. The last time I spoke to Joaquin he said he and his husband were adopting two pre-teen brothers who have been languishing for years in foster care."

Jasmine smiled. "So it all ended in happily ever after."

"For them it has. And it will happen for us, Jazz. What we have to do is recognize and get around the roadblocks that crop up when we least expect."

Jasmine lowered her arms. "Right now I'm really not looking forward to getting into another relationship. I wouldn't mind dating different guys, but my head is not ready for anything serious."

"So, you were really serious about not wanting to marry again."

"I am *very* serious."

Nydia's eyelids fluttered slightly. "But, weren't you happy when you first married Raymond?"

"I'd convinced myself that I was happy, but when I

look back, I realize I was always the one making concessions, while Raymond did whatever the hell he wanted to do. My first mistake was to tell him that I wanted to be married by age thirty, because I didn't want to wait until I was well into my thirties to start a family. I suppose he saw me as the goose that laid the golden egg because I had a successful decorating business and owned a condo in a luxury building in a trendy Manhattan neighborhood."

Nydia pushed out her lips. "He sounds a lot like Danny, except that at least he was established in his career."

Jasmine nodded. "That's why I married him. He has the gift to judge whether an item is authentic or a fake with a single glance. And when it came to appraising Asian artifacts he was spot-on every time. It's too bad he let the head between his legs and not the one on his shoulders define his future." She held up both hands. "Enough talk about the clowns in our past. Now how serious are you about taking over the lease in Tonya's apartment when it expires?"

"Very serious. She's already informed the building management that I'm her niece, so that means they can change the name on the lease and I'll continue to live there. I'll have to buy furniture because Tonya has promised her daughter she can have the furniture after she moves into her own apartment."

"I can't believe Samara will be graduating from Spelman next week." Jasmine met Tonya's daughter for the first time last summer when they drove from New York to New Orleans.

"Word," Nydia drawled. "By the way, I'm going to need your assistance when I go furniture shopping."

Jasmine sat straight. "You want me to decorate your apartment?"

"Why do you look so surprised? Of course I want you to do it."

"Do you realize you'll be my first client in years?"

Nydia smiled. "Let's hope I'll be the first of many, many to come."

More than an hour after entering the restaurant, Jasmine settled the bill. "I'm parked in a garage a few blocks from here. I can drop you off home."

Nydia shook her head. "Thanks for the offer, but I want to do some shopping. My cousin is hosting a divorce party and I want to bring her a gift to celebrate her newfound freedom."

Jasmine gave Nydia a skeptical look. "I've never heard of anyone throwing a divorce party."

"This will be my second one."

"What do you bring to the party?"

"Sex toys like vibrators and dildos."

Pinpoints of heat stung Jasmine's face at the mention of sex toys. "Oh, I see," she whispered.

Nydia's eyebrows lifted a fraction. "You've never used a vibrator?" she whispered.

"No."

"When was the last time you slept with a man?"

Jasmine paused. "It's been almost three years."

"Don't you have urges?"

"Sometimes, but—"

"Say no more," Nydia said, interrupting her. "This is a conversation we'll have the next time we meet." Leaning closer, she hugged Jasmine. "Thanks for dinner. The next one is on me. And don't forget to text to let me know how it went with Cameron."

Jasmine pressed her cheek to Nydia's. "I won't." She and Nydia parted, and she walked in the direction of the indoor garage several blocks away.

Thirty-five minutes later she maneuvered into the underground parking garage across the street from her building and waved to the parking attendant in the booth. She had seriously contemplated selling the Yukon Denali because it was a gas-guzzler, and the only time she used it was when visiting her parents on Long Island. Also, her visits were becoming more infrequent because her retired high-school principal father and former trauma-nurse mother were busy volunteering for various charities.

She parked in her assigned space, walked to her building, nodded to the doorman on duty, and then headed for the elevator in the air-cooled lobby. She'd bought the one-bedroom unit in the luxury high-rise two years before she married Raymond, and despite his consistent urgings she had refused to add his name to the deed. The condo had been her first and most important big-ticket purchase and she had not wanted to share it with anyone—not even her husband. Making him a partner in her decorating business was a no-brainer once she changed careers, but after her divorce was finalized she reclaimed her maiden name.

Agreeing to have dinner with Cameron was certainly going to be interesting, although initially there had been something about the well-dressed businessman Jasmine had found disturbing whenever she discovered him staring at her; yet, despite this she still found him attractive. Classically handsome features in a deeply tanned face radiated good health, while flecks of gray shimmered like gold in his thick, fashionably styled light-brown hair. It was when she met his steel-blue eyes that she felt slightly uncomfortable. It was as if there was no warmth behind the penetrating orbs. But her uneasiness faded once he smiled. The iciness in his eyes had disappeared and after a while she had felt comfortable talking with him.

Jasmine smiled when she realized it had been years since she had had a date. Her smile was still in place as she retrieved her mail from the mailbox before she stepped into the elevator car. She punched the button for the eighteenth floor, the doors closed, and the car rose swiftly to the designated floor. Within seconds of opening the door to her apartment Jasmine felt the buildup of heat. When she had left earlier that morning she hadn't bothered to turn on the central air-conditioning. Spring had come early and unlike in recent years the temperatures had not fluctuated between warm and cool. Most morning temperatures began in the mid-sixties and by late afternoon were close to eighty.

She slipped out of her shoes, leaving them on the mat in the entryway next to a bleached-pine table. Walking on bare feet, Jasmine switched on the living-dining room air-conditioning unit, and then repeated the action in the bedroom. She flopped down on a chair and rested her feet on a matching footstool. She hadn't bothered to close the drapes covering the windows spanning the width of the bedroom. It was her time to sit and watch the lengthening shadows cover Manhattan like someone pulling down a shade to conceal the fading light.

There had been a time when she loathed sitting alone in the dark, but now she welcomed it. And she did not realize how much she had come to look forward to sharing dinner with Nydia because she could always count on her friend to lift her spirits. Before Tonya moved to New Orleans they had all met once a week, but now that there was only the two of them they switched to meeting twice a month.

I'm going on a date. It was her time for new beginnings and starting over and that meant a new attitude—something she intended to embrace with open arms.

Chapter 2

The rear door opened and Cameron Singleton stepped out of the town car when it stopped in front of Cipriani Club 55. He had made certain to leave his hotel in time to get to the restaurant before Jasmine arrived. "I'll call you when I'm ready to go back," he told the driver.

Cameron had flown into New York on Saturday night and Sunday afternoon he reconnected with eleven of his fraternity brothers living in the tristate area when they gathered for brunch in Harlem. They were still awaiting the arrival of others from different parts of the country, which would swell their confirmed total to fifteen.

It had been more than a quarter of a century since his college graduation and over the years he'd lost some of his friends because of illness, accidents, and a few who had died in combat. Several had had more than one marriage and the result was a loss of interest in attempting to revive what had been and would never be again. But Cameron, having never been married and now forty-eight, still reveled in his single status.

Over the years he had dated a number of different women, although there were occasions when he was content to be alone for long periods of time. He had earned the reputation of being a serial dater, yet the epithet did not affect him because he enjoyed living his life without restrictions and/or entanglements. What few knew was that his reluctance to marry stemmed from his parents' turbulent marriage. They couldn't live together, but were miserable whenever they separated. Cameron lost count of the number of times they had reconciled, and the irony was that in a few months they would celebrate their fiftieth wedding anniversary.

Ten minutes later a taxi maneuvered up to the curb and the rear door opened. Cameron went completely still. He held his breath as he stared at the beautifully formed feet of a woman wearing a pair of strappy stilettos touch the sidewalk before his gaze moved up and lingered on smooth, bare brown legs. A hint of a smile parted his lips when he saw Jasmine Washington for the first time in nearly seven months.

She looked different than he remembered. Back in October she'd worn an orange gown that concealed her legs and feet, but now the slimness of her body was blatantly on display in a de rigueur sleeveless little black dress with a scooped neckline and slightly flared skirt ending at the knees. Hair that had been pinned up in a sophisticated twist behind her right ear now bounced above her shoulders in a mass of curls.

Galvanized into motion, Cameron approached her. Everything about Jasmine enveloped him: her perfume, the flawless complexion that shimmered like burnished silk, the slightly slanting dark eyes, and the tiny heart-shaped beauty mark high on her right cheekbone, the pert nose, and the full lush mouth that other women paid plastic surgeons exorbitant sums of money to achieve. And the slight expression of shock that momentarily froze her delicate features faded when she recognized him.

Lowering his head, he pressed a kiss to her cheek. "You look incredible. Thank you for meeting me."

Jasmine stared up at him through her lashes, clearly unaware of the seductiveness of the gesture. "Thank you for inviting me." She shifted the black cashmere shawl and small evening purse to her right hand when Cameron took her left.

He gave her a sidelong glance as he led her to the entrance of the restaurant, his gaze lingering on her profile. Cameron did not know what it was about Jasmine that made him feel slightly off-balance; when he had first approached her at Hannah and St. John McNair's wedding reception he felt her tension as surely as it was his own. Once they had shared a dance, he'd asked to take her out to dinner. She told him that wasn't possible because she was leaving to return to New York the following afternoon.

Undaunted, he asked for her number while explaining that he traveled to New York every May. Jasmine offered him her number probably believing he would forget her. Well, he hadn't forgotten her, because not only did she look different from any other woman he'd dated, she also appeared more sophisticated *and* more mature.

The door opened and they were greeted by the maître de. "Good evening. Welcome to Cipriani."

Cameron smiled. "Thank you. The name is Singleton. I have a seven o'clock reservation for two in Terrace 55."

The man nodded. "Mr. Singleton. I'll have someone escort you to your table."

Cameron gave Jasmine's fingers a gentle squeeze. Three minutes later they were seated at a table on the colonnade terrace overlooking Wall Street. He stared at her as she glanced around the dining room. "Have you eaten here before?" he asked.

"Yes. The company I used to work for occasionally held their holiday and retirement parties here."

There was something about Jasmine he found mesmerizing and while he knew it was rude to stare, he was past caring. He didn't know if it was the perfection of her face, the black dress flattering the slender curves of her lithe figure, or the fluidity of her body language that indicated she was unquestionably confident in her femininity.

"Who did you work for?"

"Are you familiar with the name Wakefield Hamilton?" she asked, answering his question with one of her own.

"Yes. I remember Hannah mentioning she once worked for them." As her financial manager, Cameron was more than familiar with his client's resources. But when he'd asked Hannah about Jasmine, she had refused to give him any feedback. She said a grown man didn't need her as a go-between if he was interested in her friend.

Jasmine settled back in her chair as she studied her dining partner and found him even more attractive than she had remembered. The sprinkling of lighter strands in his thick hair, parted on the left, appeared more gold than gray. A lean jaw, strong firm chin, and balanced features all made for an arresting masculine face. His light-blue eyes were an exact match for his custom-made shirt with French cuffs bearing his monogram, and she knew from the cut of the tailored dark-gray suit that it had not come off a store rack.

"Hannah did work for them, and so did I. It's a private international investment bank," she explained. "Last year they merged with another bank and moved the entire company to south Jersey."

"You weren't willing to commute?"

"I wasn't given the opportunity to accept or reject commuting. None of us who were downsized were aware of the merger until we were told to retrieve our personal effects and then escorted out of the building."

He grimaced. "That's cold."

She scrunched up her nose. "That's one of the pitfalls of working for someone else. Even though we were given a generous severance package and health insurance coverage for a year it still didn't lessen the pain of having the rug pulled out from under us. And as the assistant director of personnel I had no idea the merger was taking place."

Cameron whistled softly. "Talk about a sneak attack."

"Amen," Jasmine said under her breath.

Their conversation was preempted when the sommelier handed Cameron a binder with a wine listing. "Will you share a bottle of champagne with me?"

Smiling, Jasmine nodded. "Of course."

"Do you have a preference?"

"No, I don't."

Cameron signaled the sommelier and gave him the binder without opening it. "We'll have a bottle of Krug."

The man smiled. "Excellent choice."

"Do you come here so often that you don't have to look at the wine list?" Jasmine asked Cameron.

He smiled, revealing a mouth filled with straight, white teeth. "I usually eat here whenever I come to New York."

"And how often is that?"

"Once or twice a year."

"For business or pleasure?"

Cameron stared out the window for several seconds. "Always pleasure." His gaze swung back to her. "The first time I came to New York, I admit I was a little intimidated moving to a city with a population in the millions, but after I completed my freshman year I couldn't wait to get back. I shared a two-bedroom apartment with another student, and we eventually became fraternity brothers. His concentration was accounting, while I majored in finance and economics."

"I've never been able to grasp the principles of economics. It's the only high school and college course that I barely passed," Jasmine admitted.

"Where did you attend college?" he asked.

"Unlike you, I didn't leave home. I grew up on Long Island and commuted into the city to the New York School of Interior Design."

Cameron found this disclosure puzzling. Jasmine had said she worked in the bank as a human resource manager. "You're an interior decorator." The query was a statement.

"Yes."

"What made you decide to go into HR?"

"That's a long story."

His impassive expression did not change. "Is that your way of telling me it's none of my business?"

Jasmine's jaw dropped, apparently taken aback by his accusation. "No. If I didn't want to talk about it I would've said so."

Reaching across the table, he placed his hand over hers. "Forgive me for prying."

She smiled. "There's nothing to forgive. When did you get in and how long do you plan to stay?" Jasmine asked, deftly changing the topic.

Cameron withdrew his hand and leaned back in his chair. "I flew in Friday afternoon, and I'm not scheduled to fly out again until Sunday night."

"What is it you do in a week?"

"Most of the guys who come into town early always meet for Sunday brunch. This year we ate at Chocolat."

Her eyebrows lifted slightly. "Are you talking about the Chocolat Restaurant Lounge in Harlem?"

He nodded. "Yes. Are you familiar with the place?"

"Yes. It's my favorite place for Sunday brunch."

"It was my first time eating there," Cameron said. "I must admit I was very impressed with the food, service, and the decor. Every time I come back and visit Harlem I find the area changed."

"It's undergoing an incredible gentrification like Brooklyn. The word is Brooklyn is the new Manhattan."

Cameron nodded again. "Give it a few years and it will be almost impossible to afford to live in either place."

"Have you ever thought about living here permanently?"

Jasmine's query caught him slightly off-guard. "Not really."

"You claim you like New York, so why wouldn't you want to live here?"

A beat passed before he said, "I like New York, but not enough to relocate. What about you, Jasmine?"

"What about me?"

"Would you ever consider living somewhere other than New York?"

She bit down on her lower lip, bringing his gaze to linger there. "I've thought about it."

"What's stopping you?"

Her answer was preempted when the wine steward approached the table with two flutes and a bottle of chilled champagne. He expertly uncorked the bottle, half-filled one of the flutes with the sparkling liquid, and handed it to Cameron, who gave it to Jasmine.

She took a sip and smiled. "Excellent."

Cameron nodded, silently acknowledging his approval. Once the flutes were filled, he raised his in a toast. "I raise my glass to wish you your heart's desire."

Jasmine blinked slowly, and then lifted her flute. "If we do meet again, why, we shall smile. If not, why then this parting was well made."

He went completely still. Why was she toasting about parting when he had hoped this wouldn't be their last encounter during his weeklong stay. "Are you saying you'll never go out with me again?"

She took a sip of wine while staring directly at him. "Don't you recognize the Bard?"

He shook his head as a sheepish expression flitted over his features. "I must admit I slept through most of my literature courses. Shakespeare in particular."

"Shame on you," Jasmine teased, smiling. "And to answer your question. I didn't say I wouldn't go out with you again. Remember, we met the first time last October and our parting was amicable even though I felt as if you did come on a little strong."

Cameron lowered his eyes as he stared at his left hand splayed on the tablecloth. "I'm sorry about that." He smiled. "Does this mean we'll get to see each other again before I go back home?"

Reaching across the table, Jasmine rested her hand atop his. "Let's get through tonight's dinner before we fast-forward to the next date."

He was momentarily speechless in his surprise. When he had sent Jasmine the text message he wasn't certain whether she would reply, or if she did, if she would accept his dinner invitation. Cameron had known and dated enough women in his life to recognize there was something different about Jasmine that made him want to know her better.

"You're right. There are times when I tend to get ahead of myself."

Jasmine's eyebrows lifted slightly. "How long have you been plagued with impulsivity?"

Much to his chagrin, Cameron laughed softly. He was more than aware of his negative personality traits, but being impulsive wasn't one of them. There were times when he had been accused of being moody, controlling, and possessive, but never reckless or impetuous.

"It appears it only occurs when I'm with you." He felt Jasmine's hand tremble slightly atop his before she removed it.

"What is there about me that makes you so reckless?"

He angled his head and smiled. "I don't know. And that's what I'd like to find out."

Jasmine sat straight. "That's not going to happen over one dinner date."

"You're right, but perhaps over time I can get to figure it out."

"You come to New York once or twice a year, while I doubt whether I'll come down to New Orleans for more than a couple of weeks once I find permanent employment."

"You're not working?"

"Not at the present time," she admitted in a quiet voice. "I'd accepted a temporary, per-diem position with a social services agency to help with a backlog of cases assisting families transitioning from homeless shelters to permanent housing, but that ended last week. Right now I've decided to take the summer off and wait until September before looking for a permanent position."

"Do you plan to spend the entire summer here?" Cameron asked.

Jasmine shook her head. "No. I'm coming down to your neck of the woods for my friend's wedding, and if it doesn't get too hot, then I'll hang out there for a couple of weeks with Hannah and St. John."

Cameron flashed a Cheshire cat grin. "If we get along well tonight, then I'd like to extend an invitation to act as your guide once you come down."

Jasmine wanted to tell Cameron that again he was getting ahead of himself, but decided not to call him on it. Even though she had accused him of coming on too strong, there was something about him that radiated strength and confidence—two traits she found attractive in a man. "I'll definitely keep that mind," she said. "I'm leaving here the end of the month, and I plan to stay until the seventeenth of June."

"When's your friend's wedding?"

"It's the second Saturday in June."

Cameron nodded. "I'll make certain to rearrange my work hours to take you around."

"You don't have to do that."

He put up a hand. "It's okay. I've been told that I work too much, so now I have an excuse to get out of the office."

Jasmine didn't have the opportunity to form a reply when their waiter approached the table to take their dining selections. She chose an asparagus salad with beets and goat cheese, and a main course of Mediterranean grilled branzino with mixed vegetables. Cameron decided on tuna tartare with a frisée salad, grilled salmon, and vegetables.

She listened intently as he outlined the activities he'd share with his college buddies. After Sunday brunch they'd traveled to Atlantic City to stay overnight to gamble and attend several shows. Cameron admitted they had overindulged and once they returned Monday afternoon most were too hungover and had to scrap their plans for that night and the next day.

"Tomorrow we're scheduled to drive up to Connecticut to golf."

"How many are in your squad?" she teased.

Throwing back his head, Cameron laughed. "Initially we had twenty-two, but we're down to fifteen. We are a motley crew of middle-aged frat boys trying to recapture our youth, and so far we're failing miserably."

Her salad and Cameron's appetizer were set on the table, and Jasmine could not help but smile when she tried to imagine forty-something men challenging each other to see how much they could drink and still remain upright. "That's the distinct difference between men and women. We are less likely to challenge one another in what I call a pissing contest to see who comes out the winner."

Cameron sobered. "You have other ways of competing."

"How's that?"

"It all comes down to physical appearance. Many sororities accept or reject girls based on how they look, while jocks are only concerned with having dudes on their teams that will help them win."

Jasmine's eyes met and fused with Cameron's penetrating light-blue orbs. She took another sip of champagne before the waiter refilled her glass. "I suppose we all have our biases."

"You're right, even though some biases are more dangerous than others."

"What's on your agenda for Thursday?" she asked, again deftly changing the topic.

"We have tickets for a game at Yankees Stadium. Friday is free day because that will give everyone time to prepare for Saturday night's finale. Those who have wives and girlfriends usually arrive on Friday to join their significant others."

"What's happening Saturday night?"

"We have a formal dinner cruise up the Hudson River to the Adirondack Mountains before we reverse direction to dock at Chelsea Piers."

"How long will that take?"

"Twelve hours."

"What about your girlfriend?" Jasmine asked, as she wondered why Cameron was asking to take her out when he had someone committed to join him on the dinner cruise.

"What about her?"

"Is she coming in Friday?"

A mysterious smile tilted the corners of his mouth. "No, because I don't have a girlfriend."

"Why not?" Jasmine asked. "You seem nice enough to have a special lady friend."

Attractive lines deepened around his luminous eyes when his smile grew wider. "Thanks for the compliment, but right now I'm not involved with anyone."

"It doesn't bother you to attend a formal affair without a plus-one?" She had asked him what seemed like an end-less stream of questions.

"At forty-eight I'm quite comfortable going to social events without a date."

She had been unable to pinpoint Cameron's age, yet she would have thought him closer to early forties rather than approaching fifty. It was obvious he took good care of himself as evidenced by his slender physique and un-lined complexion.

"You did attend Hannah's wedding alone."

"There you go. What about you, Jasmine? Have you ever attended an affair unescorted?"

His question gave her pause and she thought back to before she married Raymond. There had only been one other man in her life, and he had been her first lover and mentor. She owed everything to twice-married Gregory

Carson, thirty years her senior, for giving her what she needed to become a much sought-after successful interior decorator.

"Maybe a few times, but I always found it uncomfortable," she admitted. "Whenever a guy who had a date would come over and ask me to dance, their woman would either give me the stink-eye, or a few would be bold enough to tell me not to dance with their man again. I wanted to tell them their man had asked me to dance, and not the other way around."

"Didn't you know they were jealous of you?"

Jasmine rolled her eyes upward. "It had nothing to do with jealousy, but insecurity. I wouldn't care how much my man danced with other women as long I knew he was coming home with me."

Cameron applauded softly. "Good for you. You're in the minority because not everyone is as confident as you are."

"Would it bother you if we went out together and I danced with other men?"

"Hell no," he drawled. "As you said, as long as we were going home together, then it wouldn't make a difference to me." Cameron paused. "Now that we're on the same page, I'd like to invite you to be my date for the dinner cruise."

Jasmine wanted to remind him that he was coming on strong again, but in a moment of madness she decided to turn the tables on Cameron. "I'll go with you, but I'd like you to go out with me Friday." There was no doubt she had shocked him when his jaw dropped.

Seconds became a full minute. "Where are we going?"

"You'll get to see Long Island's North Fork when I

take you to a restaurant where you can sample a variety of incredibly prepared seafood dishes."

He winked at her. "That sounds like the Big Easy if you're talking about seafood."

She smiled. "Seafood, yes, drinks no. The difference is go-cups are illegal in New York."

His smile matched hers. "I accept, which means we're on for Saturday. Now, if you need to buy a dress and accessories for Saturday, then I'll give you one of my credit cards."

Jasmine's expression changed as if she had been doused with ice-cold water. Did he actually believe that because she wasn't employed she could not afford to purchase something to wear for a formal affair? Not having a job did not translate into her struggling to make ends meet. The generous severance package from Wakefield Hamilton, in addition to the equity in her condo and a generous divorce settlement, afforded her financial stability if she did not drastically alter her lifestyle.

"Thanks, but no thanks." Her words were dripping with sarcasm.

"I didn't mean to insult you, Jasmine," Cameron said in apology.

She held up her hand. "Let it go, Cameron. I can assure you that I have something appropriate for the evening." She hadn't lied to him. When she had visited her favorite boutique to look for an outfit for Tonya's wedding she had been unable to decide between two dresses, and in the end purchased both.

Jasmine concentrated on eating her salad. Tonya's invitation indicated she and Gage planned to exchange vows at seven in the courtyard of her fiancé's home in the Upper French Quarter, followed by a reception in Hannah and St. John's garden. Tonya had sent her photos of the interior and exterior of Gage's house and Jasmine was awed by the beauty of the residence. It resembled Parisian-style garret with wrought-iron balconies, a lush courtyard, and upper floors offering views of the city and Mississippi River. Tonya had chosen her daughter to be her attendant, while Gage had selected his son as his groomsman.

She was looking forward to reuniting with Tonya and Hannah, and discovered each time she left New Orleans to return to New York she felt something pulling her back to the historic city. Jasmine knew it wasn't the place as much as it was her friends. She'd become so connected with Nydia, Hannah, and Tonya that she had begun to think of them as her sisters.

Jasmine waved away the waiter when he attempted to refill her glass again. "I'm good, thank you." Although she had eaten the salad she was beginning to feel the effects of the sparkling wine.

"Are you sure you don't want another glass?" Cameron asked under his breath when the man moved away from the table. "I'll make certain you get home unscathed."

"I'm not worried about getting home, because I plan to take a taxi."

"That's unnecessary because I have a driver on-call. By the way, where do you live?"

"East Eighty-Second Street. Where are you staying?"

"This year we all checked in at the Mandarin Oriental. A couple of years ago we stayed on an estate on one of the Thousand Islands that had been in one of my frat brother's family as far back as the Civil War. He claimed his three-time great-grandfather had a factory in New Hampshire that manufactured armaments for the Union army. He built the house and several outbuildings as a vacation retreat with the fortune he had made from the war."

"How did you get there?" Jasmine asked.

"We flew up to Syracuse, and then took a boat to the island. After we got there we scrapped our plans to visit Canada because we spent most of our time swimming and touring some of the other islands."

"It's nice that you guys still get together after so many years."

"We all made a pact that once any of us becomes a grandfather, we'll get together every five years."

Jasmine wondered if Cameron had an ex-wife, or had fathered children. "Most of you are nearing the big five-oh, so it's only a matter of time before someone will claim grandfather status."

"I'm not counted among them, because I don't have any kids."

This disclosure puzzled her. "You never wanted children?"

He lifted broad shoulders under his suit jacket. "I never thought of them one way or the other. Unlike some men, I didn't want to become a baby daddy, so I've always made certain to use protection whenever I sleep with a woman."

"Good for you," she said sotto voce. Jasmine wanted to tell Cameron her ex had no qualms when it came to sleeping with a woman who wasn't his wife and eventually fathered a child with her.

"Do you have children?"

She shook her head. "No. My ex-husband and I talked about starting a family, but it wasn't in the cards for us."

Cameron touched his napkin to the corners of his

mouth. "You're still young enough to become a mother or you could always adopt."

Jasmine wanted to tell him she wasn't *that* young, and in another week she would celebrate her forty-third birthday. "Look at you," she chided. "You talk about not wanting to become a baby daddy; meanwhile you're suggesting I become a baby mama."

"There is a difference. If you decide to adopt a child you'd be a single mother."

"It's the same difference. Either way I wouldn't have a man in my child's life," she argued softly.

"What if you'd had a child when you were married and it ended in divorce? You'd still be a single mother."

"True, but at least my child would know who his or her father is. I grew up with both parents and I'd want the same for my child."

"That is something none of us can control," Cameron argued softly. "Children can lose a parent either through divorce or even death and still grow up well-adjusted."

Jasmine waited until the waiter removed her salad plate before he set down her entrée, and then Cameron's before she asked, "Is that what happened to you?"

He frowned as he stared at the contents on his plate for several seconds. "No. Even though my parents are still married, there was a time when they were like oil and water." His head popped up and the coldness in his eyes wouldn't permit her to take a normal breath. The blue was replaced by a steely-gray.

"Are you saying they shouldn't have married?"

"That's not for me to say. But, there were times when I'd wished they weren't together, because they were always at each other's throats."

Jasmine knew it was time to change the topic of conversation; she didn't want to talk about babies, and it was apparent Cameron's parents had had a volatile marriage, while her own had been equally turbulent.

"How long have you known Hannah?"

"It has to be at least thirty years," he said. "I must admit there was a time when I was a teenager that I had a crush on her."

"You're kidding!"

Chapter 3

Cameron knew this disclosure would probably shock Jasmine. "No, I'm not. I'd just turned fifteen and that summer I went to work in my father's office as a gofer. Hannah walked in with her father and I couldn't take my eyes off her. Judge DuPont had come to see my dad about setting up an investment portfolio for his grandson. Hannah was ten years my senior, married and a mother but that did not stop me from gawking at her."

"Did she know this?"

Cameron lowered his eyes, and the expression crossing his features made him appear slightly embarrassed. "No."

"Not many men are willing to admit to their boyhood fantasies."

"It could be they're ashamed to admit it."

"And you're not?" Jasmine asked.

Cameron exhaled an inaudible breath. "No. I'm not

perfect—far from it, and if I realize I've done something wrong, then I try to make it right."

He did not want to tell Jasmine that he had dated a few women who were under the impression they would become the next Mrs. Cameron Singleton even when he hadn't sent them signals or any indication that what they had shared would lead to an exchange of vows. As soon as they mentioned commitment, Cameron realized it was time to end it.

He liked and respected women, enjoyed their company, and had grown confident and comfortable being seen with a different woman every five or six months. It usually took that long for him to determine whether to continue or end their liaison. And while his brothers and occasionally his father chided him for sleeping around, he said nothing to change their minds. He'd become very discriminating when it came to sleeping with a woman, because he did not want to take advantage of them. There were women he'd continued to date without taking their relationship from platonic to physical.

"How's your salmon?" Jasmine's query shattered his reverie.

"It's delicious," Cameron replied. "Right now I'm trying to detox from red meat. There are times when I crave steak and I end up eating it at least twice a week. Recently I've made it a point to include more chicken and fish in my diet."

"Do you cook for yourself?"

"No. I'm not very proficient in the kitchen."

"Who cooks for you?" she asked.

"I order in."

With wide eyes, Jasmine rested a hand on her throat.

There was no doubt she was taken aback by the revelation that he ordered his meals. "Why don't you hire a cook?"

"I have a chef. I order what I want and have it delivered to me."

"I know by the cut of your suit that you have a personal tailor. Do you also have a housekeeper and driver?"

Cameron saw a hint of laughter in her eyes. "I do admit I have a housekeeper and tailor, but I do draw the line with a driver. I like driving my own car."

"Do you also live in the Garden District?"

"No. I have a place in the Central Business District, or as the locals call it the CBD."

"I really haven't seen that much of New Orleans. The exception is the Garden District, Tremé, and Faubourg Marigny."

"So I wasn't being presumptuous when offering to act as your tour guide when you come down?" Cameron asked.

"No, you weren't," she told him, smiling.

The conversation switched to sports and Cameron was mildly surprised to discover Jasmine was quite knowledgeable about her New York sports teams. She had admitted to attending Mets' games at CitiField and braving the winter elements at MetLife Stadium to cheer on the New York Giants.

He could not remember a time he had ever enjoyed the company of a woman so much. Cameron had known within ten minutes of sitting down with Jasmine that she would never bore him. However, he did find it odd that she'd graduated college with a fine arts degree only to give it up to become a human resource specialist. He felt comfortable talking about anything with her, including the revelation that he'd never slept with a woman without using protection.

Cameron did not want Jasmine to believe he wanted her for sex. Although he had to admit to himself that he was physically drawn to her, because when he saw her for the first time it had been her face and figure that had garnered his immediate attention. And after he asked Hannah about Jasmine, he had made it known to his friend and client that he wanted to take Jasmine out, and not sleep with her. The attorney looked at him as if he had taken leave of his senses because apparently his reputation with women had preceded him. Most people, other than the women who were seen in public with him, didn't know that many of his relationships were platonic. And those he'd slept with did not kiss and tell.

He peered under lowered lids over the rim of the flute. "Are you going to give me a hint where on Long Island we're going?"

Jasmine flashed a mysterious smile. "No. It's a surprise. The only thing I'm going to say is you should wear comfortable clothing and shoes. And don't forget your sunblock, because the weather is predicted to be in the eighties. I don't want you looking like a lobster while we're eating lobster. Oh, I forgot to ask. Are you allergic to shellfish?"

"No." Her mentioning sunblock and comfortable clothing piqued Cameron's curiosity. "Are we going sailing?"

"No," she repeated, smiling. "I wouldn't invite you to go sailing when you're taking me on a river cruise Saturday."

Cameron lifted broad shoulders under his suit jacket.

"I suppose I'll have to wait and find out what the beautiful lady has planned for us."

Jasmine lowered her eyes with the compliment, and he found himself transfixed by the demure expression. There was something about the woman sitting across from him that he found worldly and innocent at the same time. Worldly because she'd been married and was not an ingénue when it came to sleeping with a man, and chaste whenever she would lower her eyes and blush when complimented.

He wondered if her husband had been her only lover or aside from him if she hadn't had much experience with the opposite sex. The questions tumbled over themselves in his head and Cameron knew if he didn't stop ruminating about Jasmine's past he would ruin his chances of possibly cultivating a friendship with her. He had to let things unfold naturally. Their conversation segued to the high number of movie sequels and Broadway revivals, and both agreed there was a dearth of new artistic talent in Hollywood and along the Great White Way.

Jasmine stared out the window. "I'm ashamed to admit although I live here I rarely attend a Broadway show or movie opening."

"You don't like live theater?" Cameron asked.

Jasmine rested an elbow on the table and cupped her chin in the heel of her hand. "Not as much as I enjoy old school music."

"Like old school rap?"

"Some. But mostly R&B similar to Luther Vandross, Keith Sweat, Marvin Gaye, Joe, Dru Hill, and Maxwell. And I love the soundtracks to *Waiting to Exhale,* and *Soul*

Food. In other words, I prefer to listen to music rather than go to see someone perform."

"I like both," he admitted. "When you asked me how many times I come to New York other than to meet with my frat brothers, the only other thing that would bring me here is a live play or concert. Last year I managed to see *Hamilton.* I flew up, saw it, and then took a redeye back to New Orleans the same night because I had a meeting at eleven the next morning with a new client."

Jasmine's smile spoke volumes. "Now, that's one play I wanted to see, but sadly I couldn't get a ticket."

"If I'd known you then I would've asked you to come with me."

"Maybe another time," she said cryptically.

Cameron knew without a doubt there would be another time. When he'd sent Jasmine the text he'd hoped she would agree to meet him. Now, not only were they sharing dinner but she had also invited him to accompany her to Long Island, and had agreed to become his plus-one for a yacht party.

He'd found Jasmine different from the other women he'd dated when it came to poise and confidence. Some women, despite their age, retained their adolescent tendencies when they were overly flirtatious, seductive, and concocted schemes to make him jealous—all which he found offensive and a turn-off.

A wry smile twisted Cameron's mouth when he realized he'd had to wait until he was nearly fifty to find a woman with whom he hoped he could have an ongoing relationship lasting more than a year. The only drawback was the distance between them. More than thirteen hundred miles separated them, and he knew he couldn't relocate. Despite her unemployed status, he had no idea

whether Jasmine would be willing to move to New Orleans. Jasmine had accused him of coming on too aggres-
sively, so he decided not to broach the possibility of her
moving to his hometown.

The waiter returned to the table and refilled both
flutes. This time Jasmine did not cover the glass with
her hand. Cameron took a long swallow, while silently
complimenting himself on securing not one, but two
more dates with Jasmine during his stay. He ate slowly
because he did not want the evening to end. There was so
much he wanted to know about her but decided to hold
off making further inquiries as to why she had given up
her career as an interior decorator. He wanted her to feel
comfortable enough with him to divulge it on her own.

All too soon for Cameron, dinner ended with he and
Jasmine both declining dessert and coffee. "Is there any
place you'd like to go before I take you home?" he asked
Jasmine.

"No, thank you."

He reached into the breast pocket of his jacket and retrieved his cell phone. He spoke quietly into the speaker,
before signaling the waiter for the check. Cameron settled the bill and escorted her out of the restaurant where a
shiny black town car sat idling at the curb. Nightfall had
descended on the island of Manhattan and there was
hardly any pedestrian traffic in the Financial District.

The driver got out and came around to open the rear
door and Jasmine managed to slide gracefully onto the
rear seat without exposing too much leg. Cameron got in
next to her, his left arm resting over the back of the seat.
She went still when his fingers caressed the nape of her

neck, and then relaxed as he moved closer. It had been a long time since a man had touched her in a display of affection. And she had to admit that it felt good.

Jasmine closed her eyes. Her initial uneasiness as to whether she would share dinner with Cameron vanished when he proved to be a wonderful conversationalist, and she wanted to tell him he truly was a son of New Orleans because he and Harry Connick, Jr. shared the same speech pattern.

"Where do you want me to drop you off?" Cameron asked her.

She opened her eyes gave him her address and he in turn told the driver. She found it impossible to ignore the warmth from Cameron's body, which was a blatant reminder that it had been much too long since she'd been this physically close to a man she was attracted to. There had been a time when Jasmine realized her ex's duplicity had so turned her off to the opposite sex that she found the notion of sleeping with a man abhorrent. However, something about Cameron was different. Everything about him was a turn-on from his fastidious grooming to his undivided attentiveness. He was well past forty which made her wonder why he hadn't married. Was he a confirmed bachelor because he'd loved and lost or did he prefer living his life without having to be responsible for another person?

Jasmine forced herself not to think of becoming involved with Cameron beyond the coming weekend. After Sunday morning she would not see him again until she returned to New Orleans for her friend's wedding. And she didn't know why she'd invited him to accompany her to visit her aunt and uncle except that she wanted to offer him a little New York hospitality. She hadn't told him where they were going because she wanted it to be a surprise. It was a place where as a child she'd always spent the last two weeks of her summer vacation.

The ride from the Financial District to the Upper Eastside was accomplished in record time and Cameron leaned forward as the driver maneuvered along the curb in front her apartment building. "Please wait here for me."

The doorman approached the car and opened the rear door as Cameron got out, and then he turned to assist Jasmine. She smiled up at him. "Thank you for a wonderful evening."

He leaned in and dipped his head. "I'll see you to your door."

"That won't be necessary."

Cameron reached for her hand, threading their fingers together. "I was raised whenever I date a lady to make certain she gets home safely."

"I am home, and the building's safe because there's a doorman and anyone who doesn't live here has to be announced."

He gave her fingers a barely perceptible squeeze. "Just because I'm walking in peaceably with you doesn't show anything. What if I had ordered you not to scream or I'd carry you away on my pirate ship."

Jasmine smothered a giggle. "Why are you being so melodramatic? It's apparent you've watched too many movies featuring kidnappings."

Cameron chuckled softly. "How did you know?"

She sobered quickly. "You do?"

He nodded. "Yes. My television is always tuned to the Investigation Discovery Channel."

"What about the Bloomberg Channel?"

"That, too," he confirmed. "Do you watch much television?" Cameron asked as they walked in the direction of the building's elevators and entered an empty car.

Jasmine, easing her hand from Cameron's loose grip, put some distance between them as she moved against the opposite wall of the elevator car, and punched the button for the eighteenth floor. "There are times when I watch too much," she admitted as the car rose quietly and quickly upward. "I've OD'd on programs featuring home renovations, decorating, and flipping properties and countless DYI projects."

Cameron smiled and attractive lines fanned out around his luminous eyes. "What's the expression? You can take the girl out of the business but you can't get the decorating business out of the girl."

She lowered her eyes. It was obvious Cameron wanted to know why she'd switched careers, and although she'd revealed the details behind her failed marriage to her former coworkers, Jasmine was reluctant to talk about it to anyone else. And especially not to a man she was certain she would see again once she returned to New Orleans for Tonya's wedding. Whenever she thought about her relationship with her ex-husband she still could not believe she had been that gullible and trusting, and had allowed her obsession with being a wife keep her from seeing what was so obvious. She'd even lied to herself when she'd suspected Raymond of cheating on her. It was only when she saw the emails and text messages on his phone that she was forced to face reality: her husband had fathered a child with another woman.

"That sounds about right," she said, meeting Cameron's eyes.

"Have you given up decorating altogether?"

"Yes. At least for now." The elevator stopped and the

doors opened and Cameron stepped out, allowing Jasmine to precede him down the carpeted hallway to her apartment. "A friend has asked me to help her decorate her apartment, but that's still months away." She stopped at her door, opened her evening bag and took out a set of keys. Turning, she smiled at Cameron. "Thank you again for a wonderful dinner. I'll text you tomorrow to let you know what time I'll pick you up Friday." Going on tiptoe, she kissed his cheek. "Good night."

Cameron nodded. "Good night, Jasmine."

He turned on his heel and retraced his steps to the bank of elevators as she unlocked the door to her apartment, and once inside she slipped out of her shoes. It was then she allowed herself to exhale. She didn't know why, but she felt as if she'd been holding her breath from the moment she recognized Cameron as he stood outside the restaurant. There was something about the man that kept her on edge, as if her nerves were stretched taut while in his presence.

He hadn't done anything to make her feel ill at ease, so it had to be something of her own doing. And Jasmine didn't know what possessed her to invite him to accompany her on a drive to Long Island, except that she wanted to even the playing field for his inviting her to have dinner with him at one of her favorite restaurants.

She draped the shawl over the chair next to the table in the entryway and walked on bare feet to the bedroom. It took minutes for her to slip out of her dress and underwear and enter the en suite bathroom to brush her teeth and remove her makeup. A quick shower followed by the regimen of slathering a moisturizer over her still-damp body completed her nightly ablution.

Jasmine returned to the bedroom and, opening a drawer

in a chest-on-chest, she selected a floral cotton sleep tank and matching shorts. It wasn't even ten o'clock and much too early for bed. When, she mused, had her life become so mundane? She had too much time on her hands now that she was unemployed again.

When she was laid off with more than two dozen employees without prior warning, she had been more shocked than the others because as the assistant human resource specialist, she never heard or saw anything in writing that a merger was being finalized. It had been the second time during her tenure that the bank's executives had blindsided her. The first was when the director of HR resigned and Jasmine had assumed she would be promoted to head the department. She'd managed not to reveal her disappointment when the nephew of a board member was hired to replace her former supervisor. Then it all had become clear to her once the downsizing went into effect. Her new boss had managed to conceal every detail of the merger and layoffs because of his direct access to the board of directors.

She shook her head to rid her thoughts of the past. It had been a year since life as she knew it had changed drastically, and now it was time for her to plan for her future. Although she was unemployed again Jasmine knew she had options. She could either apply for another position as a human resource specialist, or return to her former profession as an interior decorator. Or she could accept Hannah's offer to invest in the DuPont Inn. Becoming a part-owner of a lodging establishment was tempting because it would harken back to when she ran her own business.

A slow smile parted her lips when she recalled Nydia's request that she decorate the apartment she was subletting from Tonya. It would the first time in years that she would take an empty space and fill it with furnishings that suited a client's taste and their personality. Thinking of Nydia reminded her she had to text her friend to let her know about her date with Cameron.

She retrieved her cell phone, climbed onto a stool at the kitchen's breakfast bar, and sent her friend a text message. The condo had undergone several renovations since she first purchased the unit what now seemed eons ago. She'd had walls removed to allow for an open floor plan and the expansive dining and living rooms flowed together. The kitchen had been remodeled, and Jasmine had also updated the bathroom off the entryway. Her bedroom, with breathtaking views of the East River, was spacious enough for an en suite bath and sitting area.

Five minutes later her cell chimed and Nydia's name and number appeared on the screen. "What do you want to know?" Jasmine asked, smiling as she answered.

"How did it go with Daddy?" Nydia asked.

"Well."

"Just well, *mija*?"

Her smile grew wider. "It went very, very well. I'm seeing him again on Friday, and he invited me to join him and his friends for a yacht party Saturday night."

"*Coño*," Nydia drawled. "What did you do to him?"

Jasmine laughed. Nydia would regularly intersperse English and Spanish whenever they were together. Jasmine grew up with her father speaking English, while her mother spoke Spanish and Tagalog. The latter she perfected whenever she spent summer in the Philippines with her mother's relatives.

"I didn't do anything except be myself."

It was Nydia's turn to laugh. "We'll it's more than apparent that he likes you. But, the question is, do you like him?

"I do," Jasmine said without hesitation. "I must admit initially I felt a bit uneasy because he can come on a little too strong."

"That's called confidence, Jasmine. Cameron's mature and definitely confident enough to go after something he wants."

"And that is?"

"You, *mija*. He was staring at you at Hannah's reception like a starving man who hadn't eaten in days. And I'm certain I'm not the only one that noticed it."

"That's because he was curious," she said.

"Yeah, right," Nydia drawled. "Although I'm younger than you, I'm willing to bet that I've had more experience with men than you, and I'm going to say it even though you may not want to hear it."

Jasmine went completely still when she encountered silence on the other end of the connection. She didn't want Nydia to tell her something she didn't want or need to hear. "What is it?"

"The man's going to put something on you that will rock your world."

Throwing back her head, Jasmine laughed until she could hardly catch her breath. "Do you really think I'm going to sleep with him?" she asked once she recovered from laughing hysterically.

"Well, you should. It's been much too long since you've slept with a man, so if it feels right with Cameron, then go for it."

Jasmine closed her eyes at the same time she exhaled an audible sigh. "That's not going to happen."

"Why not? Do you find him repulsive?"

"Of course not," she said much too quickly. The truth was she found Cameron very attractive.

"Then what's stopping you, *mija*?"

"He's a stranger."

"Every man is a stranger until you sleep with him."

Jasmine frowned. "That's where you're wrong, chica. I slept with a man who lay next to me practically every night and I didn't get to know him until it was too late."

"That may be true, but the difference is you're not married to Cameron. He's only going to be here for a short time, so have a little fun and then send him on his way."

"Why do you make it sound as if I'm planning to use him for sex?"

"And why shouldn't you? Men use us, don't they?"

"True."

"What's the expression? 'What's good for the goose is good for the gander.'"

Jasmine knew Nydia was right. She had offered an older man her virginity and in return he had helped to advance her career. It had become a win-win for both. He had claimed a young woman as his constant companion and he made it possible for her to establish her name as an up-and-coming decorator in a male-dominated design field.

"You're right," she said after a pregnant pause.

"Well, what are you going to do about it?"

Jasmine felt a shiver of annoyance creep up her spine. "I'm not going to set out to seduce a man because it's been a while since I've had sex."

"A while? Didn't you tell me it's been almost three years? It's a wonder you don't have cobwebs growing you know where."

Jasmine laughed again. "Stop it!" She sobered. "What about you, Nydia? What are you doing now that you're not seeing Danny?"

"I have a vibrator. I haven't used it yet, but at least I have it if I feel the urge to take care of my own sexual needs."

Jasmine grimaced. She did not want to think of inserting a foreign object into her body in order to have an orgasm. There had been a time when her sex drive was very strong, but after uncovering her ex's deception it was as if something inside her died.

"I prefer a man to a vibrator."

"Well, you have a man, so what are you going to do about it? Jump the man's bones and give him something he'll remember for the rest of his life. Don't forget he came onto you and not the other way around."

"That doesn't matter. I've never seduced a man."

"Let's take the word seduction out of the equation. What if it just happens?"

"Then it does, Nydia."

"Does this mean you're open to kicking it with Daddy?"

A slight frown creased Jasmine's forehead. "Why do you keep calling him Daddy?"

"I call all fine-ass men Daddy or Papi. And Cameron's definitely a Daddy. Hannah's St. John is a Daddy and Tonya's Gage is a Papi."

"You're right about that," she agreed. There was something about Cameron she found enthralling, but that still did not translate into her seducing the man. If she saw him in New Orleans for an extended period of time, and if their relationship underwent a change from friends to friends with benefits, then they could enjoy whatever each other offered.

"What are you wearing to the yacht party?" Nydia asked.

"I haven't decided yet. Remember, I couldn't decide between two dresses to wear to Tonya's wedding and bought them both."

It had been the only time when Jasmine found herself in a quandary as to what to select to wear to a formal event. Most times she knew what she wanted and within an hour of walking into a shop would leave with her purchases. Looking for shoes never posed a problem because her closet was filled with shoes in varying styles and colors ranging from sandals and athletic footwear to serviceable pumps and designer stilettos.

"You have fabulous taste in clothes, so whatever you wear will be stunning," Nydia said.

"Thank you."

"How do you plan to wear your hair?"

"I'll definitely pin it up."

"If you need your hair done, then I'll ask my mother if she'll do it for you."

"Thanks for the offer, but I don't need anything that fancy." Except for going to the salon for a haircut or trim, Jasmine usually styled her own coal-black wavy hair to suit the occasion. However, she planned to schedule a mani-pedi and a facial with a popular Second Avenue spa with operating hours that extended to midnight, and call her stylist for a trim.

Jasmine chatted with Nydia for another few minutes, and then said good night. She slipped off the stool and walked into the living room and sat on the loveseat facing the expanse of wall-to-wall, floor-to-ceiling windows. She always enjoyed sitting in the darkened room to look out at the lights on the bridges spanning the East River linking Manhattan with Queens and Brooklyn. It had become her time to reflect and heal.

When she'd decided to divorce Raymond, Jasmine would've been willing to give him everything he wanted to gain her freedom and independence—except the condo. No matter how much he pleaded and begged for her to put his name on the deed to the property she refused to relent. It had been her first and only big-ticket purchase and after being handed the keys to the unit, she and Gregory celebrated at his favorite restaurant before returning to his penthouse to make love. She hadn't known that would be the last time. Two months later he died in his sleep from natural causes. Losing her mentor left her devastated, and it wasn't until she met antiques dealer Raymond Rios she was able to shake off the sadness that shadowed her whenever she found herself alone.

Jasmine sat in the dark until she felt her lids drooping and knew it was time she get up and go to bed before falling asleep on the loveseat. She left the living room and slipped into bed as she recalled Nydia's suggestion that she sleep with Cameron, and when the accountant asked her if she had urges, she hadn't been reticent when she said sometimes. It was as if her desire for making love waned as soon as she discovered her husband's infidelity. Although she wasn't the first woman with an unfaithful husband, the pain of knowing he'd denied her the opportunity to become a mother when he had a child with another woman continued to haunt Jasmine. And she wouldn't have been the only woman forced to accept the reality that her husband had fathered a child outside their marriage. What she refused to accept was his deceptiveness when he underwent a procedure which denied her the possibility of ever bearing his child.

Turning over on her belly, she closed her eyes. Jasmine had promised herself not to dwell on the past and now she was ruminating on what was and would never be repeated. She was rapidly approaching forty-three, she would never have children or want to remarry. And she had more than twenty years before she could even contemplate retiring.

Pounding the pillow under her head, she willed her mind blank and within minutes fell asleep, shutting out the image of the man she would see again and the suggestion of her friend to seduce him.

Chapter 4

Friday morning Jasmine maneuvered up to the curb in front of the Mandarin Oriental to find Cameron waiting for her. Missing was the tailored suit and imported footwear. It was apparent he'd taken her advice to wear comfortable clothing: khakis, matching deck shoes, white golf shirt, and a navy-blue cap with a Yankees logo. He'd perched a pair of sunglasses on the bridge of his nose to protect his eyes from the rays of the brilliant May sun.

She tapped the horn to get his attention. A slight smile parted her lips when he came over to the vehicle, opened the passenger-side door, and sat beside her. His warmth, the now familiar scent of his cologne washed over her when he leaned closer to press a kiss to her cheek.

"Good morning," he whispered in her ear.

"Good morning, Cameron." Jasmine did not recognize

her own voice which had dropped an octave at the same time her pulse raced wildly throughout her body. His seemingly perfect teeth sparkled in a face that was even more tanned than it had been when they shared dinner at Cipriani.

Waiting until he secured his seatbelt, Jasmine signaled, and then pulled out into traffic when she saw an opening. She was grateful that she was forced to concentrate on the roadway ahead of her rather than the man who made her feel something she had believed long dead—a spark of desire. She wasn't certain whether it was because of her conversation with Nydia or if it was the man himself.

Jasmine was not an ingénue when it came to interacting with men. After all, she had been a successful decorator in a world dominated by men. However, it wasn't the same when it came to having a relationship with a man. There had only been Gregory and Raymond, and now she was thinking about cultivating a relationship with Cameron. She did not have to be a genius to acknowledge that Cameron perhaps wanted more than friendship. And with her rapidly approaching forty-three she realized she had nothing to lose.

She lived in New York and he lived in New Orleans, and it would not be the first time Jasmine engaged in a long-distance liaison. The difference this time was that she would not marry her lover, and she doubted that Cameron at forty-eight would want to give up his bachelor card. Her mantra had become *once bitten, twice shy.*

"How was golf?" Jasmine asked as she headed for the East Side and the Queens-Midtown Tunnel.

Cameron took off his sunglasses and placed them on

the dash before he removed his cap and tossed it onto the seat behind him. "It was good. I'll never make the pros, but I did have fun."

Jasmine gave him a sidelong glance. "How many holes did you play?"

"Nine. Most of the guys aren't serious golfers."

She decelerated and stopped at a red light. "And you are?"

Cameron met her eyes when she glanced at him. "I can say that I'm more serious than the others. I belong to a country club and I participate in many of their charity events. Do you play?"

Jasmine shook her head. "No, but my parents do."

"Do they still live on Long Island?"

"Yes," she said. "But I don't know for how much longer. They've complained constantly this past winter about the cold and snow and that their house requires too much maintenance."

"Are they retired?" Cameron asked.

She nodded. "My father was a high-school principal and my mother an ER trauma nurse. Daddy has to watch his diet because he's always been plagued with hypertension and my mother is a borderline diabetic, so she also monitors her diet and exercises regularly to avoid having to take insulin."

Cameron stretched out his legs and shifted into a more comfortable position. "Where do they want to relocate to?"

"North Carolina. My father still has family there."

Cameron's eyebrows lifted slightly. "So there's a little country in the girl," he teased.

Jasmine laughed. "There's a lot country in this girl. As a kid I used to divide my summer vacations spending three weeks in North Carolina and three in the Philippines. Then the last two weeks of the summer would be spent with my aunt, uncle, and cousins on Long Island."

"Is that where we're going?"

She nodded again. "Yes. My aunt and her husband own and operate a bed-and-breakfast overlooking Long Island Sound. Eight years ago they bought a fifteen-acre parcel of land adjacent to the property and set up a farm-to-table restaurant."

"Isn't that similar to what Hannah is planning to do with the DuPont Inn?" Cameron asked.

Jasmine paused before answering his question because she wasn't certain how much Hannah had divulged to her financial manager. "I know her plans include a café for those who stay over in the inn and an onsite restaurant for the general public. As for a farm-to-table I don't believe there's enough land on which to farm much beyond herbs, tomato, or peppers." She paused again. "Tonya mentioned she plans to do most of her shopping for her restaurants at the French Market."

"Hannah told me Tonya is a phenomenal chef."

"She is." Jasmine told Cameron about her first trip to New Orleans with her former coworkers. "It was my first time sampling the local cuisine, cocktails, and music and within days I was ready to pack my bags and move there."

"What's stopping you?"

Cameron was asking a question Jasmine had pondered a number of times since Hannah had asked her to invest in her new venture. She had offered Jasmine a ten percent share in the DuPont Inn if she agreed to come onboard to assist in managing the inn.

"My parents and my condo."

"Why your parents?"

"I'm their only child and now that they're getting older I don't want to live that far away from them."

"If they relocate to North Carolina you wouldn't be that far away."

"That's true," Jasmine confirmed.

"What's up with your condo? You don't think you'll be able to sell it?"

Jasmine tapped the horn lightly when the vehicle in front of her lingered once the light changed from red to green. "I know I'll be able to sell it once it's listed, but . . ." Her words trailed off.

"But what?" Cameron questioned when she didn't continue.

"I'd rather sublet it than sell it because I can use the equity *if* or when I decide to start up another decorating business."

Cameron sat straight. "Are you serious about decorating again?"

She smiled. "I'm thinking about it. Why?"

"You may be sitting next to a potential client."

Jasmine gave him a quick glance. "You need a decorator?"

Cameron paused, and then said, "Not right away, but in the very near future."

"How near?" Jasmine asked.

"Probably in the next few months," he said. "I'll be closing on a property sometime at the end of the month, but it has to be restored before I'll be able to move in."

"Is it in New Orleans?" Jasmine asked.

"Yes. It's only blocks from where I now live."

"You must really like the CBD."

Cameron smiled as he stared out the windshield. "I do.

Some folks like the Garden District because of the big houses, and others prefer the Upper and Lower French Quarters, but I've always been partial to the CBD."

"What's the appeal?"

"It reminds me a lot of lower Manhattan with narrow streets lined with office buildings, banks, and Victorian warehouses. You can also find skyscrapers belonging to financial institutions and oil companies. There are a number of hotels, museums, and galleries, and an outlet at the Riverwalk with more than one hundred and twenty stores."

Jasmine gave him a quick glance. "Did you say outlet?"

"I did."

"Now you're singing my song. I love shopping at outlets because there are so many of my favorite shops in one location. There's an outlet in Riverhead, Long Island that I visit at least two or three times a year."

Cameron slightly reclined the seatback, stretched out his legs, and crossed his feet at the ankles. "Is it anywhere near where we're going today?"

"We'll pass it on the way. Are you thinking of doing some shopping?"

"I hadn't planned on it, but if I think of something maybe we can stop on the way back."

There came a comfortable pause before he asked, "How long will it take us to get there to your aunt's place?"

"Barring delays, we should get there in about two hours."

Cameron stared out the windshield as Jasmine headed toward the Queens-Midtown Tunnel. "Tell me about your family." There was so much he wanted to know about the woman who had intrigued him the instant he spied her at Hannah's wedding.

"What do you want to know?" she asked.

"How did your parents meet?"

"My father saw combat in Vietnam and—"

"I thought you said your mother is Filipino," Cameron interrupted.

"She is. My father met her in Manila. He was drafted during the Vietnam War, and his unit was shipped to Philippines. A typhoon hit the islands and his unit's deployment to Vietnam was delayed more than a week. My mother was a first-year nursing student at that time and she was recruited to help with injured civilians when my father offered to carry one of her elderly relatives who'd suffered a broken leg to a nearby mobile hospital. They struck up a friendship and Daddy gave her his military address and home telephone number and told her to write him. She never wrote, but after she graduated she called and left a message with her address with his mother to thank her son for saving her grandmother's life."

"What happened after that?" Cameron asked, totally engrossed in the story.

"By that time my father had returned to civilian life and had enrolled in college as an engineering student. Of course he was shocked to hear from someone he hadn't known more than a couple of days. There was something about Marta Avila he couldn't forget, so Richard Washington decided it was time for a reunion. Their mutual attraction for each other hadn't waned and after spending a month courting Marta, my father proposed marriage. They were married in the Philippines and had another ceremony once they got back to the States for his family.

"My mother got pregnant right away, and a couple of weeks after she delivered me she went back into the hospital to undergo a procedure which would prevent her from having any more children. Meanwhile Daddy got a position teaching at a specialized New York City high school and after a couple of years he bought a house on Long Island. I was two when Mom was hired by a local municipal hospital. She eventually applied for citizenship, earned a graduate degree in public health and went on to head the Trauma Center. After nearly twenty years of teaching, my father was hired as an assistant principal in a high school within walking distance of where we lived."

Cameron thought about how uneventful Jasmine's parents' marriage was when it had taken years before his parents finally called a truce and stopped their verbal and psychological rivalry. And as the eldest of their four children he had been the one to witness the hostility, while wondering why they would stay together when they were complete opposites.

Whenever his father moved out of the house to stay in the country club, Cameron felt as if he could exhale normally for the first time. When his father returned, he never knew what he would encounter. Either his parents were glaring at each other and exchanging barbs, or they were hugging so tightly he didn't know where one began and the other ended.

He'd reached adolescence and his father decided it was time to have a man-to-man talk with his eldest son, and Cameron knew he'd shocked his father when he angrily told Nathan Singleton there was nothing he could tell him about how to treat a woman because he hadn't been the best role model. He and Nathan engaged in a hostile stare-down before the older man walked away without saying a word. It was another month before Cameron apologized to his father for his tone, but refused to retract what he'd said because his father had shown him how *not* to treat a woman. And once he'd begun dating he made it a practice never to raise his voice at a woman or engage in a verbal exchange about something on which they would never agree. He had lost count of the number of women he'd stopped seeing because he'd found them too argumentative.

"Do you have any brothers or sisters?" Jasmine asked, breaking into his musings.

"Yes. I have two brothers and a sister."

"Are they married?"

"Yes. Leigh is forty-four with three boys. Preston is forty and he has a son and a daughter. Evangeline is thirty-eight and is the mother of twin girls."

"Your parents are lucky to have so many grandchildren."

Cameron heard the wistfulness in Jasmine's voice, and wondered if her parents had missed the opportunity to become grandparents. "They treat their grandbabies as if they were a part of a royal family. I'm ashamed to say they're spoiled rotten."

Jasmine met his eyes when she glanced at him. "Is Uncle Cameron also guilty when it comes to spoiling them?"

He smiled. "Guilty as charged."

Cameron wanted to tell Jasmine that there were times when he missed not fathering children when interacting with his nieces and nephews. He'd watched them grow from infants to toddlers, and now tweens. His brother and brother-in-law bemoaned the approaching time when their daughters would begin dating, and Cameron always reminded them there was good and bad karma and they had to reap what they'd sown. Preston had had a new girlfriend every few months until he met his match when a girl he really liked refused to go out with him. He chased her relentlessly until she gave him an ultimatum: she wouldn't sleep with him unless he married her. He married Madison and gladly turned in what he'd called his tomcatting card to become a husband and father.

"You said you divided your summers between North Carolina, New York, and the Philippines. Which did you like best?" he asked.

Jasmine decelerated as she entered the tunnel. "It's a toss-up. I enjoyed going to Elizabeth City, North Carolina, because I got to see my cousins. We'd get up early and go swimming or berry-picking and between my aunties and my grandmother I learned to cook Southern cuisine. The weeks I spent in Manila were with my grandmother who taught me Tagalog and Spanish, and how to prepare traditional Filipino dishes. My last two weeks of the summer were on Long Island's north shore where my father's youngest sister had once been a private-duty live-in nurse and cook for an investment banker who had a former beauty pageant winner-wife who'd been diagnosed with brain cancer. After she passed away, he gave Danita the house, which had been a wedding gift to his wife, because she had been his late wife's constant companion when she'd been unable to do anything for herself.

"My aunt rented out rooms to tourists over the summer months, while during the off-season she attended culinary school to perfect her cooking skills. Once she graduated she reopened the house as a bed-and-breakfast. She married a fellow chef and that's when they decided to expand and open the restaurant in a converted barn." Jasmine paused, smiling. "I loved spending those weeks on the North Fork because I had a bedroom that overlooked the Sound."

Cameron stared at Jasmine's delicate profile as she maneuvered through the tunnel. Although he'd grown up in a privileged home, he envied the woman sitting less than a foot away. Her summers were filled with love from family members who contributed to her becoming a well-rounded adult.

Cameron knew when he took a woman out on their first date that it would either lead to a second or it would be their last. But something told him when he'd asked Jasmine to dance with him at Hannah's reception that she was different from any of the other women he'd dated or had been intimately involved with. Before that he'd spent the better part of an hour watching her interact with those sitting with her. He had also noticed her body language when a man held her too close when dancing. Her ringless fingers indicated she wasn't married or engaged, which had given him the opening he needed to approach her. Cameron did not want to pat himself on the back for his good luck in spending more time with Jasmine than he'd originally planned, but he intended to enjoy every moment they had together.

Tapping a button on the steering wheel, Jasmine turned on the satellite radio and tuned the station to hits from the eighties.

"You like disco." Cameron's question was a statement. He remembered her saying she liked old school music.

"Not all of it. One year my school had a lip-sync talent show and I performed 'Last Dance'."

Cameron tried imagining Jasmine belting out a Donna Summer hit. "Who would you be if you had the choice of being three female performers?"

Jasmine met his eyes for a second. "I'd have to pick Tina Turner, Christina Aguilera, and Whitney Houston."

"If you had to choose one, then who would it be?"

"I can't choose just one. I love Tina Tuner for her energy and longevity. I went with my mother to see her perform at Jones Beach when I was in junior high school and it was as if I had been holding my breath during her entire performance because she was just that mesmerizing. When it comes to Whitney Houston's voice, I always felt it was like a gift from heaven. She could sing the alphabet and make it sound wonderful. Last, but definitely not least is Christina Aguilera. She has the reputation of having one of the most skillful and powerful voices in today's music industry. Now, if you had to be three male performers, who would you be?" she asked, turning the tables on him.

"I would be Mick Jagger," he said without hesitating. "Now that's longevity. Mick will be singing and prancing across the stage when he's eighty."

"He's almost eighty, Cameron. Did you know he recently became a father for the eighth time at seventy-three?"

Cameron grimaced. "No. He should've been celebrating becoming a great-grandfather at that age."

Jasmine giggled. "He's already a great-grandfather."

He shook his head. "It looks as if he has no intention of slowing down. Then of course I would've loved to have been Michael Jackson, because he's the ultimate showman."

"I agree."

"I was so taken with him that I even learned to moon-walk," Cameron admitted.

"You didn't!"

"Yes, I did. Of course it took nearly a week before I could slide backward without losing my balance." Cameron didn't tell Jasmine that he'd practiced incessantly because he'd wanted to impress his friends.

"And who's your third one?" she asked.

"Marvin Gaye."

Jasmine gave him a quick glance. "You're kidding, aren't you?"

"No. I have everything he's ever recorded. My only regret is I never got to see him in concert."

"I'm really surprised with you being from New Orleans that you didn't select a jazz musician."

"I didn't because I couldn't," Cameron confessed. "They are too numerous to pick a favorite."

Jasmine accelerated as their conversation about music genres and performers continued when they left the city's skyscrapers behind. In between their discussion there were pauses where they were content to listen to music without talking, and Cameron realized Jasmine didn't feel the need to talk when she didn't have anything to say.

The passing landscape changed from apartment buildings and condos to single and multi-family homes with trees and lawns. There was a slight delay getting onto the Long Island Expressway and he noted the signs indicating the number of miles to Riverhead. He found Jasmine to be an excellent driver as she merged into traffic and maneuvered past other vehicles and tractor trailers into the HOV lane.

"I can't believe people do this every day in order to get to work," he remarked.

"There was a time when folks called the LIE the longest parking lot in the world before they added more lanes. If I lived out here, I'd commute into the city rather than spend hours in bumper-to-bumper traffic."

"I hear you," he said under his breath.

Fortunately Cameron did not have that problem. He lived within walking distance to his office in a building on Carondelet Street in the CBD. Days when he wasn't scheduled to meet clients he would walk if it wasn't too hot or humid in order to take in the sights. Although a native of the Big Easy, Cameron never tired of his native city. Whether it was the food, drink, or the music, the essence that made New Orleans so unique was a part of his DNA. Even when he left the city to travel abroad or to other places in the country it was as if after a few days something intangible would pull him back home.

"Sorry about that," he said, when he'd attempted to smother a yawn with his hand.

"What time did you go to bed last night?"

Cameron smiled. "It wasn't last night, but this morning. We got back from Connecticut around ten, but no one wanted to go their suites, so we all hung out in the hotel lounge until around two. I was still too wound up to sleep, so I sat up watching an all-news cable station, and didn't doze off until around four."

"If I'd known this I would've picked you up later this morning."

"Well, I didn't know I was going to stay up that late."

"Recline your seat and take a nap. It's still going to take a while before we get to Peconic."

Cameron smothered another yawn. "That's okay, I'll—"

"Please do it," Jasmine ordered softly, interrupting

him. She tapped the steering wheel again and changed the station to one featuring classical music.

He wanted to tell Jasmine that he wasn't going to collapse because he'd had less than seven hours of sleep. "Yes, ma'am." Cameron reclined the seat, crossed his arms over his chest, and closed his eyes. The smooth motion of the vehicle lulled him into a state of complete relaxation, and much to his surprise he fell asleep.

Jasmine slowed when she heard the siren and then saw the flashing lights of a police car behind her. Once she saw an opening, she changed lanes and came to a complete stop and smothered a groan.

When she called Danita to tell her she was coming out for a visit, she'd told her aunt she planned to arrive before eleven. During the height of the summer season, she usually left Manhattan either late Friday night or before sunrise Saturday morning to avoid the traffic delays that resulted from those driving east to spend the weekend. Once she informed Danita that she was unemployed, her aunt extended an invitation for her to come and work with her. Jasmine would have considered it if it hadn't been for the isolation during the winter months. After Labor Day business slowed appreciably and Danita and her husband, Keith closed the bed-and-breakfast and restaurant in late November and did not reopen for business until Memorial Day weekend. During the off-season they traveled abroad, perfecting their culinary skills and/or visiting their medical doctor son and attorney daughter.

Slumping back in her seat, she chanced a glance at

Cameron. His chest rising and falling in an even rhythm indicated he'd fallen asleep.

Jasmine knew she had rejected the attention of men who'd been interested in her because she'd developed a mental list of her ideal man. And when she'd disclosed this to Nydia, her friend turned on her like a rabid dog declaring all men were alike under the skin. Then she reminded Jasmine that although her ex-husband and Hannah's ex weren't in the same racial classification, both were cheaters. And if Hannah had decided never to date a black man then she would not have married St. John McNair.

Nydia's explanation did give Jasmine food for thought, because she knew she was being not only biased, but close-minded. Smiling, she thought about her former coworkers. It had taken less than a year since they'd found themselves unceremoniously discharged from their positions at the bank and now two of the four were embarking on new lives with husbands.

And she truly believed Nydia when she declared she liked being single and at thirty-two she was willing to wait until hell froze over before becoming involved in another relationship. Jasmine had told herself she also enjoyed being single, but there was a difference. Nydia was looking for a relationship and she wasn't. Jasmine wasn't against dating, but drew the line when it came to a committed relationship. She wanted to be the one to establish the rules whether to continue or end the relationship. Never again would she give another man control over her life as she had with Raymond.

Her gaze shifted from Cameron to the road. He wanted to take her around when she returned to New Orleans and

Jasmine planned to tell him she was looking forward to having him as her tour guide. She would enjoy his company and when she returned to New York she would have even more wonderful memories of the historic colorful city.

Traffic had begun moving at a snail's pace, but at least it was moving. It took more than forty-five minutes before she was able to accelerate and maneuver into the HOV lane again. A box truck and several cars had rear-ended one another as flares and automobile parts littered the roadway, tow trucks were positioned behind police cars and waiting to hook up the damaged vehicles.

Jasmine had to agree with Cameron. There was no way she wanted to commute by car to and from work. She had driven to downtown Brooklyn for the temporary position because she found parking at a nearby garage. When she'd worked at Wakefield Hamilton she'd taken the subway to work and occasionally rode the bus back home because she loathed being sandwiched in between hot sweaty bodies during the summer months. The one time a man attempted to touch her behind, she reached into her handbag and took out her keys and stabbed the back of his hand. Then she warned him in no uncertain terms that his face was next. When the train stopped he got off at the next stop, but not before he let loose with a string of expletives that stunned those in the car and others standing on the platform. It was another month before she took the subway home for fear of running into the pervert again.

Jasmine exhaled an inaudible sigh when she finally left the expressway and drove along a local road. The drive which should've taken two hours was now closer to three. She passed acres of farms and several vineyards, before turning off on the path leading to her aunt and uncle's property. The three-story Victorian house with a broad front porch sported a new coat of navy-blue paint and white shutters.

Several years ago Keith purchased a quartet of greenhouses which had allowed him to grow his fruits and vegetables months before the spring planting, and when they reopened for business their menu included ripened farm-to-table ingredients. And before the summer season ended Keith and Danita set up a farm stand to sell off the surplus produce.

There were only two cars and the van bearing the D&K Bed-and-Breakfast logo in the restaurant's parking lot. Jasmine pulled into a space close to the entrance. She turned off the engine and gently shook Cameron. "Wake up," she crooned, not wanting to startle him. "We're here."

He sat up, raised his seat, and stared at her. "I can't believe I fell asleep."

Jasmine's lips parted when she smiled. "That's because you needed to sleep." She undid her seatbelt. "Are you ready for some Long Island hospitality?"

His smile matched hers. "You bet."

Chapter 5

Jasmine was out of the car before Cameron could come around to assist her. He was glad she'd suggested he take a nap because he suddenly felt energized. He'd gotten up early Thursday morning to meet his buddies to board the charter bus that would take them to Connecticut for a day of golfing. By the time they'd arrived they weren't able to play for several hours, and they passed the time eating brunch. Twelve hours later they returned to the hotel for a late-night dinner. Most were too wound up to retire for bed, so they gathered in the lounge as each one continued to reminisce and catch up on what had been going on in their lives.

Cameron had taken his share of ribbing when several of his frat brothers accused him of being marriage-phobic, joking that every year he'd come with a different woman as his plus-one. A few had intimated he was living an alternative lifestyle, while Cameron was forthcoming when he said if he was, then he would be man enough to come out. He knew if he'd revealed the circumstances behind his parents' turbulent marriage his friends would've been less critical of his reluctance to marry; and he did not want to remind his former college roommate that not only had both of his marriages failed, but he was now was engaged to a woman younger than his eldest son. He wasn't one to criticize anyone when it came to their personal relationships because at forty-eight he still hadn't had one that lasted more than a year. Despite tiring of the topic of discussion he had remained to listen without further contributing to the conversations.

However, there was something about Jasmine from the first time he'd spied her at Hannah and St. John's wedding that garnered his attention and he couldn't take his eyes off her. And it was only after talking to her that he'd found her so wholly different from the other women he'd asked out. Although she was polite, he found her aloof and indifferent, and he had attributed that to her not knowing who he was, while most women he'd dated were local and more than familiar with the Singleton name.

The Singletons had settled in Louisiana even before the territory achieved statehood. His ancestors had made their fortune in shipping cotton and sugar cane to northern and European cities. During the Civil War, when the Union army blocked the mouth of the Mississippi, their generals had commandeered his great-great-great-grandfather's ships to transport armaments to supply General Sherman's troops for their March to the

Sea campaign. Archibald Singleton was secretly a spy for the Union because he did not own slaves, and had believed in preserving the Union.

Once the mode of transportation changed from shipping to railroads Archibald's sons went into insurance and banking. They managed to hold on to most of their fortune during the Great Depression and slowly regained their status as one of the wealthier New Orleans families. Cameron's father had developed a sixth sense when investing in the stock market, while Cameron as a certified wealth manager worked tirelessly to assist his clients when planning portfolios for retirement and estate planning.

He approached Jasmine and she took his hand, lacing their fingers together. "The restaurant doesn't open for dinner until the Memorial Day weekend, so we're going to have to eat at the B and B."

His gaze shifted to the barn-converted restaurant painted in the distinctive red. "Was this barn always here?" Cameron also noticed the solar panels on the roof.

"No. My uncle had it moved here. It saved him tons of money because he didn't have to build a structure from the ground up. Keith also added the greenhouses so he could have fresh vegetables during the six months the restaurant's open for dinner. After the Thanksgiving weekend they close down until the following spring."

"What about the bed-and-breakfast?"

"It also closes down."

He whistled softly. "Working six months out of twelve is a sweet deal if you can get it."

Jasmine gave him a sidelong glance. "You have to remember they have to be available 24/7 for their guests. Folks check in at two in the afternoon and check out at eleven the next day. And before they check out they're served breakfast. Those who stay more than one night can elect to eat dinner at the restaurant, which means my uncle has to be there to cook and supervise the restaurant staff."

"What time does the restaurant close?" he asked.

"Ten o'clock during the week, and midnight on the weekends. My aunt and uncle are in their mid-sixties, and there's going to come a time when they won't be able to keep up the pace of running two businesses simultaneously."

"Do they have children?"

Jasmine nodded. "Yes. Their son is a doctor who lives with his family in Texas, and their daughter is an attorney for a nonprofit advocacy program in upstate New York." She squeezed Cameron's fingers. "I don't know about you, but I'm ready for lunch."

Cameron eased his hand out of hers and rested it at the small of her back. "Lead on."

He followed Jasmine as she led him to the Victorian-style house several hundred feet away from the restaurant with a shingle identifying it as the D&K Bed-and-Breakfast. A plaque next to the front door verified the house had been built in 1892. Ceiling fans, hanging baskets overflowing with ferns, and red, white, and blue rockers on the porch invited one to come and while away the time.

It had only taken a single glance for Cameron to realize why Jasmine enjoyed ending her summers in the historic structure. A chime sounded when she opened the front door. Seconds later a tall, slender woman with a dark-brown complexion and graying twists under a white bandana appeared. Jasmine extended her arms and hugged the woman he assumed was her aunt.

*   *   *

Jasmine kissed Danita's cheek. She smelled of sugar and cinnamon. "I'm sorry we're late. There was an accident on the LIE."

Danita peered over Jasmine's head at the tall man glancing around the entryway. "That's to be expected. After you introduce me to your friend and you guys wash up we'll sit down to eat."

Jasmine beckoned Cameron closer. "Cameron, this is my aunt Danita Moore. Aunt Dee, Cameron Singleton. He's visiting from New Orleans and I wanted to show him some Long Island hospitality while he's here."

Cameron extended his hand. "It's a pleasure to meet you, Mrs. Moore."

Danita took his hand. "I'm glad to meet you, too, Cameron. But, please call me Danita."

He nodded. "Then Danita it is. This house is beautiful."

Danita smiled at Jasmine. "I can't take any of the credit because my very talented niece is the decorator. Guests who stay here always talk about how they feel as if they've stepped back in time because of the furnishings. Jasmine can give you a tour after we eat lunch."

Cameron's eyebrows lifted slightly when he met Jasmine's eyes. "I'm definitely looking forward to it."

Jasmine gave her aunt a saccharine smile. She could always count on Danita singing her praises as an interior decorator, while her aunt had been responsible to referring several clients to her. Although she enjoyed working as a human resource specialist, Cameron suggesting she consider decorating his new home had her considering resuming her former career.

"Is that who I think it is?" asked a deep masculine voice.

Jasmine turned to find her uncle walking into the entryway. "Yes it is, Uncle Keith." She wasn't given time to catch her breath when Keith wrapped his arms around her waist and lifted her off her feet. Like his wife, he'd covered his head with a bandana. The man her aunt married had been drafted by the NFL as a second-round defensive end. But his professional football career ended after three years from an off-season car crash in which he broke both legs. When he recovered he sat on the bench for the next season, and once his contract ended he gave up football and enrolled in culinary school where he announced to anyone who would stand still long enough to listen that he'd found his purpose in life: cooking and the woman who would eventually become his wife.

He planted a noisy kiss on Jasmine's cheek. "It's about time you paid us a visit."

She kissed her uncle's gray stubble. "Some of us do work," Jasmine teased. Keith set her on her feet. "You're looking good, chef," she said truthfully. Although he'd recently celebrated his sixty-fifth birthday, Keith's golden-brown complexion was still clear and unlined.

"I've been working out lately and lost some weight, but I still have to get rid my little friend that doesn't seem to want to leave me." Keith patted his rounded belly over a bibbed apron. "Enough about me, Jazz. How about you introduce me to your boyfriend?"

Jasmine wanted to tell Keith that Cameron was a *friend* and not her boyfriend.

Cameron, who'd been watching the interaction between Jasmine and her uncle, approached them, hand extended. "Cameron Singleton. It's nice meeting you."

Keith took the proffered hand. "Keith Moore." The older man narrowed his eyes. "Who dat?"

Cameron smiled from ear to ear. "Yeah! How did you know?"

"The minute you opened your mouth I knew you were from New Orleans. My college roommate was from the Big Easy. Whenever anyone asked if they'd seen Who Dat everyone knew exactly who they were talking about."

"Have you ever been to Nawlins?" Cameron asked.

Keith nodded. "A few times. I swore an oath to stay away from that place because it's detrimental to my health. I ate too much, drank much too much, and definitely didn't get enough sleep."

Danita came over to join them, looping her arm through Keith's. "Whenever we close for the season, my dear husband starts talking about going down to New Orleans, but I manage to overrule him because he knows he can't eat and drink like he used to when he was younger."

"I don't think any of us can," Cameron said in agreement, "but if you guys decide to visit, I'd like to act as your host and take you to places outside the city. And if you come late-fall, then I'll be able to get tickets to see the Saints or Pelicans." He had several clients who had season tickets for the local professional football and basketball teams.

"Hey now," Keith drawled, smiling. "I like you, Cameron. I'm sure Dee and I will take you up on your offer. Right, Dee?"

Danita kissed her husband's cheek. "We will definitely talk about it, because we still haven't decided where we're going during the off-season. I don't mean to change the subject, but we prepared lunch, and I'd like to sit down to eat before it gets cold. Cameron, Jasmine will show you where to wash up so we can eat."

Jasmine took Cameron's hand. "Come with me." Waiting until they were out of earshot of her aunt and uncle, she said, "It sounds as if you've become the Crescent City's official host."

He followed her into a bathroom off the parlor. "I love my city, its history, people, and traditions, so I don't mind sounding biased when I talk about it."

Cameron had been truthful with Jasmine. Despite having lived in New York while attending college and vacationing abroad, he still couldn't shake his infatuation for his birthplace. He equated New Orleans to a woman and he was enthralled with her physical beauty, smell, and the sound of her voice. He found staring out the window of his suite at the slow-moving, muddy waters of the Mississippi mesmerizing. The aroma of fresh fruit, vegetables, and spices filling the stalls of the vendors at the French Market was intoxicating. The sounds of jazz, blues, and funeral dirges were imprinted on his brain like a permanent tattoo.

His mother's family settled in Louisiana when it was still a swamp and a French colony. The LaSalle family arrived from England in 1814, two years after Louisiana was admitted to the Union, and set up a steamboat business. It wasn't his mother who talked about her ancestors but his maternal grandmother who had been obliging about those on her family tree who managed to maintain a modicum of gentility while circumventing the law when it came to nefarious activities.

He met Jasmine's eyes in the reflection of the mirror over twin sinks. "Do you think your aunt and uncle will come down once they close for the season?"

Reaching for a guest towel, Jasmine dried her hands before handing Cameron one. "I'm not sure. My uncle can be very persuasive when he wants to be, but in the end they both compromise."

Cameron smiled. Even if he didn't get to see Jasmine again after she came down for her friend's wedding, he wondered if she would be willing to accompany her aunt and uncle once they closed the B & B and restaurant for the winter season. "When you told your aunt and uncle that you were bringing company, did you tell them it would be a man?"

Turning slowly, Jasmine stared directly at him. "No. Why?"

"Their expressions said it all. It was obvious they were slightly taken aback."

"You're right about that," Jasmine admitted. "Whenever I tell them I'm coming out with someone it's usually my former coworkers, Tonya and Nydia."

His eyebrows lifted slightly. "So, you never come here with a man?"

Jasmine's expression was impassive. "The last man they saw me with was my ex-husband, and that was more than three years ago." She closed her eyes for several seconds. "I'll tell you later about my ex."

Cameron felt as if he'd won a small victory when Jasmine offered to tell him about her failed marriage without him prying.

He followed Jasmine out of the bathroom, through a formal living and dining room and down a narrow hallway to the kitchen. Cameron was temporarily stunned by the space with French doors spanning two walls, a huge wood-burning fireplace taking up half of another wall, and the last with a massive commercial Viking stovetop and grill. Shiny copper pots were suspended from a rack over the stove. Mouthwatering aromas wafted from warming dishes on a side table hewed from a tree trunk.

"We're eating buffet-style today," Danita announced. "So grab a plate and dig in."

Cameron wanted to tell Danita she didn't have to tell him more than once because he'd only had two cups of coffee earlier that morning. Keith uncovered the dishes to reveal steamed dumplings, soft-shell crabs, crab cakes, lobster tails, grilled prosciutto-wrapped asparagus, grilled shrimp, and bite-size spareribs. There were also bowls of Caesar and potato salads, and couscous.

"Don't be shy, son," Keith urged, when Cameron filled his plate. "I made just enough for the four of us, which means I don't intend to have leftovers for tomorrow. Whatever we don't eat, I'll box up for you and Jasmine to take back with you."

"Do you cook like this every day?" Cameron asked.

Keith shook his head. "Not for Nita and myself. We have another two weeks before we'll open for business, and she always makes breakfast for her guests, while I do most of the cooking, along with my assistants, for the restaurant." He uncorked a bottle of rosé. "I support our local wineries, so if you haven't sampled Long Island wines, then here's your chance."

"Do you shop locally?" Cameron asked after he seated Jasmine, and then sat beside her.

"Yes," Danita answered as she set down her plate. "There was a time when we bought our vegetables from farmers in the area, but after Keith suggested we grow our own we were able to save a lot of money."

Cameron savored each delicious morsel he put into his mouth as he listened to Keith explain how he had decided to open the restaurant after some of their guests extended their stay for more than one or two nights, and occasionally complained about having to leave the premises to eat dinner.

Keith took a sip of wine. "I didn't want to wait for approval from the town for the variances to build a new structure, so I found the abandoned barn and arranged to have it moved here. It took a couple of months to renovate it, and the following spring we were open for business."

Cameron touched the napkin to the corners of his mouth. "What made you decide, other than saving money, to grow your own produce?"

Keith smiled. "My grandfather had a watermelon and peach farm in Georgia. And when I was a boy he taught me everything I needed to know about farming. I suspect he wanted me to take over the farm once he retired, but I'd decided early on that I did not want to become a farmer. I'd excelled in high-school football and got a full athletic scholarship to the University of Georgia."

"So you were a Georgia bulldog."

"Woof, woof!" Keith said, grinning from ear to ear. "Where did you go to school?" he asked Cameron.

"Columbia."

Keith whistled. "I'm impressed. So, my niece has an Ivy Leaguer for a boyfriend."

Cameron nodded. "I'm the lucky one, because I never thought I'd meet someone like her who has brains, beauty, and talent."

"How long have you known each other?" Danita questioned.

Cameron shared a glance with Jasmine. The set of her

delicate jaw indicated she wasn't too pleased being the topic of conversation. "Jasmine and I met last fall at friend's wedding."

"Is that the friend who's been after you to move to New Orleans and help run her business?" Keith asked.

A moment of silence ensued before Jasmine said, "Yes."

"I've been after my niece to come and manage this place, because Keith and I are going to give ourselves another seven or eight years before we retire completely," Danita said.

Jasmine flashed a brittle smile. "You both have other nieces and nephews that would be willing to pick up the slack once you retire. What about your brother's son, Uncle Keith? Brent has been complaining for years that he's tired of working in the criminal justice system and is looking to get out. If he can supervise correction officers, then it should be a cakewalk for him to manage this place."

Keith appeared deep in thought. "I keep forgetting about Brent. Jazz may be right, Nita. Brent can also cook his ass off, so it would be easy for him to learn to prepare some of our more popular dishes."

Danita's expression mirrored indecision. "We'll talk about it later."

Cameron felt like a voyeur where he had been drawn into the lives of Jasmine's family members. He held up his wineglass. "This wine is excellent."

Keith nodded. "If you and Jazz aren't in a hurry to get back to the city, then I'll take you to a local winery where you can sample a few varieties. You can also arrange for whatever you want to be shipped back to New Orleans."

Lines fanned around Cameron's eyes when he smiled. "Now, that sounds like a plan. Did you enjoy Georgia U?" he asked, deftly changing the topic of conversation from one which he suspected was uncomfortable for Jasmine.

Keith's head moved and up down like a bobble-head doll. "I loved it because I was living out my dream to play football. I was good enough to be drafted to the NFL but my pro ball career ended after a couple of years when a drunk driver hit me head-on and I broke both my legs. I was in a funk for a couple of months after my contract ended, and I thought about going back to college to get a graduate degree and coach high school or college ball when my sister suggested I go to culinary school because I always loved to cook. I took her advice and that's when I met the love of my life." Keith winked at Danita when she lowered her eyes.

"She told me she'd inherited a house out on Long Island and was thinking about turning it into a bed-and-breakfast. I told her I was willing to invest in her business venture, but only as her partner and husband."

Reaching for his wineglass, Cameron touched it to Keith's. "Smooth move."

Danita rolled her eyes upward. "He wasn't that smooth. I made him wait a year before I told him I would marry him."

"Don't they say good things come to those who wait?" Cameron intoned.

"I hear you!" Keith drawled. "What about you, Cameron?"

"What about me?"

"Have you ever been married?" Keith asked.

"No."

Danita gave her husband an incredulous stare. "Keith! Why are you in that man's business?"

"The man said no, so it's obvious he didn't mind my asking," Keith said defensively.

Cameron stared at his plate. He knew Keith was curious as to his relationship with his niece. The older man had referred to him as her boyfriend and while he wanted it to be true, it was hardly the case. Although it was only the second time they'd gotten together, he felt as if he had known her longer.

Jasmine knew it was time to end what would be an inquisition where her uncle would ask Cameron a litany of questions—some he may not have wanted to answer. She rested a hand on his. "Whenever you're ready, I'll show you the house."

Cameron pushed back his chair, rising to his feet, and easing back Jasmine's chair. "I'm ready."

She waited until they were near the staircase leading to the second story, and then said, "I'm sorry about my uncle interrogating you."

"There's nothing for you to apologize for, Jasmine. There's nothing in my life or past I feel the need to hide. In other words, I'm an open book."

A mysterious smile touched the corners of Jasmine's mouth. "Are you a page-turner or one I'm tempted to close after reading the first page?"

Cameron angled his head. "That's something you're going to have to discover for yourself. After all, you'll have the rest of today, tomorrow, and Sunday morning to read as much as you can before I leave."

"We'll see, won't we," Jasmine countered.

She doubted whether she would know everything she wanted or needed to know about Cameron because she'd married and slept next to a man for nearly a decade and had no inkling that he was leading a double life. With the exception of traveling for a client, Raymond came home every night, made love to her at least twice a week, never forgot her birthday or their anniversary, and always ended their telephone calls with *I love you.*

Jasmine decided to take Nydia's advice and enjoy her time with Cameron and once he left New York she would continue her life as usual. It would be the second time within a year that she wouldn't work the summer, and come fall she would know whether she would continue as a human resource specialist, or resurrect her career as an interior decorator.

"How many rooms are in this house?" Cameron asked as they climbed the staircase.

Jasmine peered at him over her shoulder. "There are five bedrooms and seven baths. A man who owned a Brooklyn beer distillery built the house as a summer retreat for his family. He lost his fortune during Prohibition and decided to move out here permanently and take up farming. The property changed hands over the years until an investment banker bought it as a wedding present for his bride. Once my aunt decided to convert the house to a B and B, and asked me to decorate it, I suggested she fill it with period pieces."

"Were the original pieces antiques?" Cameron asked when he followed Jasmine down a carpeted hallway.

"Yes. Much to my disappointment I wasn't able to locate the dealer who'd purchased them. It took me a year of going to estate and garage sales to exhaust my list of antique dealers here on the island and in the tristate to find something comparable to the period. Personally I find the rooms in Victorian homes rather tacky. They were overcrowded because the occupants tended to flaunt their wealth."

"Are you saying less is better?"

She smiled over her shoulder at Cameron. "For me, yes. A room is a blank canvas and it's up to the decorator to fill it up with items that reflect his or her client's personality. There are four guest rooms here on the second floor, while my aunt and uncle have claimed the suite on the first floor for themselves. Each room is identified by color: green, blue, red, and yellow." Jasmine opened the door to the bedroom suite at the end of the hall. "This is our yellow room."

She waited outside the door while Cameron entered. Pale yellow walls provided a backdrop for mahogany furnishings indicative of classic English designs coupled with rich, exotic influences from the South Seas, Africa, and India. Varying shades of yellow were reflected in the bed dressings and raw silk drapery. A queen-size four-poster bed with an exotic peacock motif on the duvet in a rich palette of yellow and cinnamon-red matched the one on the full-size bed in an alcove behind a decorative screen. All of the suites had triple dressers, armoires with large flat screen television, were wired with Wi-Fi, and had sitting areas with overstuffed loveseats. The original plank floors were scraped, refinished, and covered with rugs with deeply hued colors that contrasted with the suite's dominate shade. The adjoining bathrooms had twin vanities, claw-foot tubs, shower stalls, commodes, and bidets.

"Your aunt and uncle must have invested a lot of money in this place to have it look like this," Cameron said after leaving the last bedroom.

Jasmine nodded. "My uncle used the money he'd invested from his days playing football, while my aunt took out a mortgage on the house. They worked hard the first couple of years to make a go of it, and then after a while when it became fashionable to vacation on Long Island during the summer months things turned around."

"What about staffing?"

"They hire many of the kids who attend the Long Island University Southampton College. Classes end mid-May, so most are available beginning the Memorial Day weekend and up until Labor Day."

"Where do they live?"

"Uncle Keith converted a section of the barn into living quarters for employees. It's set up dormitory style for men and women. The students always move back on campus during the school year until the summer season begins."

Cameron took Jasmine's hand when they retraced their steps. "Why wouldn't you want to run this place after your aunt and uncle retire?"

"I grew up in the suburbs and I don't want to retire in the suburbs. Once I went to college in Manhattan I realized it was where I wanted to live. People complain about the noise, traffic, and pollution, but for me it's like an aphrodisiac. Any and everything I want is in New York City where I have easy access to museums, restaurants, theaters, parks, and public transportation."

Cameron paused when they moved off the last stair. "Spending six months here and six months in the city sounds like a wonderful arrangement to me. There could come a point in time when you may want to retire here."

Jasmine shook her head. "I doubt if that is going to become a reality. The views from the house are spectacular, but there's little or no activity during the winter months. And if it wasn't for year-round locals this part of the island would be as quiet as a tomb. I'll probably follow my parents and move south so I don't have to concern myself with snowstorms and bone-chilling winters. Until then I plan to enjoy being a city girl."

Cameron wanted to tell Jasmine if she moved to New Orleans, then she would have restaurants, live music, museums and easy access to public transportation at her disposal. But again he was getting ahead of himself. He'd attempted to figure out what it was about Jasmine that made her different from the other women in his past, and now he knew it was her ability to allow him to be himself. There wasn't a need to try and impress her, because she was confident enough in her own right to say exactly what was on her mind.

"You've done an incredible job decorating this place, Jasmine."

She patted his shoulder. "You're quite the silver-tongued devil. You haven't seen every room."

"I've seen enough to know that I want to commission you to decorate my house once the renovations are completed."

Jasmine gave him a long penetrating stare. "I'm not going to commit to anything until I come down for

Tonya's wedding. Once I see what I have to work with then I'll give you my answer."

Cameron's expression did not reveal his relief in getting Jasmine to at least consider decorating his new home. Walking into the bedroom suites felt as if he'd entered a portal into the past. He'd been invited to enough historic residences in New Orleans, and to him they were more like museums than homes. But for those who checked into D&K Bed-and-Breakfast for a few days, it was an opportunity for them to escape to a place where they were able to imagine what it would be like to experience a world at the turn of the century.

The formal living and dining rooms, and the parlor, were as inviting as the bedroom suites. Lamps, tables, chandeliers, and area rugs had turned the house into an exquisite showplace that could be featured in interior design magazines.

His future home was a three-story converted Victorian warehouse with a rear courtyard and a garage with enough space for three vehicles. He planned to use the first floor for entertaining family, friends, and clients, and the two upper floors for his personal use. It would be the third time in his life he would change residences. The first was when he rented a house in the Lower French Quarter blocks from Esplanade Avenue, which he eventually purchased as a gift to himself for his thirtieth birthday. Ten years later he sold the property and bought a boutique hotel in the CBD, and converted a number of rooms into condos. Now he was moving again—and he swore it would be his last move.

"Are coming with me and your uncle to the winery?" he asked Jasmine.

She shook her head. "No. Go and enjoy yourself. I'm going to stay here and maybe go shopping with my aunt."

Cameron leaned down to kiss her, but caught himself in time. "I'll see you later."

Jasmine smiled. "Later."

Turning on his heel and whistling a nameless tune, he returned to the kitchen. Jasmine taking him to meet her family had become a pleasant surprise and he hoped it was a prelude to more good things to come.

Chapter 6

Jasmine stared at Cameron's broad shoulders and trim waist as he walked away. It was obvious by his toned physique that he either worked out regularly or carefully monitored his diet. He'd hinted she would uncover a lot about him over the next two days, but what Cameron failed to realize she knew everything she needed to know about him. He had been informative about his marital status; he liked golfing, had a personal chef, and kept close contact with his college buddies. The only other thing she needed to know, if or when she agreed to accept his commission, was his preference for decorating styles.

It wasn't that Jasmine hadn't found Cameron attractive, charming, and engaging. He was all that, yet she could not see herself becoming romantically involved with him, because there was no room in her life for a relationship—even if it was a long-distance one. And for her there was still the issue of where she wanted her career to go. Did she want to continue in human resources or return to decorating? Jasmine recalled Tonya's lament after they were downsized from Wakefield Hamilton about starting over at the bottom in a restaurant's kitchen despite her vast experience as a professional chef, so when Hannah suggested Tonya invest in the DuPont Inn to own and operate her own eating establishments, the talented cook quickly accepted the offer.

Hannah had extended the same offer for Jasmine to invest in the new venture not as a decorator, but to assist her managing the inn where she would be responsible for benefits, payroll, and time management. She'd balked because she didn't want to leave her parents or sell her condo, but now that she was unemployed for the second time within a year Jasmine knew she had to make a decision before summer's end; however, if she hadn't been solvent, then she wouldn't have the luxury of taking the summer off.

Fortunately she hadn't had to touch the severance pay she'd received from Wakefield Hamilton, while the monies she received in the divorce settlement from the sale of her design business and the equity in her condo had provided Jasmine with certain financial stability if she did not dramatically alter her current lifestyle. A hint of a smile parted her lips when she recalled her ex's face when the judge awarded him ten percent of the business instead of the fifty he had asked for. After all, she had been the one to start up and grow the company before marrying Raymond. He'd left the courtroom infuriated and into the arms of his baby's mama who'd sat in the back row witnessing the proceedings. She refused to make eye contact with the woman who'd slept with her husband and given him the child Jasmine had always wanted. With that phase of her life behind her, Jasmine went home and slept for more than twelve hours, and when she woke felt as if she'd been reborn.

"There you are. I was wondering where you'd disappeared to."

Jasmine turned and smiled at her aunt. "I was just thinking about something."

Danita returned Jasmine's smile. "I hope it was about your boyfriend."

Jasmine's smile faded. She knew it was time she settle the matter of her relationship with Cameron. "Come sit with me in the parlor. I need to talk to you about Cameron." Waiting until Danita sat on a brocade armchair, Jasmine sat on a matching one.

Of all of her father's siblings, she was closest to his youngest sister. Danita had been the one she'd confided to about sleeping with a man old enough to be her father, and she'd been the first one she told when she uncovered her husband's infidelity. There were times when she felt more like Danita's daughter than her niece.

"What about Cameron?" Danita asked after a comfortable silence.

"He's not my boyfriend."

"He's your husband." Danita's question was a statement.

Jasmine rolled her eyes upward. "No. He's not my husband, and he'll never be my husband."

"Is there something wrong with him?"

"There's nothing wrong with him. It's just that I don't intend to marry again. Cameron is a friend. We met at a mutual friend's wedding and he told me that he comes to New York every May to reconnect with his college frat brothers. A couple of days ago he took me out for dinner, and I thought I'd repay the favor by bringing him out here."

Danita's eyebrows lifted slightly. "So, there's nothing going on between the two of you?"

Jasmine slowly shook her head. "Absolutely nothing."

Taking off her bandana, Danita pushed it into the large patch pocket of her apron. "I'm willing to bet that Cameron would like something to happen."

Jasmine went completely still. "Why would you say something like that?"

"Open your eyes, Jazz. Don't you see how the man stares at you?"

"What's that supposed to mean?"

"That he wants to be more than friends. I'm certain you've heard the song "Hungry Eyes," from *Dirty Dancing.* The man has hungry eyes whenever he looks at you. Keith mentioned it to me when you and Cameron were upstairs."

"He stares a lot."

"That's because he likes what he sees and wants more than friendship, Jazz."

"What he wants and what he gets are two different things."

Danita met the younger woman's eyes. "Are you still angry with men because of what Raymond did to you?"

Jasmine shook her head. "I'm so over him."

"I don't think so," Danita accused softly. "If you were then you'd be willing to start dating again, or do you intend to spend the rest of your life alone? After Jaelynn's funeral, Mark told me not only could he not bear to live in this house because there were too many memories of the good times he and Jaelynn shared here, but he never wanted to love another woman as much as he'd loved his late wife. Four years later I got an invitation to his wedding. The man was babbling incoherently because he was so happy his fiancée was pregnant with their first child. As devastating as it was for him to watch Jaelynn change from a young vibrant woman to one as helpless as a newborn, he has been given a second chance at love."

"Maybe he proposed marriage because his girlfriend was pregnant."

"Stop it, Jasmine! Men nowadays don't feel compelled to marry a woman because they've gotten her pregnant. Every time you turn around you hear a woman refer to a man as her baby daddy, or she's his baby mama."

"Maybe Mark married again because he didn't feel complete unless he had a wife," Jasmine rationalized. "Some men like the idea of ownership when they say 'my wife.'"

"I doubt that. I'd just passed my state boards and was hired at a small, private hospital on the Upper East Side when Mark brought his wife in for an evaluation because she'd begun falling. And once she was finally diagnosed with an inoperable brain tumor she asked if I'd be her private-duty nurse. Mark's father was on the hospital board, so he arranged for me to take a leave and I moved out here to take care of her. The man drove into the city every Sunday night and drove back on Fridays, until he finally installed a computer so he could communicate with his office and clients.

"I'd watch his face whenever he stared at his wife and I knew that he was in love with her and not just her beauty, and that's when I told myself if I could get a man to look at me like that I'd marry him. And when I met your uncle and the first time he smiled at me I knew he was the one. You've had two men look at you that way, and neither was the one you married."

Jasmine temporarily found herself at a loss for words. "What are you talking about?" she asked, once she recovered her voice.

"I'm talking about Gregory Carson and Cameron Singleton. When you introduced Gregory as your mentor I knew you were sleeping together because I'd noticed the sly glances and the proprietary way he'd touch your arm or waist. And when you told me Gregory had been instrumental in helping you get your condo I wanted to say something, but figured it was none of my business. Once you opened up and confided in me about your relationship with him I wanted to tell you that I knew he was your lover, but pretended to be surprised. Now, let's talk about Raymond."

"I'd rather not," Jasmine countered.

A slight frown appeared between Danita's eyes. "Well, I'm going to have my say, and then I'll never speak of him again. The man is nothing more than a parasite. He saw you as a lamb he could fleece. You had a thriving business, a luxury condo, and he played on the fact that you both shared Filipino ancestry. I swore to my brother I'd never say anything to you, but I had to talk Richard off the ledge when he threatened to shoot Raymond for what he'd done to you and blame it on PTSD from Vietnam."

Jasmine's eyes grew wide. She could not imagine her even-tempered, soft-spoken father shooting anyone. "I don't believe it."

Danita made a sucking sound with her tongue and teeth. "Believe it, and if you ever mention it to him I'll deny I said anything."

Jasmine pantomimed zipping her mouth closed. "My lips are sealed."

"Let's talk about Cameron. I've just met Mr. Cool Breeze, but he looks and smells like money so I doubt he's going to try to pimp you."

"You're right about the money aspect. Cameron's a CFA."

"What's a CFA?"

"It's a chartered financial analyst. In other words, he's a portfolio manager."

Danita chuckled. "I told you he smells like money. Call it women's intuition, but there's something about him I like."

"I'm not saying I don't like him, Aunt Dee."

"Then what's stopping you from becoming more than friends?"

"We live more than thirteen hundred miles apart."

"That's BS and you know it. You dated Raymond when you two lived eight thousand miles apart. All you have to do is hop on a plane to New Orleans and you're there in a matter of hours, so stop making excuses. And now that you're not working you can go down and spend the summer, and that way you'll find out if you want to continue to date Cameron or call it off completely."

A shiver of annoyance eddied over Jasmine's body. Her aunt was being pushy. "You sound like Nydia."

"I'm glad I do," Danita retorted, "because until you start seeing someone else you're not going to get out of the funk where you keep rejecting men who are attracted to you. You're young, beautiful, and talented, and there's no reason why you shouldn't enjoy the company of the opposite sex. I'm not saying you should jump into bed with them, but you need to have some fun. What's wrong with going to a movie, a ballgame, or just taking a walk through Central Park?"

"There's nothing wrong with any of those things."

"Then why aren't you doing them, Jazz? Keith and I love running this place but there comes a time when we can't wait for the Thanksgiving weekend to close down, so we can have time for ourselves. Our kids are grown and out on their own and that means we can travel, register for cooking classes in different countries, and act like young lovers when we kiss and hold hands in public. And now that I don't have to worry about getting pregnant making love with Keith is better than ever."

Jasmine grimaced. "That is too much information."

"Is it? I'm more than twenty years older than you and I'm doing what you should be doing."

"You're right, Aunt Dee."

Danita waved her hand. "Please don't tell me I'm right and not do it."

Jasmine knew it was time to enlighten her aunt. "I'm Cameron's date tomorrow night for a yacht party with his college frat brothers."

Danita gave her an incredulous stare. "You mean to tell me I've been beating my gums about you going out and now you tell me the man's introducing to his friends?"

"Yup," Jasmine said smugly.

"I take back what I said. I hope you're wearing something that will have him salivating."

Amusement flickered in Jasmine's eyes when she thought of the dresses she had to select from for her date with Cameron. "I bought two dresses for my friend's wedding, but I still haven't decided which one I'll wear. Either way, I have a dress for the yacht party and the wedding."

"Speaking of weddings, Keith and I will cater one next weekend. The bride wants a Western-style wedding so when she saw the barn she decided it was the perfect place to hold her reception."

"How many parties do you cater during the season?" Jasmine asked.

"It averages about a couple of dozen. Catered parties make up almost half of our annual revenue. I want to add a few new appetizers to this season's menu. After taking a few lessons in Thailand, I told Keith we should include a few Asian dishes."

Jasmine smothered a moan. "When you say Asian appetizers I fantasize about spring rolls and shrimp fritters."

Danita nodded. "I had what the Thai call shrimp in tuxedo with a sweet chili sauce and they were so good I wanted to cry tears of joy."

"Filipinos call them shrimp lumpia." Jasmine searched her memory for the ingredients to make the appetizers she'd eaten as a child in the Philippines. Three hundred years of Spanish rule resulted in a fusion of Asian and Spanish cuisine of which she never tired, along with the dishes indigenous to the American South.

Danita sat straight, her gaze fusing with Jasmine's. "Do you know how to make them?"

"Yes. Why?"

"I have all of the ingredients so I'd like you to help me make some."

Jasmine's eyes grew wide. "Now?"

Danita stood up. "Yes, now. We can make a few of your Filipino shrimp recipes before *our men* get back."

Jasmine wanted to tell her father's sister that Cameron wasn't her man but didn't want to rehash or defend her decision not to commit to a relationship because she did not trust men. She was a hopeless romantic and she knew becoming involved would be detrimental to her emotional wellbeing. She tended to think with her heart and not her head.

"What else do you want to make?" she asked her aunt.

"You mentioned shrimp fritters, and I have loads of them in the freezer."

"They're called *ukoy*. Do you have butternut squash?"

Danita nodded. "There may be a few ripe ones in the greenhouse."

"Let's go, because it's been a long time since I've had shrimp *lumpia* and *ukoy*."

"Where do you park your car?" Cameron asked as he left the RFK Bridge and headed toward downtown. He'd offered to drive back from Long Island to Manhattan after spending an enjoyable afternoon with Jasmine and her relatives. He and Keith had visited a winery and after a winetasting he ordered several cases of red, white, and rosé shipped to New Orleans. Jasmine's uncle suggested he come back the end of August for the Shinnecock Indian Powwow which was one of the largest Native American Gatherings on the East Coast. Cameron told him he couldn't commit at this time, but would definitely consider it.

"There's an underground on the corner across the street from my building. Why?"

"I'm going to park this beast and take a taxi back to the hotel."

Jasmine gave him a sidelong glance. "Why would you want to do that when I could drop you off, and continue uptown?"

"Are you trying to get rid of me?" he teased.

Jasmine's mouth opened and closed before she said, "No. Why would you say that?"

"It's only seven-thirty and I thought we could hang out together a little longer."

He'd spent nearly twelve hours with Jasmine and her family and he hadn't wanted it to end. Her aunt and uncle were inviting, unpretentious, and obviously very much in love with each other. Keith had openly admitted he was more in love with his wife now than he'd been when he first married her, and Cameron was open when he admitted he had never been in love and would only marry if he was in love with a woman.

She smiled. "Is this when I invite you up to my place for coffee or a nightcap?"

His teeth showed whitely in his face as he flashed a wide grin. "It is."

"Okay. When you turn onto my street there's an underground garage near the corner opposite my building."

Cameron felt as if he'd won a major victory. It was apparent Jasmine trusted him enough to allow him inside her apartment. During the drive to the city he'd expected her to talk about her ex, but when she didn't he decided not to bring up the subject, and complimented himself on his ability to quell his impulsiveness when it came to Jasmine. His inner voice told him that she would reveal everything in her own time *and* at the right time.

During the long drive back to the city both had been content to listen to music rather than talk, and for Cameron this was a first for him just to relax and enjoy the music and the presence of the woman sitting next to him. Perhaps it was because he was a bachelor living alone that he'd come to covet his privacy and solitude. His mother had accused him of shunning marriage because he was selfish and predicted he would eventually die a lonely old man with nothing to contribute to the world except a tombstone. He'd kept mum when he wanted to tell Belinda LaSalle Singleton that she had stayed in a marriage that had been doomed from the start, and continued to stay with a man because she did not believe in divorce.

"Why did you call Black Betty a beast?" Jasmine asked, breaking into his thoughts.

"You named your vehicle Black Betty?"

"Yes. You don't name your cars?"

"No," he replied, "and why Black Betty?"

"The day I drove her home from the dealership Queen's "Black Betty" was playing on the radio, so that became her name."

"She must suck up gas like a sponge in city driving."

"She does," Jasmine admitted. "That's why I only drive her when I'm going on the highway."

"Do you really need a vehicle this big?"

"Not now. I bought it when I still had my decorating business."

"Wasn't that before you went into human resources?"

Jasmine shook her head. "Even though I was working in HR, I still had a decorating business."

He shot her an incredulous look when stopping for a red light. "How were you able to manage both?"

There came a noticeable pause. "I didn't. My ex took over the business for me." There came another pause before Jasmine said, "I'd gone to Manila to visit relatives and look for pieces for a client who had become enamored with anything from Southeast Asia. That's when I met Raymond Rios, whose family owned an import/export business. He had an uncanny gift for appraising whether an object was authentic or a reproduction with a single glance. What had begun as friendship turned into a long-distance romance and after a year we married in a traditional Filipino wedding and then in an American ceremony once we were back in the States.

"We ran the company together for about seven years until I decided to change careers, leaving Raymond to control the decorating business. Once I was out of the picture I discovered not only had he cheated on me, but unbeknownst to me, he'd had a baby with another woman. Meanwhile he'd been telling me he wasn't ready to become a father. I was really devastated when he finally admitted after his son was born he had a vasectomy and that meant we'd never have children together."

"The sonofabitch!" Cameron said under his breath. "How did you find out that he'd been cheating?"

"Raymond had two cell phones. One that was personal and the other for business. He'd gone out and left the business one at home and called me to ask if I'd seen it, and if I did, then pick up his voicemail messages because he was expecting a call from an important client. That's when I heard a woman's voice asking him to bring home some disposable diapers because she was running short. She ended the message with something that was too salacious for me to repeat. It was apparent she'd called the wrong phone. There were also text messages about when he could see her and others when he promised to give her money. I couldn't believe he could be that stupid and give her both numbers. I don't how I stayed so calm, but when he came home later that night I told him I knew about his baby mama, and that I was filing for divorce. We continued to live together until I had him served with separation papers charging him with adultery. That's when he packed his clothes and moved out."

"Where did he go?"

"The only place he could go. He moved in with his baby mama who lived in public housing with her three other children all from different daddies."

Cameron laughed loudly. "Talk about going from the penthouse to the outhouse."

"That he did. Of course he sued me for half the business, Black Betty, and a share of the equity in the condo, but thanks to advice from Hannah he wound up with only ten percent of the business, which I'd sold before the divorce was finalized. He wasn't entitled to the condo because I never put his name on the deed even though he'd begged me to over and over."

"Had you put his name on anything?"

Jasmine shook her head. "No. The business, condo, and Black Betty were all in my name, because my grand-mamma had preached to me not to give a man what I'd worked for no matter how good he made me feel."

For Cameron, it had been his grandmother who had provided him with a place of refuge when the arguments between his parents escalated to the point where he feared it would lead to physical confrontation. "Grandma does always know what's best for their grandbabies."

"I'm a witness to that," Jasmine said in agreement.

"Hannah was your divorce attorney?" he asked.

"Not in the legal sense."

Cameron listened when Jasmine said that she'd suspected her lawyer was being paid off by her husband

and one call from Hannah threatening to report him to the bar association which could've jeopardized his license ended it.

"How did she know he was being paid off?"

"It probably was because he told me Raymond was entitled to a lot more than ten percent of the business, and that I was leaving him practically destitute because he had a child to raise and educate. I knew I sounded cruel when I told him I wasn't the child's mother and therefore it wasn't my responsibility to provide support for him."

"And you weren't, Jasmine. If he made the baby with another woman then it was incumbent on him to take care of it and raise it with her. He waded out into the waters of adultery and unlucky for him he got caught in the undertow."

"Have you ever cheated on the women with whom you were involved?"

Jasmine's question caught Cameron completely unaware. "No. I've never been able to juggle more than one woman at the same time."

"Good for you."

"Does this mean I passed your test?" he teased.

Jasmine shook her head. "Only the first part. I have a three-part examination before you can earn your certification."

Cameron laughed. "Damn, woman. That's sounds cruel."

"Do you blame me after what I've been through?" she asked.

He sobered quickly. "No I don't. If my brother-in-law did to my sister what your ex did to you I definitely would've knocked the hell out of him." Cameron signaled, and then maneuvered around the driver holding up the flow of traffic. "How long have you been divorced?"

"It'll be three years in July."

"How long did it take you to get back into the dating pool?"

"Almost three years."

Cameron gave her a quick glance. "Am I your first?"

"Yes. Only because you're the first who refused to accept rejection."

He smiled. "I suppose there's something to be said for perseverance."

"That's only half of it," Jasmine said cryptically.

"What's the other half?"

"We live thirteen hundred miles apart."

Cameron felt some of his confidence waning much like someone taking the air out of a balloon. "Are you saying you're not willing to agree to a long-distance relationship?"

"Right now, I'm not willing to agree to *any* relationship, Cameron. I like you and enjoy your company otherwise I wouldn't have agreed to become your date for tomorrow night. I have trust issues when it comes to men, so I'm reluctant to become that involved. I'm certain you've dated women because you enjoy being with them, but not enough to plan a future."

"Are you saying you never want to marry again?"

"That's exactly what I am saying," she said emphatically.

Cameron wanted to tell Jasmine they were more alike than not, because his reason for remaining single had nothing to do with an unfaithful partner but from seeing firsthand how a union fraught with anger and resentment had scarred him as a child and young adult.

"It looks as if we're both on the same page when it comes to marriage," he said after a comfortable pause.

"Someone you loved cheated on you?" she questioned.

A wry smile parted his lips. "Not at all. And if she did, then I wouldn't blame the entire opposite sex for one woman. I—"

"I'm not blaming all men for what my ex did to me," Jasmine said, interrupting him.

"I didn't say you did. You're the one who assumed I'm anti-marriage because a woman cheated on me."

"If not that, then it would have to be your parents' marriage," she said perceptively.

Cameron had promised Jasmine she would know everything about him before the end of the weekend, and that meant being straightforward. "You're right. I grew up believing parents don't agree on everything, but my folks not only argued, they seemed bent on emotionally destroying each other. I'd lock myself in my bedroom and put a pillow over my head so I wouldn't hear their yelling. If that didn't work, then I'd hide in a closet, refusing to come out until they promised they would stop fighting with each other. That would last for maybe a week, and then it would start up again."

Jasmine rested a hand against his that was holding the steering wheel in a death-grip. "I'm sorry, Cameron. No child should grow up having to experience that."

He reversed their hands and threaded their fingers together. "It's unfortunate that it took an accident where my mother almost lost her life for them to come to their senses."

Jasmine's audible intake of breath reverberated in the vehicle. "What happened?"

"Fifteen years ago my mother was in a car accident

that resulted in severe head trauma. The doctors put her into a drug-induced coma to reduce the swelling on her brain, and the chief doctor of the department of neuro-surgery predicted that if she did come out of the coma she wouldn't be the same. It was a wake-up call for my father who refused to leave her bedside, except to go to the hos-pital chapel to pray for her full recovery. Within weeks he went from a controlling, bombastic, arrogant tyrant to a humble, repentant husband. Miraculously she came out of it without any lingering adverse effects. After spending two months in the hospital, she came home and she and Dad were like loving newlyweds and have been that way ever since. This August they will celebrate their fiftieth wedding anniversary."

Jasmine smiled. "Good for them. I assume they real-ized fighting wasn't worth it when they may lose some-one they really love."

Cameron nodded. "That's what Dad said after he brought Mom home. He'd married her because he loved her but he also wanted to control her, and my mother is too independent to allow a man to have that kind of power over her."

"Why didn't she divorce him?"

"My mother doesn't believe in divorce, and I suppose she stayed in the marriage because she thought it would eventually get better. Regrettably it took a near-death sit-uation for it to get better."

"What's the expression? *Better late than never.*"

Lines fanned out around Cameron's eyes when he smiled. "You're right about that. The few times I at-tempted to intervene in my parents' brouhaha, my mother cautioned me to stay out of it because she didn't want to involve her children in something she could handle on her own. She could be like a rabid coon when cornered, which meant she could give it *and* take it."

"I'm glad they were finally able to save their marriage."

Cameron brought Jasmine's hand to his mouth and kissed the back of it. His parents were fortunate to have been given a second chance, while it hadn't been the same with Jasmine. He concentrated on driving, as he replayed the events that led to Jasmine's divorce and her reluctance to trust men. He'd registered the pain in her voice when she mentioned her ex-husband's duplicity. His cheating on her was traumatic enough, but to have a child with another woman while denying his wife the possibility of becoming a mother was loathsome. Well, in the end Jasmine had become the victor because she had denied the scheming leech what he wanted. If it had been up to Cameron he'd have made certain that the man only got one percent instead of ten.

He maneuvered around the corner to her street, found the underground garage and when Jasmine leaned over to press a remote device attached to the underside of the driver's visor he recoiled as if burned when her breast brushed his forearm. The flesh between his thighs stirred and he pressed his knees together in an attempt to suppress an erection. The barrier went up and he drove through.

"My space is 52," Jasmine said as he deliberately slowed to less than ten miles an hour to give himself time for his hard-on to go down. He found her assigned space and parked.

Cameron shut off the engine, got out and came around to help her out, and then reached behind the passenger seat for the cooler Danita had packed with leftovers. Grasping the handles of the cooler in one hand, he rested his free hand at the small of Jasmine's back. She waved to the attendant in the booth at the entrance as he led her out of the garage and across the street. It was a warm spring night and the sidewalks were teeming with people taking advantage of the unseasonably balmy weather.

Spring and fall were his favorite seasons to visit the city where he'd attended college. Cameron had planned to return to New York for his graduate studies but chose Loyola University instead for an MBA with a specialization track in finance. He'd registered for courses in investment and venture capital investment, and financial decision modeling.

Jasmine greeted the doorman on duty with a friendly smile when they walked into the lobby. She retrieved her mail while Cameron punched the button for the elevator. They stepped into the car and rode to the eighteenth floor, and when she opened the door to her apartment and he followed her inside Cameron was stunned with the panorama unfolding before his startled gaze. Jasmine's condo was a palette in varying shades of white: walls, area rugs, chairs, sofa, drapes, and tables, and he wondered if her life since her divorce was absent of color and sterile as her home.

Chapter 7

Jasmine took the cooler from Cameron. She knew he was shocked to see the all-white furnishings. "I redecorated after my divorce."

"Why white, Jasmine?"

She slipped out of her shoes and left them on the mat in the entryway, and then set the cooler on the floor. "White is romantic, intimate, and it can be fragile or strong. But if you look closely, the dining area table and chairs have a pale-green patina. It's the same with most of the tables." She touched a wall light switch and the pendants in the living and dining areas illuminated whites and off-whites, creams, palest-greens, oyster-grays, and blues. Creamy moth orchids overflowed from milk-glass pots lining a table in front of wall-to-wall windows spanning the living and dining rooms. He realized the walls weren't at first glance white but a cool icy-blue.

"Exquisite." The single word was a whisper.

"You like it?"

"I'm at a loss for words," Cameron admitted. "Before you turned on the lights I thought everything appeared so sterile, but that's not the case. I can see the blues, greens, and gray."

"The downside is keeping everything clean."

Cameron kicked off his running shoes, leaving them on the mat beside Jasmine's. "It's obvious your place isn't child-proof."

Jasmine watched Cameron as he walked over to the entertainment unit with a large flat screen, audio components with a sound bar, and shelves cradling family photographs. "I definitely would not have selected white furnishings if I had children, because I'd have to have the chairs and sofas reupholstered every few years and have washable paint."

He turned and stared out the wall-to-wall, floor-to-ceiling windows, hands clasped behind his back. "The views from up here are spectacular."

She nodded. "Most times I don't draw the drapes because I love looking out the windows."

"I can see why you didn't want to give up this place."

"I'd only give it up to buy a larger unit in the building."

Cameron turned to face her. "Are there two- or three-bedrooms units available?"

"Why? Are you thinking of purchasing one?"

He laughed softly. "No. I couldn't see myself having two residences unless I had to do business in New York and New Orleans."

* * *

Cameron approached Jasmine, reaching for her hand and cradling it in his larger one. She tilted her chin, meeting his eyes. "Tell me about your new home."

"What do you want to know?"

"What's the total square footage?"

"I believe the architect said it was about six thousand."

Jasmine whistled softly. "That's really big."

"It's a three-story Victorian warehouse. Each floor is a little over two thousand square feet."

Jasmine felt a jolt of excitement. Her favorite projects were decorating former lofts and warehouses into beautiful spaces for living and entertaining. "I can't wait to see it."

"And I can't wait for you to see it," Cameron said, smiling.

"Have you decided what decorating style you want?"

"No. You're the professional, so I'm going to leave that up to you."

She gave him a long, penetrating stare. "That's not going to help me because I like to create a style that will be compatible with my client's personality. If I were to decorate a basketball player's home, then the style would be in keeping with his physicality, and if he is a larger-than-life celebrity."

"I can assure you that I'm not a celebrity, nor is my personal life over the top."

"Are you a workaholic?"

Cameron's smile vanished, replaced by astonishment. "Why would you ask me that?"

"Just answer the question, Cameron."

He angled his head, wondering what Jasmine was contemplating. "Sometimes. But that's usually when I'm setting up an investment portfolio for a new client. I'll stay in the office hours after everyone else leaves because I won't want any distractions."

Jasmine blinked slowly. "I'm asking because I'll probably recommend you have a home/office where you can work during off-hours. Statistics show an employee eating lunch at his or her desk while working on a project is no more productive than one who will leave the office for a lunch break."

"Have you exchanged your decorating hat for your HR hat?" he teased.

"Right now I'm wearing both. It's apparent you have enough room in your house for an office, so why not install one?"

"I'll definitely consider it." Cameron did not want to tell Jasmine that he would eventually assume full responsibility of running the Singleton Investment Group once his father retired on his seventy-fifth birthday, which was less than six months away. "What made you decide to go into HR? From what I've seen of the bed-and-breakfast and your condo you're a very talented decorator."

"Come with me to the kitchen. I'll tell you everything over coffee." She picked up the cooler.

Cameron followed Jasmine into the kitchen, and sat on a stool at the breakfast bar in the state-of-the-art space with brushed-nickel appliances. He watched Jasmine wash her hands in a stainless-steel sink, empty the cooler and place containers of leftovers in the built-in French-door refrigerator-freezer, and then open a narrow cabinet and take out a jar filled with coffee beans. The bleached-pine cabinets matched the plank flooring.

"How do want your coffee?"

His eyebrows lifted slightly. "I get a choice?"

Jasmine winked at him. "Of course you do. You can have coffee, espresso, cappuccino, macchiato, or a latté."

It was obvious she was a coffee connoisseur with a DeLonghi coffeemaker/espresso machine. "I'll have what you're having."

"I'm having a cappuccino with double espresso and steamed milk foam. I have cream if you prefer that instead of milk, and if you want a sprinkle of cinnamon or chocolate powder."

Cameron stared at Jasmine, and then burst into laughter. "Why do I feel as if I'm in Starbucks?"

Jasmine's laughter joined his. "Because you're looking at a trained barista."

He sobered quickly. "You are?"

She nodded. "My uncle bought an espresso machine several years ago and taught me how to use it. That's when I figured out it was cost-effective to purchase my own machine rather than spend an average of five or six dollars a day on specialized coffees."

"It must come in handy when you're entertaining," Cameron said, raising his voice slightly when Jasmine ground the beans in a grinder.

"It does," she agreed. "I still keep in touch with several women from our high school and three times a year we have a girls' night out. We'll usually meet at a restaurant and sometimes I'll host a dinner and sleepover. That's when we eat too much, drink too much, and stay up half the night talking and laughing."

"Where does everyone sleep?"

"I have a queen-sized bed in my bedroom, and the sofa converts to a full bed, and the loveseat to a twin."

"Do they always come into the city?" Cameron asked her.

"Yes. They still live out east so coming into Manhattan is a change of scenery for them. I grew up with a lot of kids who never ventured off Long Island until they were adults. Once I graduated junior high I told my parents I didn't want to spend my summers in North Carolina or the Philippines. That's when Mom and I, if she didn't work a weekend shift, would go to early mass, then take the railroad into the city where we'd have brunch. After that we visited museums and art galleries, or botanic gardens in different boroughs. It wasn't until my junior year in high school that I realized I wanted to be a decorator."

"What made you decide to go into human resource management?"

"I was thinking of expanding my business and that meant hiring and training employees, researching labor-relations, employee benefits, compensation and family-leave. So I went back to school while Raymond ran the business. A month before I graduated one of my professors told me about a position with a private investment bank looking to hire someone for their HR department. I called and emailed my resume and transcripts, believing they would never contact me for an interview. Not only did I have the interview but they also hired me. The salary and benefits package they offered was impressive, so I decided to accept the position, work there a couple of years, and get the experience I needed to grow my company. Two years became three and eventually six. Once Raymond and I were legally separated I sold the business and continued with Wakefield Hamilton until the merger."

"It looks as if everything worked out for you in the end."

Jasmine flashed a Cheshire cat grin. "Yes, it did." She added water to the coffeemaker. "You can turn on the television while I finish making the coffee."

Cameron slipped off the stool. "Is there anything in particular you want to see?"

"No. You can put on the ballgame if you want."

He smiled. Now he knew for certain Jasmine was someone he could hang out with. "Yankees or Mets?"

"It doesn't matter."

Cameron knew if he were to spend any appreciable time with Jasmine they would have a lot of fun. He would enjoy taking her to sporting events, concerts, and plays. But then he would have to compromise when accompanying her to museums, which he found as exciting as watching paint dry. He had a few clients who'd become art collectors with the hope that what they'd acquired would become invaluable. Cameron tended to caution, while not pressuring his clients, to invest conservatively and most of them followed his advice which increased their net worth.

Picking up the remote, he turned on the television, scrolled through the guide until he clicked on the Yankee game. Jasmine walked into the living with large cups of coffee topped with foaming milk. He took both cups from her, waiting until she sat, and then handed her one.

"I can really get used to this," he said as he took the seat beside her.

Jasmine touched her cup to his, smiling. "I expect the same treatment when I come to New Orleans."

Cameron winked at her. "I promise not to disappoint you." He lost track of time as they sat together drinking coffee while watching the game. He draped an arm over Jasmine's shoulders and let out an inaudible breath when she did not pull away.

Jasmine smothered a yawn. "Coffee at night always makes me sleepy, so forgive me if I fall asleep on you."

Cameron kissed her hair. "There's no need to apologize. After all, I fell asleep during the drive to Long Island."

"That's different. You're my guest."

"I thought I was your boyfriend. At least that's what your aunt and uncle called me."

Jasmine shifted slightly. "That's because I didn't tell them I was bringing a man with me and they just assumed we were a couple."

Cameron stopped himself before asking her if they would ever become a couple—if she was someone with whom he could have a comfortable ongoing relationship. "I would probably assume the same," he said instead. "It's getting late and you need your sleep." Cameron stood, gently easing Jasmine to stand. Standing in her bare feet, the top of her head barely reached his nose.

"What time are you picking up me tomorrow?"

"Six. The boat sails at seven, so I'd like us to be there before six-thirty."

Jasmine massaged the back of her neck. "I'll be ready. Do you want me to call down to the lobby and have the doorman hail a taxi for you?"

Cameron cradled her face in his hands, his eyes moving slowly over her features as if committing them to memory. "Don't bother. The weather's nice, so I'll probably walk back to the hotel."

"Be careful."

Lowering his head, he brushed a light kiss over her

mouth. "I will." He kissed her again, this time a little longer. "I really enjoyed today."

"I'm glad, because I did, too."

"I'll help you clean up before I leave."

Jasmine pulled his hands away from her face, and looped her arm through his. "There's nothing to clean up except to put cups in the dishwasher. Come. I'll walk you to the door."

Cameron sat on the chair in the entryway and put on his shoes. Walking back to the hotel would give him time to sort out his feelings for a woman who had him counting down the time until he would see her again.

He rose to his feet when Jasmine opened the door. "Good night, sweets."

Going on tiptoe, she kissed his cheek. "Good night."

Cameron took the elevator to the building lobby and walked out into the warm night. He made his way down Second Avenue and then toward Columbus Circle. Instead of meeting his frat brothers and their significant others for a scheduled gab session in the hotel bar, he wanted to take a shower and just hang out in his room. He managed to make it to his room without encountering anyone in his group and hung the DO NOT DISTURB placard on the doorknob.

The day had been one where he had experienced a gamut of emotions: impatience when he stood outside the hotel waiting for Jasmine to arrive; surprise once she revealed they were going to spend the day on Long Island; uneasiness when meeting her aunt and uncle because he wasn't certain how they would react to him; pleasantly surprised that he and Keith had bonded so quickly during their tour of the winery; shock and horror once Jasmine revealed the details of her failed marriage; and the unfamiliar feeling of an awakened sense of himself and his rightful place and purpose in the world.

Walking into Jasmine's apartment was akin to entering an ethereal garden that calmed a restlessness he had denied for years. She admitted to redecorating the space in an attempt to discard everything that reminded her of her ex-husband, and begin anew. She had been betrayed by a man she loved and trusted, while he'd denied her the prospect of having his child. It was apparent her ex had underestimated her, because Jasmine possessed an inner strength that belied her physical fragility.

Cameron had told himself he didn't need a woman for other than occasional companionship, but knew that was a lie. He had convinced himself that he did not miss fathering children, but was aware that was also a falsehood. Whenever he interacted with his nieces and nephews he was the funny, indulgent Uncle Cam whose intent was to listen to their complaints and give them whatever they wanted despite their parents' objections.

Within minutes of seeing Jasmine to her door after their dinner at Cipriani Club 55, he had asked himself what it was about Jasmine that made her different from other women. It wasn't until he saw her again that he realized it was not only her beauty that attracted him but also her intellect. She was well-spoken and her interests were varied. He wondered if they'd met ten years ago, would she have changed his views about marriage.

Stripping off his clothes, he left them in the bag for hotel laundry. Walking on bare feet, he entered the bathroom, brushed his teeth, and showered. Cameron patted his body dry and returned to the bedroom. Normally he would've sat up watching late-night talk shows or encores of baseball and basketball games, but this night was different. He got into bed and turned off the bedside lamp. His last thoughts before Morpheus claimed him were of a slender woman with a golden-brown complexion, raven-black hair, and a sensual mouth he had barely tasted when he had wanted to devour.

Jasmine had just slipped into her dress when she registered the distinctive buzzing of the intercom. She glanced at the clock on the bedside table. It was ten minutes before six. Walking across the bedroom, she tapped a button, and then closed the hidden zipper.

"Yes."

"Ms. Washington, there's a Mr. Singleton here to see you," came the voice through the speaker.

"Please send him up."

She returned to the sitting room, slipped her feet into a pair of black, silk-covered peep-toe stilettoes, and then picked up a matching cashmere shawl and small evening bag covered with bugle beads. Jasmine opened the bag to make certain she hadn't forgotten her keys and made her way to the door.

She had gotten up earlier that morning and stopped at a neighborhood coffee shop for breakfast, then made it to the nail salon for her scheduled mani-pedi and facial. She had arrived early for her hair appointment but fortunately her stylist had a cancellation and was able to take her. Jasmine walked out ninety minutes later with her hair shampooed, deep-conditioned, set, and blown out before being brushed off her face and pinned into a chic chignon.

After returning home, Jasmine took a bath in lieu of a shower because she did not want to cover her coiffed hair with a plastic cap, and afterwards devoted an inordinate amount of time to meticulously applying makeup. The last time she had attended a formal affair Hannah had arranged for professional artists to make up the faces of her bridal party.

Nydia had complimented Jasmine's fabulous taste in clothes, but what her friend didn't know was that it had come from her being an older man's companion. Her involvement with Gregory had thrust Jasmine into a revolving door of formal dinner parties, fundraisers, gallery openings, fashion shows, and art auctions—some of which required formal attire. Gregory paid for her clothes, hair, makeup, and jewelry. He also acquainted her with potential clients, while introducing her to them as his protégée. Jasmine later realized she'd been naïve because she believed no one knew she and Gregory were lovers, and when questioned as to their association she was quick to explain that he was her mentor.

There was a soft knock on the door; she opened it and for a brief moment she held her breath. Cameron stood there, resplendent in a slim-cut tuxedo, with a stark-white spread collar shirt and black-and-red striped silk tie fashioned into a Windsor knot. His tawny-brown thick hair was cut in precise layered strands, while his tanned face shimmered from a close shave.

A slow smile parted her vermilion-colored lips. "You look very nice."

Cameron stared at Jasmine like a deer in the blinding glare of a vehicle's headlights. He could not believe she could improve on perfection, but she had. His eyes moved slowly from the smoky shadow on her lids to the blood-red color on her lips that was an exact match for the lace sheath dress hugging the curves of her slender body; and then down to the black silk obi sash accentuating her tiny waist; and finally to her feet in the sexy heels. The red color on her mouth, fingers, and toes illuminated the yellow undertones in her golden-brown complexion.

He blinked slowly. "How . . . how did you know?" Cameron stuttered.

Jasmine looked up at him under lowered lashes. "Know what?"

"That my fraternity colors are black and red."

"I had no way of knowing that. I'd bought this dress several months ago, and decided to wear it tonight."

He took a step, bringing them within inches of each other. "I'm glad you did because you're beyond beautiful."

Jasmine lowered her eyes. "Thank you."

Cameron offered her his arm. "Our driver is downstairs."

He waited for Jasmine to lock the door and then escorted her to the elevator. Everything about her screamed feminine and sexy. A generous slit in the front of the high-neck, sleeveless dress revealed an expanse of smooth bare leg from ankle to knee with each step. The overhead lights in the elevator reflected off the jeweled hairpins in the elaborate twist on the nape of her neck, and the ruby and diamond studs in her ears.

"You're staring, Cameron," Jasmine said accusingly.

"That's because I have something to stare at," he countered. "Does my staring make you uncomfortable?"

"A little," she admitted.

"I'm willing to bet that I won't be the only man staring at you tonight."

Jasmine's eyebrows lifted. "And that won't bother you?"

A sardonic smile parted Cameron's lips. "Hell no, because I know you'll be leaving with me. Does that answer your question?"

She nodded. "Yes it does."

The elevator arrived at the lobby and when the doors opened Cameron held her hand as they walked out of the building and to the town car parked at the curb. The driver, who'd been leaning against the car, moved quickly to open the rear door. Lifting the skirt of her dress, Jasmine got in as Cameron removed his jacket, handed it to the driver. She moved over to her left when he slipped in to sit beside her.

"Once everyone arrives, there will be introductions. Do you want me to identify you as an interior decorator or HR manager?"

Jasmine met his eyes. "Interior decorator will do. What's on the program?"

Cameron rested his hand over hers, his thumb caressing her fingers. Everything about Jasmine seeped into him: the hypnotic scent of her perfume, the warm silkiness of her skin, and velvety timbre of her voice. "We begin with a cocktail hour with hors d'oeuvres. That's followed by a sit-down dinner that will last for a couple of hours. We always have a deejay and live band for dancing, and this year the planning committee added a stand-up comic for entertainment. We always have an open bar which will occasionally lead to overindulgence, but that's not a problem because our drivers will be at the pier when the boat docks tomorrow morning. And those who're still able to stand upright will be served a buffet breakfast."

"I can't believe you party for twelve continuous hours."

Cameron dropped a kiss on Jasmine's flower-scented hair. "I have to admit we're getting a little long in the tooth when it comes to the number of activities we try to cram into a week. I've suggested we go to a tropical island resort and kick back. We still can meet in May and avoid hurricane season."

"Why aren't you on the planning committee?" Jasmine asked.

"We rotate, and my turn isn't coming up again for another two years."

"Are all of your frat brothers in finance?"

"Just about all of them are involved in a field where they use math."

"Did you always want to be a money manager?"

"Yes, only because I knew I had a position waiting for me in my family's company. But there had been a time when I thought about becoming a veterinarian."

"Then you'd be Dr. Singleton, DVM."

Cameron chuckled softly. "My life would've been very different if I was Dr. Singleton, because I doubt whether I would've met you."

"You can't say that, Cameron."

"Why?"

"Because I believe everything is predestined. People come into our lives for a reason. Some stay long enough to help shape our future and others are just passing through. If I hadn't worked with Hannah, then we never would've met. Meanwhile you'd met Hannah when you were just a teenager. Even if you hadn't joined your father's company you still would've had a connection with her."

"So, you believe in destiny?"

"I do," Jasmine said quickly.

"What does destiny say about us?" he whispered in her ear.

Jasmine pressed her shoulder to his. "It says I'm going to decorate your new home."

Cameron stared at her, complete surprise freezing his features. "When did you decide this?"

"What happened to *thank you, Jasmine*?" she drawled.

"Thank you, Jasmine," he repeated. "But—"

"Please let it go, Cameron," Jasmine said, cutting him off.

"Okay."

She was right. He didn't need to know why she'd agreed to decorate his home. What mattered was he would get to see Jasmine for an extended period of time. The anxiety he'd felt when she made the toast at Cipriani Club 55 about their parting had temporarily shattered his confidence until she reminded him they'd parted when she returned to New York following Hannah's wedding.

Jasmine had him occasionally second-guessing himself and suddenly it became clear. She was the first woman with whom he wasn't as confident as with others in the past. In other relationships, he had been the one to control or steer things in the direction he wanted to go, but not with Jasmine. Both had agreed they weren't looking for marriage. However, he was the one contemplating a relationship when he suspected it wasn't the same for her. And Cameron knew he had to bide his time and not put any pressure on her, allowing her to take the lead. She had been deceived by a man she loved and married and that meant she now had zero trust when it came to the opposite sex. His musings ended when the driver stopped at Chelsea Piers. He spotted several of his frat brothers getting out of town cars and walking with their wives toward the moored yacht.

His driver opened the rear door and handed him his jacket. Cameron extended his hand to Jasmine and gently assisted her out of the vehicle as sunlight glinted off the precious stones in her ears. He slipped on his jacket, and then curved an arm around her waist. Her heels added an additional four inches to her height.

Cameron pressed his mouth to her ear. "I forgot to tell you that you look incredibly beautiful."

Jasmine lowered her eyes and gave him a demure smile. "Thank you."

Chapter 8

Jasmine wanted to tell Cameron that she felt beautiful—inside and out. It had been too long since she'd attended a formal event with a man, and she was glad she'd waited for a man as urbane as Cameron to fill the void. After Gregory passed away she found that she was no longer a part of the social circle in which he had been a principal player. And she'd discovered Raymond felt uncomfortable attending events whether large or intimate, so most times she went alone. The only time he'd accompanied her to a Wakefield Hamilton Christmas party he stood off to the side, refusing to interact with her coworkers.

Once they were home, he claimed he had no use for her pretentious friends whose fathers donated enormous sums for their children to attend the best colleges. It was then that she realized he resented anyone with a college education. Despite coming from a middle-class family, Raymond had been denied attending university to become an architect because of his father's pressure for him to join the family import/export business. Once his father died, Raymond relinquished his share of the company to his uncles and his ultimate goal was to leave the Philippines.

She chided herself for conjuring up memories of Raymond when she wanted to enjoy her time with the man holding her to his side. Perhaps it had something to do with her talking to Cameron about the details of her failed marriage. She made a mental promise to herself that it would be last time she would allow Raymond to become a part of her consciousness. Since meeting Cameron she had turned a page on her life and wanted only good things and good memories for her future.

"It's a beautiful night for sailing on the river," she said as Cameron assisted her up the gangplank and into the luxuriously appointed yacht, as New Age music filled the cabin from hidden speakers. The evening temperatures were in the mid-seventies with a cool breeze coming off the water.

His fingers tightened slightly at her waist. "It couldn't be better."

A young woman, dressed in black slacks and jacket, a white shirt, and a black tie, greeted them. "Welcome aboard. Your name, sir."

"Singleton."

She checked the name off on the typed sheet on the clipboard. "Mr. Singleton, you and your guest are assigned to table 4. Once you're inside someone will escort you to your table."

Cameron nodded. "Thank you. Let's go, sweets," he whispered in Jasmine's ear. "I hope you're ready to party like it's 1999. Why are you looking at me like that?" he asked when she shook her head.

"Prince, Cameron?"

"Yes, Prince. Don't you like his music?"

"Yes, but . . ." Jasmine's words trailed off.

"But what?"

Jasmine scrunched up her nose. "I didn't think he would be someone you'd like."

"Don't try and put me in a box, babe, because I just may shock you."

"I'll try and keep that in mind." Jasmine knew he was warning her not to stereotype him or she would end up with egg on her face.

She and Cameron encountered another crew member who led them to their assigned table. Three other couples were onboard, the men wearing tuxedos with black-and-red striped ties, while their dates had chosen black gowns that revealed an excessive amount of skin. Jasmine didn't know why, but suddenly she felt overdressed.

Round tables on the first deck were arranged night-club-style with seating for two. Centerpieces were oil candles and bud vases with red roses. She placed her purse on the chair and covered it with the shawl at the same time a man with bright blue eyes and thinning red hair spotted Cameron.

"Singleton, where the hell were you this morning? We missed you at brunch."

Cameron gave his former roommate a rough embrace. "I ordered room service." He rested a hand on Philip's shoulder. "I want you to meet my date." He smiled at Jasmine. "Darling, I want you to meet Philip Baxter. Phil and I were roommates and occasionally partners in crime. Phil, Jasmine Washington."

Philip stared boldly at Jasmine before extending his hand, seemingly in slow motion. "Damn! You're beautiful."

Jasmine's smile vanished, apparently stunned by his compliment. Seconds later she recovered and took his hand. "It's a pleasure to meet you, Philip."

Philip kissed the back of her hand. "The pleasure's all mine, and please call me Phil."

"Then Phil it is."

Cameron knew it was time to step in or say something that would spoil the evening for everyone. Phil was a notorious flirt, and apparently it didn't matter to him that he was engaged to marry his fiancée sometime the following year. "Where's your fiancée, Phil?"

He released Jasmine's hand and pointed to the bar. "She's getting a drink."

Cameron stared at the woman slated to become the third Mrs. Philip Baxter. Despite the twenty-year-plus age difference, Tiffany appeared to be very much in love with Phil. "Jasmine and I are going to circulate until everyone gets here."

"Don't forget to save me a dance, Jasmine," Philip called out as Cameron led her over to the railing.

"I'm sorry about Phil. He can be a little overbearing at times."

Jasmine looped her arm over the sleeve of Cameron's jacket. "There's no need to apologize. He's harmless."

"Yeah, right."

"Why would you say that, Cameron?"

"He's so harmless that he's working on his third wife."

Her mouth formed a perfect O. "It sounds like he's really been busy."

Cameron stared across the Hudson River at the New Jersey shoreline. "I love Phil like a brother, but he's always been an incorrigible flirt when it comes to women."

"Can you answer one question for me, Cameron?"

He gave Jasmine a sidelong glance, silently admiring her delicate profile. Phil was right. She was beautiful. "Only one?" he teased.

"Right now, yes. Why did you call me darling?"

Cameron turned and stared directly at her. "I did?"

"Yes you did."

He blinked slowly. "If I did, then it was the slip of the tongue. You don't believe me, do you?" he asked when she gave him a questioning look. A hint of a smile parted her sensual mouth. Cameron winked at her. "I guess you got me."

She leaned closer. "Yes, I did and I know you did it because you were marking your territory."

Cameron traced her hairline with his finger. "You're very perceptive. I don't think I'm going to get away with much with you."

Her fingers curled around his hand. "Why would you want to, *darling*? We're both over forty, and too old to play head games."

He froze. "You're over forty?"

"Yes. How old did you think I was?"

"Thirty-four or maybe even thirty-five."

"I'm forty-two," she whispered. "And before you ask, I'll celebrate my forty-third birthday next week."

"Damn!" he drawled. "Have you found the fountain of youth?"

Jasmine pressed her lips together to smother a giggle. "Don't you know good black don't crack?"

Cameron stared at Jasmine, and then burst out laughing. He splayed a hand over her back as the warmth from her body seeped into his palm. "I suppose I know now."

The number of voices escalated as more people came onboard. Moments later the blasts from the ship's horn sounded, followed by the voice of the captain announcing the crew was preparing the boat to set sail.

"Come with me, *darling.* I want to introduce you to the others."

Jasmine wanted to remind Cameron that he had called her darling again but then changed her mind. He'd called her sweets, and now darling and perhaps they were terms of endearment he was used to saying to women with whom he had been involved. She recalled her grandmother saying not to make a mountain out of a molehill because the argument wasn't worth the effort it took to get upset and it could possibly lead to ending a friendship. Jasmine smiled when she noticed that she wasn't the only woman wearing red.

Dozens of eyes were directed at her as Cameron held her waist. "I'd like everyone to meet Jasmine Washington. Darling, this motley crew wearing the striped ties are my fraternity brothers, and the beautiful women standing beside them are definitely their better halves."

One by one the men shook her hand, while their wives exchanged pleasantries. One woman gave her a critical stare. "Aren't you the interior decorator who used to work with Gregory Carson?"

Jasmine did not want to believe that someone had recognized her. After all, it had been twenty years since she had been Gregory's constant companion. "Yes."

The woman's eyes widened. "I thought I recognized you from somewhere. I used to be a cataloguer for one of the auction houses that sold a few pieces of Gregory's art collection. I'd come to his loft to view the collection, and that's when he introduced me to you as his *protégée*."

"I'm sorry, but I don't recall meeting you."

"That's because there were so many people there that night. I later discovered that Christie's sold the remaining pieces in his collection, with the exception of one. Do you have any idea who owns Pembroke's painting of his mistress Sebastiane?"

Jasmine noticed everyone hanging on to the woman's every word. "I'm sorry I don't," she lied smoothly.

She knew the painting was in the private collection of a reclusive billionaire, whose estate upon his death would donate it to MoMA. Her explanation seemed to satisfy the inquisitive woman, who accepted a flute of champagne from a waiter as the yacht pulled away from the dock. Within minutes waiters were circulating with flutes of champagne and trays of hot and cold hors d'oeuvres.

"That was quite an inquisition," Cameron said in a quiet voice.

Jasmine met his eyes over the rim of her flute. "I didn't expect to meet someone from my past," she said just before taking a sip.

Cameron held his flute, his gaze boring into her. "What was she implying when she said protégée?"

She leaned in close to him. "Let's go to our table and I'll tell you." There was enough activity for her to talk quietly to Cameron without being overheard. He escorted her to their table, pulled out a chair, and then moved the chair with her shawl and evening bag close. He placed the shawl over the back of his chair and set her purse on the table.

"He was your lover."

Jasmine turned to look at him, their noses only inches apart. "How did you know?" she whispered.

Cameron pressed a kiss on the bridge of her nose. "I don't know who Gregory Carson is or was, but Danielle looked like the cat that had swallowed the canary when she realized your connection with the man."

"He was not only my lover, but the first man I'd ever slept with." Jasmine did not know why, but she had spent the past two days revealing personal details of her life to Cameron when it hadn't been that way with others she knew. Perhaps it was because she felt she could trust him, or maybe she knew he wouldn't be judgmental.

"I take it he was much older than you?"

She nodded. "I was nineteen and he was fifty-four when I met him for the first time. He had been married twice and divorced, and was a grandfather many times. Gregory was an incredibly talented decorator who'd decorated the homes of A-list movie stars and captains of industry. Many of his interiors appeared in *Home Beautiful* and *Architectural Digest*."

"How did you meet him?"

"A professor invited him to one of my classes to judge our projects. That's when he slipped me his card and told me to call him. At first I thought he was trying to hit on me, so I threw the card away. A couple of months later he showed up at my class and asked to speak to me. When he asked why I hadn't called I told him the truth, and that's when he said he wasn't interested in sleeping with a girl younger than his daughter. He said he was impressed with my project and wanted me to work with him so he could help me develop my talent.

"I worked with him whenever I didn't have classes or when he wasn't traveling and I learned more from him in six months than I did in four years of classes. Once I graduated I became his apprentice and soon after that we began sleeping together. Meanwhile he'd begun referring clients to me and I was able to save enough to start up my own company. He'd also set up an account at a Madison Avenue boutique for me to shop whenever I needed something to wear to accompany him for a formal event."

"Did you ever think of him as your sugar daddy?" Cameron questioned.

Jasmine shook her head. "Never. He helped me professionally and I returned the favor when I became his escort because he'd tired of taking out a revolving door of women. I was still living at home at the time and when I told him I was thinking of moving into Manhattan he urged me to buy a co-op or condo. Of course I didn't have the money for either, so he co-signed for the loan for the down payment, and I only accepted his offer if he agreed to let me pay him back.

"After being handed the keys to the unit we went out to celebrate at his favorite restaurant. I never got to pay him back because two months later he died in his sleep from natural causes. I was devastated losing my mentor and it took me a while before I could even think about becoming involved with another man."

"But you did, darling," Cameron reminded her.

Her eyelids fluttered wildly. "Yes I did and much to my detriment."

"If we don't meet the bad ones, then we'd never recognize the good ones when they come our way."

Jasmine stared at the light-blue orbs shimmering like polished topaz. "You're right about that." She paused. "Are you one of the good ones, Cameron?"

He lowered his eyes. "That all depends on who you talk to. I've never mistreated or taken advantage of a woman, so hopefully I'd like to believe that will put me in the good guy category."

She smiled. "It does."

Her feelings for Cameron were changing so quickly that Jasmine couldn't explain them away. Everything about him was a turn-on from his exquisite grooming to his impeccable manners, while his overt masculinity wrapped around her like a cocoon from which she did not want to escape. In that instant she wanted to experience making love with Cameron.

"Thank you."

"There's no need to thank me. You are who you are and that's enough for me."

Cameron put the flute to his mouth and drained it. Jasmine pushed back her chair. "Let's circulate because I don't want your friends to think I'm antisocial."

Cameron rose with her, cupping her elbow. "It really doesn't matter what they think, because it will be another year before I'll get to see them again."

"Aren't you invited to Philip's wedding?"

"I'm sure I'll get an invitation once they set a date. I'll be right back. I'm going to get a glass of water from the bar."

Jasmine watched him make his way to the bar, and then turned around when someone tapped her on the shoulder. She smiled at a petite blonde woman wearing a black dress with a plunging neckline. Each time she inhaled it appeared as if her breasts would escape the revealing décolletage. The skin on her face was so smooth, so tight, it was impossible to pinpoint her age.

"Yes?"

"Jasmine, my name is Cindy. May I ask you a question?"

"Of course."

"I'd like to know where you got your dress." Jasmine gave her the name of the Madison Avenue boutique where Gregory had first set up an account for her. "I was looking for a lace dress like yours, because right now it's all the rage, but unfortunately I couldn't find anything in my size," Cindy continued. She cradled her chest in her hands. "My boobs are too big, and if I bought a larger size it would fit my chest but not my hips. Luckily you have just enough." She let go of her breasts and touched Jasmine's, causing her to take a step backward. "By the way you have a fabulous body. Were you ever nipped or tucked?"

Jasmine stared at the woman as if she had lost her mind. She didn't want to believe she was being hit on. "No!" She glanced around for Cameron and found him talking to Philip and another man. Without warning, he turned in her direction and she silently implored him to rescue her. She exhaled an inaudible breath with his approach.

He kissed her hair. "What's the matter, darling?"

"Can you help me to our table? I'm slightly woozy from the champagne."

Cameron's arm went around her waist as he led her away from the chatty woman. "Did she try to seduce you?"

Her head popped up as she stared at him in astonishment. "You know?"

"It's a fact that Cindy and her husband have an open marriage and engage in threesomes. So when I saw your face I figured she had propositioned you."

"I didn't give her the chance, especially after she touched my breast. She had one more time to touch me inappropriately and I would've invited her to the restroom and beat the living hell out of her." Her jaw tightened in frustration. "These are your friends, Cameron, and I don't want to embarrass you."

Cameron shook his head. "You won't because I have your back. I just can't believe Cindy's getting that bold."

"Why me, Cameron?"

"Everyone knows about Cindy. She probably tried to seduce you because you're the only newbie here."

Jasmine made a sucking sound with her tongue and teeth. "*If* I was going to sleep with anyone tonight, then it would be you, and not some woman or her husband."

Cameron stared at Jasmine, complete shock freezing his features. He did not want to read more into Jasmine's revelation than necessary. He knew she was upset about Cindy coming onto her, and blamed himself for not warning her. However, he loathed gossip and avoided it whenever necessary. His frat brothers weren't perfect, but they were his only link to the time when he'd gone from boyhood to manhood. He refused to comment when asked if he liked or approved of the women they'd selected as their wives or girlfriends.

Dropping an arm over her shoulders, he pulled her close. "You don't have to sleep with anyone you don't want to. And that includes me."

A mysterious smile softened Jasmine's mouth. "But, what if I want to?" she whispered. "I don't know what it is about us, but I feel as if I've known you for months instead of days. I've revealed things to you that took me years to admit to others, and that includes my family. I'd been sleeping with Gregory for almost two years before I told Danita about our relationship. She was a little upset because she thought he was taking advantage of my inexperience with men, and I had to remind her that I never would have had as much success in my career without his influence and assistance."

"What about your parents?"

"They didn't ask and I never told them even though I was certain they knew. I suppose they were in denial because they did not want to believe their young daughter was involved with a man old enough to be her father. Gregory and I never flaunted our relationship. We'd arrive and leave an affair in different cars, he'd always greet me with a kiss on both cheeks, and at no time did we ever hold hands or embrace each other while in public. And after Gregory died and I'd begun a long-distance relationship with my ex, my parents were ecstatic because I'd talked about getting married and having a family. I didn't realize until years later that Raymond was angry with me because I'd never told him how at the age of twenty-five I was able to buy a condo, have a closet filled with designer clothes, and own several priceless jewels. He also did not like the friends I'd made when Gregory was alive, and he was bitter that he hadn't gone to university. I suppose that's why he took up with a woman who hadn't graduated high school, because it allowed him to feel superior to her."

Cameron wanted to tell Jasmine she had chosen badly when she married a man who should've lauded her successes instead of trying to demean her. He had walked into her life to share in an established company where he did not have to struggle to make a go of it. "How long were you married to that clown?"

"Twelve years."

"That's a long time."

"When I look back it doesn't seem that long," Jasmine said reflectively. She smiled up at Cameron. "Let's make this the last time we talk about the clown, because the circus left town three years ago and it's never coming back."

Cameron brushed his mouth over hers in a barely there kiss. He did want to make love with Jasmine, although he hadn't made any overt overtures that he wanted to share her bed. And knowing she did not trust men because of an unfaithful husband had put Cameron on notice that if they were to make love then it would have to be her choice to initiate the act, and not his.

"I pray never to hurt you physically or emotionally," he said against her parted lips.

Jasmine's eyelids fluttered wildly. "You won't because I'd never allow it."

Lines fanned out around Cameron's eyes when he smiled. "I know that now."

* * *

Jasmine knew she'd drunk too much wine when she slowly navigated the stairs leading to the restrooms below deck. The ship's chefs had prepared dishes rivaling those served in Michelin five-star restaurants. Guests were given a choice of filet mignon, lemon and garlic roasted Cornish hen, seared beef tenderloin with cilantro and mint, rack of lamb, seared fresh tuna, or a crab, avocado, and grapefruit salad with chive vinaigrette along with an assortment of side dishes. The wait staff kept the wine glasses filled as they moved silently and efficiently around the deck seeing to everyone's needs.

The bathrooms were labeled for both men and women, and when the door opened she came face-to-face with Danielle. A noticeable flush suffused the other woman's face when she saw Jasmine. "I'm sorry I said what I said earlier tonight about you and Gregory Carson."

Jasmine smiled, trying to put the flustered woman at ease. "You didn't say anything wrong."

"Are you sure?"

"I'm very sure, Danielle."

The slightly plump woman with short highlighted dark hair exhaled an audible breath. "I thought I'd made a faux pas when I saw Cameron's face. Was he angry that I'd mentioned Gregory's name?"

"No. He didn't know Gregory."

Danielle leaned closer like a coconspirator. "You didn't tell him you and Gregory had had an affair?"

Jasmine bit her tongue to keep from telling Danielle to mind her own damn business. "What goes on between Cameron and me stays between us."

Danielle recoiled as if she had been slapped. "I'm sorry."

Suddenly she felt sorry for her sharp retort. "No, I'm sorry I snapped at you."

"I'm going to say one more thing, and then I'm going back upstairs. I know I sound biased, but aside from my husband, Cameron is the best of this bunch because he's a true Southern gentleman. It's been a few years since he's brought a woman with him, so you must be very special. And if I were you I'd hang on tight to him."

"Thanks for the advice," Jasmine said, as she walked into the bathroom, closing and locking the door behind her. She didn't need anyone to tell her that Cameron was the quintessential Southern gentleman. He reminded her of her father and how he related to her mother. Even after so many years Richard Washington continued to help his wife sit or stand. There was never a time when he didn't help Marta into or out of a car. It was what her grandmother called good home training, and Cameron had shown he had the best manners possible.

She took special care to hike up the skirt of the lined lace gown to avoid tearing the fragile fabric. Jasmine had made certain not to wear a ring or bracelet which could possibly snag the material. Three minutes later she stared at her reflection in the mirror as she washed her hands, recalling her conversation with Cameron when he admitted he was quite comfortable attending an affair unescorted. Reaching for a hand towel on a stack, she noticed several small hand-painted glazed pots filled with feminine products and another with condoms.

A knowing smile parted her lips when she remembered Nydia's declaration: *The man's going to put some-*

thing on you that will rock your world. Reaching into the pot with the condoms, Jasmine slipped two into her evening purse. "No, *mija,* I'm going to rock his world," she whispered under her breath although there was no one to overhear her.

It had been almost three years since she'd slept with a man, and she knew if or when she shared her bed with Cameron that only then would she be able to put her past behind her. Her footsteps were light as she climbed the staircase to the first deck. The crew was clearing away the remains of dinner as everyone went upstairs to the upper deck to listen to music and dance under the stars.

She found Cameron waiting for her, his eyes appearing even lighter blue in his deeply tanned face. Reaching into his pocket, he handed her a pair of black ankle socks with red gripper soles and stamped with the fraternity's Greek letters.

"They give these to all the ladies who eventually will shed their shoes once the dancing begins."

"These are adorable."

Cameron grasped her hand. "It boggles my mind that you women can stand for hours in heels that resemble stilts."

"It's takes practice, darling." Jasmine made her way up the staircase, Cameron following. She stood on the top deck, staring up at the sky. The ship had left New York City behind and without the city lights the stars seemed brighter and more numerous.

Several couples were dancing, while others had claimed deck chairs. At the far end of the deck, band members were sitting together before taking the stage. Meanwhile a deejay was spinning tunes as a bartender was taking drink orders behind a portable bar. After a glass of champagne and two glasses of wine Jasmine knew she'd reached her quota for alcoholic drinks.

"Do you want something else to drink?" Cameron asked.

She shook her head. "You must have been reading my mind because I just told myself I'm done imbibing for the night."

"It's not even midnight, so the night's not over."

"Maybe I'll wait and have a mimosa for breakfast."

Whenever Jasmine thought of mimosas she recalled the day she, Nydia, and Tonya went to Hannah's Manhattan apartment for the first time. The day had become momentous when four women from very different backgrounds became friends as they talked about new beginnings. Hannah had started over and so had Tonya, yet Jasmine was still second-guessing herself as to her future. She had promised Cameron she would decorate his new home, but she wasn't certain what she would do beyond that. He still hadn't closed on the property, which meant it probably would be months before renovations were completed.

Jasmine knew her original plan to not work the summer months and begin job-hunting after Labor Day would have to be put on hold until after the first of the year. It would become a win-win for her when over the next six months she would divide her time between the Big Apple and the Big Easy.

She recognized Cameron's cologne when he stood behind her. "I'd be honored if you would dance with me."

A shiver of awareness raced through her body when she felt his groin pressed against her hips. It was the same thing he'd said to her at Hannah and St. John's reception.

Intrigued, she'd turned to see who belonged to the drawling male voice, and when she looked into the eyes of the tall tanned man she'd wanted to run in the opposite direction, because the intensity in his steel-blue orbs excited and frightened her at the same time. It was only when he smiled that she was able to take a normal breath.

Jasmine turned around and looped her arms around his neck. "Of course I'll dance with you." She closed her eyes and melted against his lean hard body. It took only seconds for her to identify Alicia Keys singing, "Like You'll Never See Me Again," and she couldn't stop the well of emotion threatening to bring her to tears. Cameron had asked her to dance to a song where lovers weren't certain whether they would see each other again.

Cameron caught her chin, raising her face at the same time his head came down. His mouth took hers in a marauding kiss that stole the breath from her lungs. He increased the pressure and her lips parted under the onslaught. Men had kissed her, but never like this. It was if Cameron wanted to brand her his possession and if they hadn't been on a yacht in the middle of a river with others in attendance, Jasmine would have begged him to strip her naked and make love to her. The kiss ended and she buried her face against his throat. He was breathing as heavily as she was.

One of his hands slid down the length of her back and came to rest on her hip. "What are you doing to me?" he rasped in her ear.

Jasmine swallowed in an attempt to relieve the dryness in her throat when she felt his erection pulsing against her middle. "No more than what you're doing to me," she said breathlessly.

Her breasts felt heavy, the nipples were hard as pebbles. She was as aroused as Cameron. The song ended and they left the dance floor to claim deck chairs. They lay next to each other, both lost in their private thoughts. Jasmine closed her eyes as a breeze whispered over her exposed skin.

When she told Cameron she believed in destiny she wondered if fate had conspired for her to be downsized so she would travel to New Orleans to meet the man who shattered her vow not to become involved again.

Chapter 9

Jasmine lay sprawled over Cameron's body on the rear seat of the town car. "I doubt whether I'll be able to walk upstairs," she slurred.

Cameron grunted softly, not bothering to open his eyes. "Don't worry, babe. I'll carry you."

"It's going to take me a week to recuperate from one night of partying. There was a time when my weekends began on Thursday night and didn't end until Sunday morning. But that was then and this is now."

Cameron opened his eyes and rested his chin on the top of Jasmine's head. "Maybe you need to get out more."

"You're probably right about that. It's a good thing you guys only do this once a year."

"This is going to be the last year for a while. Danny

Morris told me his daughter is expecting his first grand-child, so we won't get together again for five years."

"Are you sure you'll be up to a week of nonstop party-ing when you're fifty-three?"

Cameron buried his face in Jasmine's hair. "I'll have to wait and see. A lot of things can happen in five years."

The ride from the pier to Jasmine's apartment building was accomplished in record time. It was early Sunday morning and vehicular and pedestrian traffic was light. The driver got out and came around to open the door. Cameron alighted, reached into the pocket of his trousers and handed the man a bill. "Thanks for everything."

The driver pocketed the bill, nodding. "Thank you, Mr. Singleton. Call me when you're ready to leave for the airport."

"I will." Cameron used the same car service whenever he came to New York, and always requested the same driver. Turning, he extended his hand to Jasmine. "Let's go, sleepyhead." Jasmine handed him her shoes while she gathered her shawl and purse.

"You don't have to carry me."

He lifted his eyebrows questioningly. "Are you sure?"

She placed her sock-covered feet on the sidewalk. "Yes."

Cameron took her hand, gently easing her to a stand. Everyone had danced, drank, and ate too much and when the yacht finally returned to Chelsea Pier the revelers dis-embarked as if in a trance. Rows of town cars were parked at the curb with drivers holding signs with the names of their passengers. The live band and deejay al-ternated, playing nonstop because the stand-up come-dian's flight from Chicago was canceled, and his routine would've provided a respite from the continuous danc-ing. After sailing three hundred miles up the river to the

Adirondack Mountains, the ship reversed direction. By the time the US Military Academy at West Point came into view, the crew had set up a buffet breakfast on the first deck with an omelet station, flutes of mimosas and Bellinis, chicken and waffles, pancakes, eggs Benedict, bacon, sausage, ham, and steak.

The last two reunions Cameron had come unaccompanied because there wasn't a woman with whom he felt strongly enough about to bring her with him to New York for the week. There were occasions when he embarked on what he thought of as a dating drought. He refused to see anyone and declined invitations to social events to reconnect with his inner self.

Cameron knew many local New Orleanians thought of him as a middle-aged, well-to-do, bachelor from a prominent family who'd earned the reputation of being a womanizer and serial dater, and Cameron said nothing to dispel the myth. He wasn't a womanizer or a serial dater. On average he dated no more than two women in any calendar year, but that did not stop the gossips from exacerbating the fabrication.

He nodded to the liveried doorman standing under the canopy as he escorted Jasmine inside the lobby to the elevators. She punched the button, the doors opened, and they stepped into the car. Cameron wrapped his arms around her body, pulling her close to his chest.

"Are you all right, Cinderella?"

She buried her face against his shoulder. "I can't be Cinderella because she left the ball at midnight."

"If I remember the story correctly, didn't she lose her shoes?"

"Shoe, Cameron. She lost one of her shoes and the prince found it."

Cameron smiled. "That's right. He didn't know who she was and had to search the entire kingdom before he could find the woman who could fit the shoe. He married her and they lived happily ever after."

Jasmine leaned back, meeting his eyes. "Look at you. When did you become an authority on fairytales?"

"I have nieces who are obsessed with fairytales and whenever Uncle Cam babysits them they beg me to read to them because I use different voices for each character."

"Has Uncle Cam thought about auditioning as a narrator for a recorded book?"

Throwing back his head, Cameron laughed. "I don't think so, babe. First I'd have to work with a diction coach to get rid of my drawl."

"I happen to like your drawl," Jasmine said when the elevator stopped at her floor. They exited the car. "You sound like Harry Connick, Jr."

"That's because we're homeboys."

When she opened her bag to take out her keys Cameron saw the condoms that were among other male and female personal items the boating company made available to partygoers. He recalled her statement as clearly as if she'd just said it: *If I was going to sleep with anyone tonight, then it would be you, and not some woman or her husband.* And he remembered she'd stressed *if,* which he interpreted that there was no guarantee she would permit him to make love to her. He didn't want to think of her taking the condoms because she wanted to be prepared to sleep with another man. She'd admitted she hadn't slept with anyone since the breakup of her marriage and Cameron wanted to be the one to introduce her to passion. She unlocked, opened the door, and walked inside, while he waited for her to invite him.

Jasmine turned and stared at him. "Aren't you coming in?"

"Are you inviting me?"

She gave him a stunned look. "Of course I am."

Cameron knew what he was about to say would change their fragile relationship forever. "If I come in, it's not for coffee."

Jasmine blinked slowly as if coming out of a trance. "What is it you want?" Her voice had dropped an octave.

"I want to make love to you."

He had said what he'd felt the first time he saw Jasmine at DuPont House. The physical pull had been so strong that he thought he'd imagined it. It was the only time he could remember that he'd wanted to make love to a woman after a single glance. And over the months since he'd introduced himself to her at the wedding reception, images of her face would pop into his head at the most inopportune times. It was as if he had total recall when he remembered the timbre of her beautiful voice, the scent of her perfume, and the way the light from the chandeliers reflected off her satiny golden-brown skin.

Cameron had told himself over and over he was intrigued with Jasmine because she looked nothing like the women he had dated. Yet his instincts communicated it wasn't only her physical appearance that held him enthralled but her maturity and sophistication. And once she revealed her relationship with a much older man he knew from where she had cultivated the maturity.

Jasmine extended her hand to Cameron. "Please come in and stay." He had made it easy for her not to beg him to make love to her. She'd spent days since sharing dinner with him telling herself that there was no way she was going to sleep with Cameron, but he had proven her wrong. Each time she encountered his longing stares, or the gentle touch of his hands on her body she knew she could not remain unaffected. When they'd shared their first dance on the boat she'd believed she was going to pass out from the swirling passion threatening to swallow her whole. Cameron wanted to know what she was doing to him; well, she had the same question. It had taken less than a week for him to scale and break down the wall she had put up to keep all men out of her life and bed.

She didn't know what road her life would take once she slept with Cameron because in that instant she was past caring. They could continue to be friends with benefits or revert to friends until after she completed decorating his new home.

Cameron's impassive expression did not change when he walked into the entryway. He closed and locked the door behind him. "I have protection with me," he said, reaching into his pocket and withdrawing several condoms.

Jasmine giggled like a little girl. She opened her evening purse and took out the condoms she had taken from the yacht's restroom. "I beat you to it."

Shrugging out of his jacket, Cameron placed it over the back of the chair. "So, you'd planned to seduce me?" he teased.

"No," she said innocently. "I'd planned for you to seduce me so you wouldn't brag to your buddies that I jumped your bones first."

His expression changed, becoming a mask of stone. "I never kiss and tell. Whatever we do or share stays between us."

Jasmine felt properly chastised. No matter how much someone badgered Gregory about his relationship with her, he refused to reveal anything beyond she was his protégée, and let them draw their own conclusions as to why he was always seen at public events with a much younger woman. "I agree. I'm going to give you a toothbrush and towels if you want to shower. You'll find a supply of toiletries in the vanity drawer if you need them."

"Thank you."

She went into the bathroom and selected a cellophane-wrapped toothbrush from a supply she kept for overnight guests. Opening a narrow closet, she took out towels and an oversized bathrobe from a stack. Her aunt had ordered bathrobes for B & B guests who'd forgotten theirs, but when the supplier shipped monogrammed seersucker robes rather than terrycloth, Jasmine had become the recipient of nearly a dozen bathrobes in various sizes.

Jasmine emerged from the bathroom to find Cameron sitting on the chair. "You can use this bathroom. I'm going to use the one in my bedroom because I need to take off my makeup."

Cameron stared at the gentle sway of her hips in the red dress until she disappeared from his line of sight, and then emptied his pockets. He placed the condoms, a small leather case with his driver's license and several credit cards, on the table. A money clip followed, and then the keycard to his hotel room. He undressed, leaving his clothes folded neatly on the chair, and walked into the bathroom.

He brushed his teeth and rinsed his mouth with mouth-wash, before walking into the open shower with an over-sized showerhead. The warm water sluicing over his head and body revived him as he shampooed his hair from the bottle on a shelf in the shower.

Jasmine had mentioned her friends occasionally slept over and it was apparent she was the perfect hostess because she had items on hand one would request at a hotel. His masculine pride had increased tenfold when a few of his frat brothers complimented him about his date. Several went so far as to say his taste was definitely improving and they were waiting for him to send them invitations to his wedding. Cameron had remained mute to that comment because even if he changed his stance when it came to marriage, Jasmine was adamant about not marrying again. Both were mature adults who were in control of their lives, and they had made it known to each other that their futures did not include marriage.

Cameron left the bathroom, retrieved the condoms, pushing them into the pocket of the robe, and walked in the direction of Jasmine's bedroom. The first time he'd come to her home she hadn't shown him her bedroom, and he surmised that it was her sanctuary and one had to be invited in. She had also confirmed that she had redecorated the entire apartment, which meant she wanted to rid herself of everything that had reminded her of her éx.

He slowly entered the bedroom, his eyes taking in everything with a single glance. Seeing the four-poster antique spindle bed draped in a sheer white fabric told him Jasmine was a romantic. Candles in various colors and sizes competed for space on the table in the sitting area. A club chair, covered in pale-blue watered silk, a woven basket filled with magazines, and another with books indicated the area where she spent her time reading. His gaze went back to the queen-size bed covered with what appeared to be antique white and off-white linens.

Walking over to the window, he closed the lined drapes to shut out the brilliant sunlight flooding the bedroom that contained a wall-mounted television, mahogany armoire, and matching dresser and chest of drawers. He sat down on the chair to wait for her to emerge from the en suite bathroom.

He didn't have long to wait when she walked into the bedroom wearing a delicate pale-blue nightgown ending at her knees. Cameron rose to his feet, unable to pull his eyes away from the damp hair falling around her face. He closed the distance between them and cradled her face.

Staring down into the dark-brown eyes looking up at him, he saw a glimpse of indecision and Cameron wondered if she was experiencing some apprehension about agreeing to let him make love to her. "What is it, darling?"

Jasmine's lower lip trembled slightly before she pulled it between her teeth. "Nothing," she mumbled.

Cameron shook his head. "Tell me if you really want me to make love to you? If not, then we'll get into bed together and go to sleep."

She released her lip. "No. What I mean is I want us to make love."

He lifted his eyebrows. "Are you sure?"

She smiled for the first time. Jasmine went on tiptoe and pressed her breasts to his chest. "Yes. I'm very, very sure."

Cameron lowered his hands and divested her of the

nightgown, unable to believe her clothes had concealed such a lush body. Lowering his head, Cameron trailed kisses along the column of her neck, the hollow in her throat, while the lingering scent of her body wash wafted to his nostrils.

Bending slightly, he picked her up and placed her on the bed, his body following hers down to the firm mattress. His erection was so hard it was painful, yet he knew he had to go slow because Jasmine had been celibate for a long time. His hands and mouth charted every inch of her body like a blind sculptor who wanted to commit it to his memory. Cameron tasted her skin, inhaled her fragrance, and felt himself transported to another time and space where everything ceased to exist with the exception of the woman whose soft moans and writhing threatened to have him ejaculate before he was inside her. He had wanted Jasmine for so long that he could not remember when he did not want her.

He found the condom in the pocket of the robe and tore the packet with his teeth, and then slipped the latex sheath over his tumescence. After pausing to take off the robe, he held his erection in one hand as he leaned over Jasmine. Her eyes were closed as her breasts rose and fell with every breath.

"Look at me, babe," he crooned. She complied and opened her eyes. Cameron gave her a gentle smile. He wanted to see her face when they ceased to exist as separate entities. "I'll try not to hurt you."

Jasmine felt as if someone had touched her body with a lighted match. She was hot all over, the area between thighs throbbing with a need that had to be assuaged before she screamed at Cameron to take her and end the sensual torture.

"Stop talking and make love to me," she whispered hoarsely. Seconds later, she gasped when she felt the pressure of Cameron's penis as he pushed inside her. A small cry escaped her parted lips when her celibate flesh stretched to take all of him. Either she was too small or he was larger than the other two men she'd slept with.

It had taken less than ten seconds, but to Jasmine it felt like ten minutes, before her flesh yielded to the length and girth of his erection. The discomfort ended, replaced by pleasure she had long forgotten. Cameron's hot breath in her ear and the soft groans coming from his throat turned her on as she rose off the bed to meet his measured thrusting. If she'd had to wait to make love with a man, then she was grateful that man was the one inside her. She gloried in the hard body atop hers, his swollen flesh sliding in and out of her wetness. A shiver of ecstasy washed over her, a moan slipping past her lips as she felt ready to climax. Finally letting go, her first orgasm took over, holding Jasmine captive before another Earth-shattering release rocked through her core, taking her straight to heaven.

Cameron took a deep breath, held it, and then let it out slowly as he tried not to ejaculate. He wanted this moment before taking his own pleasure. However, he could not stave off the inevitable as he surrendered to sensations shaking him from head to toe. What he'd just shared with Jasmine went beyond lovemaking. He had wanted Jasmine for so long that he could not remember when he did not want her, and now that he had her he knew it wasn't as much lovemaking as a raw act of possession. The runaway beating of his heart slowed to a normal rhythm and, reluctantly he pulled out of her warm, wet body and slipped out of bed to discard the condom in the bathroom. He returned to the bed and lay beside Jasmine, rested an arm over his face, and then turned over and pulled her to his side.

He kissed her moist forehead. "You were incredible."

Jasmine rested her leg over his as she snuggled closer. "So were you. I'm glad I waited."

Cameron knew she was referring to their making love. "That goes double for me."

He was glad Jasmine had waited for him to reintroduce her to passion, while he was glad he'd also waited for her. It had been months since he'd shared another woman's bed.

He did not want to believe he had waited until he was almost fifty to find a woman who appealed to him in and out of bed. Jasmine shifted again, this time resting her head on his shoulder. Cameron, burying his face in the damp strands, said a silent vow. Now that he and Jasmine had shared the most intimate act possible he had no intention of letting her go. Those were his last thoughts before he fell into a deep, dreamless sleep.

Jasmine wrapped her arms around Cameron's waist inside his jacket. He had wanted to stay the night but it wasn't possible because he had to return to his hotel and pack for his flight later that evening.

They had fallen asleep, waking in the late afternoon to make love again—this time it was slow, measured, as if they wanted it to last forever. And when they climaxed at the same time they had become one together. However, she did not want to think of what she had shared with

Cameron as more than two people coming together to release their pent-up sexual frustrations. Neither, in the throes of passion, had blurted out a declaration of love despite their making love.

"Text me when you touch down in New Orleans to let me know you arrived safely."

Cameron angled his head and brushed a light kiss over her mouth. "I promise I will."

Jasmine nodded. "Be safe."

He gave her a lingering look. "I will."

Jasmine was standing in the same spot long after he'd walked through the door. Now that he was gone she felt as if she was able to draw a normal breath for the first time since stepping out of the taxi to see Cameron standing in front of the restaurant waiting for her arrival.

He possessed a quiet strength radiating power and confidence he had probably spent most of his life cultivating. Everything, including his speech and body language, was precise, measured. She'd watched his interaction with his fraternity brothers and although most were around the same age, Cameron appeared more mature. The chiming of her cell phone galvanized Jasmine into action when she went into the kitchen to answer the call. Nydia's name popped up on the screen.

"Hola, mija. Que pasa?"

"That's what I should be asking you, Jazz. How did it go with you and Daddy?"

"I'm going to put you on speaker because I want to make a cup of coffee. And to answer your question, everything went well. We had a wonderful weekend."

"Tell me all about it."

Jasmine told Nydia about taking Cameron to Long Island to visit with her aunt and uncle. "The yacht party was as you say *off the chain*. Booze flowed from the time we left the pier until we returned twelve hours later."

"*Coño!* That's crazy."

"You're right. There were bars on the main and upper decks."

"How was the food?"

"It was spectacular. The prawns were huge and the deviled eggs topped with caviar were to die for."

"Shit!" Nydia said in English. "It sounds like you were hanging out with the hoity-toity."

Jasmine smiled. "As they would say in the South, they were definitely highfalutin'. The men all wore tuxedos and the women, gowns that did not come off a rack. They wore enough jewelry to light up Times Square in a black-out."

"What did you wear?"

"A red lace dress with a black obi sash."

"Nice," Nydia drawled. "What about music?"

"They had a live band and a deejay. What would really have made it better is if they'd had a Latin band." One time she'd accompanied Nydia to an event with a Latin band and she found herself on the dance floor for every number.

"I hear you, *mija*. There's nothing better than a live Latin band. Now, I want to hear all about your Daddy."

Jasmine filled the grinder with coffee beans. "What do you want to know about him?"

"Did you all kick it?"

She halted filling the coffee machine with water. "If you're asking if we slept together, then the answer is yes."

"Olé! How was he, Jazz?"

"If I had to grade him as a lover then I give him an A."

"I told you he was going to rock your world."

"Yes, you did."

"Are you going to see him again?"

"Yes. Remember we're going to New Orleans in two weeks." Jasmine wasn't ready to tell her friend that she'd promised to decorate Cameron's new home.

"Speaking of New Orleans, I just printed out my tickets. I'm really looking forward to seeing Tonya and Hannah again."

Jasmine pressed the button for the brewing cycle. "So am I. I'm curious to see what they've done with the house. The last time I spoke to Hannah she told me the permits to install the elevator were approved, so she's projecting opening in the fall."

"Word, *mija*. A lot of things have changed in one year, Jazz. You have a new man, Tonya's marrying her man, and Hannah is married to the love of her life."

"I don't have a new man. Cameron and I are friends."

"Yeah right. Friends with benefits. By the way. How old is Cameron?" Nydia asked.

"Forty-eight."

A low whistle came through the speaker. "Daddy looks good for his age. He must really take care of himself."

"It's apparent he does," Jasmine said in agreement. Cameron revealed that he regularly worked out and swam laps in his building's health club. "Do you have an outfit for Tonya's wedding?" she asked the accountant, directing the focus of the conversation away from her.

"Not yet. I was planning to go shopping next week.

Maybe I can take advantage of the Memorial Day sales. Do you want to come with me?"

"I'll let you know after I get in touch with my cousin. I'd expected her to call me before now to let me know if she's coming down from Buffalo so we can hang out together."

"Isn't she a lawyer?"

"Yes."

"Let me know one way or the other if you're going to have time. You know I take forever to select something. I can try on ten dresses and end up walking out of the shop without a single one."

Jasmine opened the refrigerator and took out a container of cream. "That's because you're indecisive. How long did it take you to finally kick Danny to the curb?"

Nydia grunted softly. "Much too long. I've said it over and over, if he'd cheated on me I would've stopped seeing him right away. I'm willing to put up with a lot things from a man, but if he cheats on me then I'm done."

"I hear you."

Once Jasmine discovered her husband was cheating, she'd asked herself if she'd done things differently, would it have kept him from straying. That notion lasted less than twenty-four hours before she dismissed it. She had done nothing wrong and she refused to heap blame on herself for someone who had the morals of a feral alley cat.

"Now that you're kicking boots with Cameron, do you plan to spend some time in New Orleans this summer?"

"I don't know, Nydia." She really didn't know how much time she would spend in the Crescent City, because

Cameron did not have a definite timetable for when the renovations for his new home would be completed.

"I'm going to let you go. I have to go to the laundromat before it closes. I either go early in the morning or just before closing time, because I can't stand it when it's crowded. People bring their children with them and they're running up and down like it's a freaking playground."

"I told you before that you can always come over and use my washer and dryer."

"Thanks but no thanks, Jazz. That would be schlepping laundry bags on the bus or subway and schlepping them back. And you know it's not cost-effective for me to buy a car. I can't see myself getting up every other morning to move a car from one side of the street to the other."

"Why don't you use Über to come down and I'll drive you back. You're on the east side and only a couple of miles away, so it shouldn't cost you that much to take the car service."

"I'll think about it."

Jasmine wanted to tell Nydia she was being indecisive again. She and Nydia chatted for another few minutes before hanging up. It was only five, too early to retire for the night, so she decided to put in several loads of laundry herself before the hamper overflowed.

She took a step and grimaced. She felt a slight ache from muscles she hadn't used in years. After she finished her coffee and the laundry, Jasmine planned to take a leisurely soak in the bathtub. She reached for the phone, scrolled through her contacts and tapped her cousin's number. Amelia had sent her a text several weeks ago informing her she was planning to come down and spend some time with her before going out east to see her parents.

"Please don't kill me, Jasmine," Amelia said after the break in the connection.

"I'm not going to kill you. I just want to know if you're coming down as planned."

"I can't because the agency is closing and I have to look for another job."

"What happened?"

"The CEO and his business manager mistress emptied out the agency's bank account and fled the country. I'm going to update my resume and look for a position with a downstate law firm. I've had enough of nonprofits at this time in my life."

"What about your apartment?" she asked her cousin.

"My lease is up at the end of July, and hopefully I'll be able to find something before then."

"If you get a job downstate, then you can stay with me until you're settled."

Thanks, Jazz. That's one problem I won't have to worry about."

"It's the least I could do for my favorite cousin." Amelia was two years her senior and as kids, both had waited patiently for the last two weeks of summer to play together.

"You're the best."

"Keep me in the loop about your job-hunting."

"I will. Talk to you later."

"Later," Jasmine said in parting.

Now that she knew Amelia wasn't coming she could plan her vacation. Slipping off the stool, she walked over to the laptop on the countertop. Jasmine booted up the computer and began searching carriers flying to New Orleans. She checked the flight Nydia had selected and found it was sold out. After forty minutes she narrowed it down to two possible flights. It appeared as if she was going to see Cameron again sooner than she had anticipated.

Chapter 10

Cameron massaged his forehead with his fingertips. He'd asked his siblings to meet at his apartment to finalize the details for their parents' upcoming anniversary celebration, but after more than an hour, they couldn't decide the venue. SAVE THE DATE notices were sent to Nathan and Belinda's friends, family members, and business associates and time was fleeting when it came to choosing a place for the gathering.

His brothers and sister's squabbling reminded him of his mother and father's verbal altercations, and he wondered if history was repeating itself with another generation that thrived on bickering. He thought about Jasmine and how well they'd gotten along. Even though they hadn't agreed on everything it hadn't escalated into a war of words.

"Stop it," he demanded. The two words were spoken barely above a whisper but he must have gotten through because the other three in the room turned and stared at him. "We're never going to solve anything screaming at one another."

His sister glared at him. "I thought we'd agreed on hosting it on one of the riverboats."

Cameron looked at Evangeline. Lines of strain bracketed her mouth and he wondered if the responsibility of trying to keep up with two hyperactive twin preschool girls was wearing her down. She was only thirty-eight, yet she claimed more gray in her dark-brown hair than Cameron who was ten years her senior. "We talked about it, Evie, but so far it's not written in stone."

Evangeline's dark-blue eyes narrowed. "We can't keep meeting and not decide where we're going to hold the party."

"I agree with you," Cameron said. "Let's make this the last time we meet because folks will have to know at least a month in advance where it's being held."

Preston Singleton sandwiched his hands between his knees. There had been a time when people mistook him for his older brother because he and Cameron looked enough alike to be twins. However, unlike Cameron, he was married and the father of a pubescent son and daughter. "Let's end the back and forth and hold the party here."

Leighton Singleton slapped his thigh. "Why didn't I think of that? I think we've settled on the venue."

It was Cameron's turn to glare. Leighton told anyone who would stand still long enough to listen that he was the Singleton maverick. After graduating college he'd declined his father's offer to join the family's investment company, electing instead to accept a position with a local bank. The decision proved advantageous for Leighton when he fell in love and married the bank president's daughter.

"Hold up, Lee. That doesn't settle anything. You—"

"What's the matter, Cam?" Leighton asked, interrupting him. "You own the fucking hotel."

Cameron's frown deepened. There had always been a below-the-surface sibling rivalry between them, but he'd hoped it had been left behind years ago. He counted slowly to ten before replying. "Yes, I own the hotel but have you thought maybe there could be other events that were booked for the same night?"

A rush of color suffused Leighton's face as he lowered his eyes. "I guess I forgot about that."

Evangeline rounded on Leighton. "I meant to tell you before, but you're going to have to stop cursing around my girls, because I don't want them to grow up with sewer mouths."

Leighton nodded. "I'm sorry, Evie."

Cameron was glad his sister had chastised Leighton, because if he had said anything to him it probably would have escalated into an all-out verbal barrage. He stood up. "Let me check with the banquet manager to see if she's booked anything for that night."

He picked up the phone and dialed the extension, watching his brothers and sister as he waited for someone to answer. "Good evening, Cameron. How can I help you?"

"Good evening, Rachel. Can you please check your calendar and let me know if you've booked anything for August 17."

"I have one party. Do you need a room, and for how many?"

"Yes. My siblings are throwing a fiftieth anniversary celebration for our parents, and we're estimating we'll have at least a hundred guests."

"I can put you into the Parisian ballroom. It's large enough to accommodate a hundred, and if you have less then we'll close off a portion for a more intimate setting."

"Please book it, Rachel. I'll get back to you later after we decide on the menu."

"You've got it, Cameron."

Cameron ended the call. As the owner of the boutique hotel, he'd made it a practice to keep a low profile. He had hired a more than capable general manager to run the hotel without his interference. "That's it," he said, sitting down on the loveseat next to his sister and resting an arm over her shoulders.

Preston shook his head. "Why didn't we consider Cam's hotel before?"

"We didn't," Evangeline said, "because you guys kept talking about boats and gambling. We're celebrating our parents' anniversary and I believe it should be more dignified than a Vegas-style party. I'll design mock-ups of several invitations for your approval before having them printed and mailed."

Leighton pushed to his feet. "I guess that does it." Cameron, Preston, and Evangeline also stood up. "Mom and Dad will celebrate their big five-oh at the Louis LaSalle."

Evangeline hugged Cameron and kissed his cheek. "Thanks, big brother."

He smiled. "You're welcome, little sister."

Cameron waited for them to leave, and then went into his bedroom to change into his swim trunks. He'd returned to New Orleans late Sunday night, sent Jasmine a text message that he'd arrived safely, and once he returned to his apartment in the hotel, he'd managed to shower before falling completely on his face, called the front desk to schedule a wake-up call, and crawled into bed and slept undisturbed.

Much to his disappointment, his ten o'clock appointment had canceled and if he'd known in advance that he did not have a consult with the new client, he would've stayed overnight with Jasmine. He had another disappointment when his sister called to say everyone in her house had come down with a stomach bug and couldn't make their meeting for later that evening. It was another four days before all were available to meet again.

However, his disappointment was short-lived when thinking about Jasmine. She'd turned out to be more than he could've ever imagined. Cameron tried not comparing her with the other women he'd known, but it wasn't as easy as he wanted. And the one notion that kept popping into his head that if he'd met her years ago he probably would've proposed marriage. And if they had married he knew for certain they would've had children.

He didn't know why she had come into his life—maybe to make him aware that not all marriages were like his parents, whom he'd one time referred to as the Squabbling Singletons.

Cameron knew he'd wanted to get as far away from home as possible when he selected colleges out of the state. He'd been accepted in several colleges in California, Michigan, and New York, and chose the latter. Living and studying in New York gave him the respite he needed to escape the toxic environment his parents seemed to revel in. It was as if they were emboldened as they challenged each other to see if who would come out the winner in their latest verbal battle of the sexes.

After he returned to New Orleans for his graduate studies Cameron moved in with his grandmother with the excuse that she should not have to live alone. Grandma La Salle saved him from what would have become an emotional breakdown because he loved both his parents and blamed both for their love-hate relationship. He'd told his grandmother if parents were aware they were scarring their children with their negative behavior then they would attempt to change. But his parents were too selfish to change until tragedy forced them to change. It took a long time for Cameron's emotional pain to fade, yet unfortunately he'd been scarred for life, fearful if he married, his union would then mirror his parents.

Cameron was more than cognizant of the negative traits and weaknesses in his personality and although he wasn't prone to arguing he could be possessive and controlling. There were times he could be overly frank, irritable, and moody which did not bode well for whomever he was interacting with.

Cameron scooped the keycard to the health club off the dish on the triple dresser and slipped his hand through the elastic band. He had bought the small hotel a year after the city was hit with Hurricane Katrina when the then-present owner did not have the money to make the necessary repairs. He made an offer and the man accepted it. It took more than six months to restore the hotel to its former elegance. Cameron changed the name to the Louis

LaSalle to honor one of his mother's ancestors and converted several of the suites into condos which were sold within months of the prospectus becoming available. Many tourists preferred staying at the LaSalle rather than in the larger hotels in the city because of the personalized service.

He took the private elevator to the lower level and inserted the keycard to the area with a workout room and Olympic-size pool. He'd come at the right time. Only two people were swimming laps in the heated pool. Cameron shed his jeans, t-shirt, and flip-flops and stepped into the shallow end and began swimming, his body slicing through the water like a sleek fish. He preferred swimming to lifting weights to stay in condition. It would take at least a week for him to detox from the food and alcohol he'd indulged in during his time in New York.

Cameron lost count of his number of laps across the pool and as he hoisted himself out of the water he was breathing heavily. Good news greeted him when he returned to his apartment suite to find a voicemail from the agent handling the sale of the warehouse. They had a closing date.

Two days later Cameron walked out of the lawyer's office with the keys to his new property. He wanted to call Jasmine and share his excitement with her but stopped himself. Except for her text telling him she was happy he'd arrived safely there hadn't been any further communication from her.

Reaching in the breast pocket of his lightweight jacket, he took out his cellphone and tapped the number for the architect he'd hired to oversee the renovations. "C and C Architects. How may I direct your call?"

"I'd like to speak to Bram Reynard."

"Who's calling?"

"Cameron Singleton."

"Hold on, Mr. Singleton. Let me see if Mr. Reynard is available."

Cameron slowly made his way to the lot behind the building where he'd parked his car, leaning against the bumper while he waited for Bram to pick up the call.

"I hope you're calling me with good news, Cam."

Cameron smiled. "I am. I just closed on the warehouse, so I need you to give me an approximate date when the renovations will be completed."

"What's the rush? Are you looking to get married and want to give your wife a new house?"

Cameron's smile faded with the mention of his getting married. "No. It's just that I'd like to move in before Christmas. Is that possible?"

"I don't see why not," the architect confirmed. "I'll send the plans and rendering to your email so you can look at what I've proposed. This will be the time when you decide what you want and don't want. Keep in mind if you want to make changes later it's going to cost you. I'll be working closely with the engineer and the contractor to give you exactly what you have in mind."

"Thanks, Bram. I'll check my email when I get back to the office."

"I'll give you a few days to look them over, and then I need you to get back to me. I'd like to start work before it gets too hot."

"No problem, Bram." Cameron had just ended the call

when a ringtone chimed indicating someone was sending him a text.

Jasmine: Made plans to come to the Easy on the 29ᵗʰ

Cameron: Where are you staying?

Jasmine: I'm staying with Hannah and St. John

Cameron: I can make arrangements for you to stay with me

Jasmine: I've already committed to them.

Cameron: I understand. Make certain you let me know when you're available for some R&R.

His mouth tightened in frustration. He hadn't told Jasmine that he owned a hotel and could put her up in one of the rooms.

Jasmine: Will do. See you soon

Cameron: You bet

He returned the phone to his pocket. It looked as if all of his plans were falling into place at the right time. He now owned a home where he planned to spend the rest of his life, and the woman with whom he'd found himself mesmerized and enthralled was coming to his hometown for an extended stay.

Cameron got into his car to drive to his office, but quickly changed his mind when he headed for Marigny. He slowed, stopping in front a brick Southern-style farmhouse. Twin fans were suspended from the ceiling of the second-story veranda. The front door opened at the same time he alighted from the low-slung sports car.

Hannah McNair stood on the porch, shading her eyes with her hand. "To what do I owe this unexpected visit?"

Cameron lowered his head and pressed his cheek to Hannah's. "I came to ask you something."

"Come inside where it's cooler. Would you like something cold to drink?"

He shook his head. "No thank you."

He followed the tall, slender platinum blonde whom he'd had a boyhood crush on so many years ago. Hannah hadn't changed much over the years. Although her body had filled out with womanly curves, her face had remained virtually unchanged. There were a few laugh lines around her green eyes, but other than that there were few discernible lines or wrinkles in her pale, flawless complexion. Once word got out that she was marrying Dr. St. John McNair, women from twenty-six to sixty were saddened that the handsome college professor was off the market.

Hannah led him to the rear of the house to an air-cooled sunroom. "Please sit down."

Cameron waited for her to sit, before he folded his body down into the dark-green rattan cushioned chair. The space was an oasis of light and color, with massive potted plants. Last December, the McNairs had hosted a New Year's Eve open house and he'd stopped by to wish the newlyweds the best. When Hannah noticed he'd come unaccompanied, he realized he'd shocked her when he revealed the simple truth: he hadn't found the woman with whom he wanted to ring in the year.

"I'm sorry for stopping by without calling first."

Hannah shook her head. "Don't apologize, Cameron. You and I have never stood on ceremony. After all, you know what I'm worth down to the last copper penny. Now, tell me what's wrong."

He froze. "What makes you think something's wrong?"

"I'm not old enough to be your mother, but I've raised a son who had the same look on his face as you have now, when he fell in love with the woman who eventually became his wife."

"I'm not in love."

"You think not, Cameron. And I know who she is."

Cameron could not believe he was that easy to read, or maybe Jasmine had told her about them. "Who is she?"

"Jasmine Washington. When you danced with me at my wedding reception and asked about Jasmine I told you that you're a big boy and didn't need me as a go-between if you wanted to meet her. Should I assume you have?"

He nodded. Cameron detested lying almost as much as he disliked verbal confrontation. "Yes."

"When?"

He told Hannah about the dates he'd had with Jasmine, but not about their sleeping together. "I know she's coming down and will stay with you but . . ."

Hannah lifted pale eyebrows. "But what?" she asked when Cameron didn't finish saying whatever he wanted to say.

Suddenly he felt like a gauche teenage boy meeting a girl who he'd fantasized about. "I like her because she's different from any other woman I've ever known. But that's something I haven't told her."

A smile parted Hannah's lips. "I think you more than like her, but I'm going to warn you that you can't come on too strong or you will send Jasmine running in the opposite direction. She had quite a contentious divorce with a sonofabitch of a husband, so she's rather distrustful of men. If you want my advice, then it's to give her time to come around on her own. Even if your relationship reaches the stage where you're sleeping together please don't take that as a signal she wants something more permanent."

A frown creased Cameron's forehead. "Are you talking about marriage?"

"Yes. Even if you stop tomcatting and decide you want to settle down there's no guarantee Jasmine will want the same because she's been there, done that."

"That's not going to happen because we both agree marriage is not a part of our future."

"She told you that?"

There was no mistaking the shock in Hannah's voice. "Yes. We were open with each other about marriage."

"So, you want to have a relationship with her without making it permanent? What's the expression: why should you pay for the cow when you can get the milk free?"

Sudden anger lit Cameron's eyes, turning them a frosty gray. "I'm not going to take advantage of her."

"Aren't you when you want her in your life without offering an alternative?" Hannah argued softly. "What if she changes her mind and decides she wants to be married? Are you going to tell her 'sorry, baby but I don't believe in matrimony'?"

"No!"

"No what, Cameron?" High color darkened Hannah's fair complexion. "You can't have it both ways." Her voice had softened. "I've known Jasmine a lot longer than you have and identify with her because we both had cheating-ass husbands. The man screwed her in and out of bed, so I'm warning you I'm not going to stand by and let you do the same to her. Either you do right by her or let her go, because you don't have the best reputation when it comes to women."

Cameron stared at Hannah in shock. He hadn't known

her husband had cheated on her, and she had judged him unfairly. "I've never messed over a woman."

"Listen to yourself, Cameron. How many women have you dated in the past let's say five years? Eight? Ten? Or maybe a dozen?"

"I'm not going to dignify that with an answer."

"Then don't!" Hannah spat out. "Just don't hurt my friend or you'll have to answer to me."

Cameron sat straight. "Don't threaten me, Hannah."

Her eyes gave off green sparks. "I just did." She blew out a breath. "Look, Cameron, I don't want to spoil a good business and personal relationship with us arguing about Jasmine. I'm just begging you to treat her good. She deserves to be happy."

He nodded. "I usually don't make promises I know I can't keep, but I promise you I will not hurt her."

Hannah gave him a long, penetrating stare. "I don't know why, but I believe you."

Cameron closed his eyes and exhaled an audible breath. "Thank you." He pushed to his feet, extended his hand, and helped Hannah stand. Angling his head, he kissed her cheek. "Thanks for the pep talk."

"Anytime. I'll walk you to the door."

"By the way, where's your husband?"

"He's at the college meeting with some of his colleagues. He's been invited out to the West Coast to meet with folks who film historical documentaries. I'd rather he not go because this will be our first summer together as husband and wife, but I didn't tell him that."

"How's the work coming on the inn?" Cameron asked.

"It's going well. Most of the rooms are finished and after that they'll begin installing the elevator. Once it's operational the contractor said he'll begin converting the guesthouses."

"Are you still projecting a fall opening?"

Hannah walked with him as far as the porch. "Yes. We've set a tentative date for mid-October."

"I'm sure the inn will be beautiful. It's true when folks say the DuPont House is one of the most magnificent homes in the Garden District."

Hannah rested a hand on Cameron's shoulder. "And I have you to thank for suggesting I invite investors when Tonya decided to open a restaurant on the property. Now if I can only convince Jasmine to help me run it I'll be as happy as a pig in slop. I've given up on Nydia handling the finances because she's wedded to New York City and doesn't want to relocate."

"You'll find someone eventually."

"I know that, but I need someone I can trust."

"I hear you," Cameron drawled. He kissed Hannah's forehead. "Thanks again for the honest talk."

"You're welcome."

Cameron slipped behind the wheel of the Porsche, shifted into gear, and drove in the direction of the CBD. The sign atop a bank building displayed the time and temperature. It wasn't quite noon and the mercury was already at eighty-seven degrees. He maneuvered into his assigned spot behind the office building and shut off the engine. The calendar said it was still spring, yet the heat and humidity registered differently.

Cameron reached for his jacket off the rear seat and quickened his steps as he headed to the front of the building. He nodded to the man sitting behind a desk monitoring everyone arriving and leaving the office building. The office of Singleton Investments was located on the second floor of the four-story building, and Cameron always opted to take the stairs rather than the elevator.

"Good afternoon, Rebecca," he said greeting the receptionist. "Do I have any calls?"

Rebecca's head popped up. It was apparent she'd gotten too much sun. The end of her nose was brick red. The natural redhead took great pains to constantly slather on sunscreen, and wear long sleeves and wide hats during the summer months.

"Good afternoon, Cameron. One call came in for you but I routed it to Preston."

He smiled. "Thank you. Is my father in?"

"Yes. In fact, he asked me if you were back."

"I'll go and see him." He made his way down the carpeted hallway to Nathan's office. After he'd agreed to join the firm, Cameron had insisted he did not want his office close to his father's. His relationship with Nathan at that time was fragile, but had strengthened gradually over the years once Cameron moved out of his parents' home. And their bond was finally cemented after Belinda's car accident when Cameron stepped into the role as consoler for his father and the entire family.

He knocked lightly on the open door. "You were looking for me?"

Nathan Singleton rose to his feet, smiling. Although he was nearing seventy-five, Nathan was still a fine figure of a man. Tall and slender with a full head of silver hair, he was usually mistaken for a man ten years younger. Cameron had inherited his patrician features and eye color.

"I wanted to know how it went."

Cameron closed the door and sat on a leather chair next to the desk. "It went well. I'm now in the possession of my new home."

Retaking his seat, a network of fine lines fanned out around Nathan's eyes as he smiled. "Congratulations. I suppose this will be your last move?"

"Oh yeah. I like living in the hotel because everything I need is at my disposal, but I still feel like a guest."

Nathan leaned back in the executive chair. "That was one of the best investments you've ever made." He held up a hand. "I know I tried talking you out of it because I thought you were squandering your money but you proved me wrong."

Cameron didn't want to relive the arguments he'd had with his father when he informed him that he was going to buy the storm-damaged property. "No one is right all of the time, but fortunately for me it worked."

"When do you think you'll be able to move into your new place?"

"Hopefully it will be before the end of the year. And once the renovations are close to completion I'm going sell the hotel." Cameron knew he'd shocked his father with this disclosure as evidenced by his stunned expression.

"Why would you sell it?"

"Right now I'm running two businesses—this one and the hotel."

"But you have a general manager for the hotel."

"That's true, Dad, but I'm still responsible for everything that goes wrong. Running the hotel is twenty-four-seven, while we have structured hours here. And what's going to happen when you retire and I take over? I'm not going to run myself into the ground trying to keep a foot in both camps."

Nathan closed his eyes, appearing to be deep in thought. "What if I stay on for another year?"

Cameron shook his head. "No, Dad. You've put in enough years running this company and it's time you enjoy the rest of your life. Take Mom on an around-the-world cruise and give her the opportunity to see a lot the countries she's been talking about. When I saw Hannah's cousins at her New Year's open house they said they were taking an around-the-world cruise lasting nearly two hundred days. You and Mom can do something comparable to that even if you want a shorter trip."

"That's something to think about. Your mother deserves that and more for putting up with my shit all those years."

"Thirty-five years to be exact," Cameron said.

"That's a long time, son. I'm surprised she took it."

"Have you forgotten that she didn't roll over and just take it?"

Nathan grunted. "That's because she was rather feisty."

"Was?" Cameron questioned. "Mom's still feisty and I'm glad she is because if she wasn't you would've broken her spirit. And there may have come a time when I would've knocked the hell out of you for the way you treated my mother."

"Once you started growing and putting on muscle I was afraid you would challenge me."

"I didn't because Mom warned me not to interfere because she didn't want me involved in what went on between her and her husband."

"I'm ashamed of how I treated her because my father had done the same thing to my mother."

Cameron wanted to remind his father that his mother took the verbal abuse because she didn't have any options other than being a housewife. "Have you had lunch?"

"No. Why?"

"I feel like celebrating and I need a partner in crime."

Nathan laughed. "Say no more, son. Where are we going?"

"I don't know. We'll figure it out on the way."

The older man picked up the phone and dialed his assistant. "Cameron and I will be out of the office for the rest of the day, and all our calls should go to Preston."

Cameron patted his father's back when he reached for his jacket off the coat tree. "When did you start playing hooky?" There was a running family joke that Nathan had two wives: Belinda LaSalle and Singleton Investments.

"I just decided today will be the first of many more to come," Nathan said as he put on his jacket. "You just reminded me that you'll be taking over the company in less than six months, so it's time I prepare for the inevitable. I'm going to take my wife away for as long as she wants, and when we return I want to spend time with my grandchildren so they can really get to know their grandpa."

"Don't go and get sappy on me, Dad."

"I do have a softer side, Cameron."

"That's okay as long as you don't become a marshmallow."

Nathan shuddered. "Please don't mention marshmallows. I remember one time I put one in my mouth and someone bumped me and it got stuck in my throat. If my brother hadn't punched me in the back I would've choked to death."

"They do make the miniature ones."

"Big or small I want nothing to do with them."

Cameron placed an arm over his father's shoulders and led him down the back staircase to the parking lot. "My car or yours?" He loved his two-door Porsche 911, while his father drove a Cadillac Escalade.

Nathan cut his eyes at him. "Mine." Reaching into his jacket pocket, he tossed the fob to Cameron. "Your old man is going to relax until we get where we're going."

Cameron knew his father hated riding in his sports car because he claimed it was too low to the ground. "There's a restaurant in Baton Rouge I want to try. You game, Dad?"

Nathan secured his seatbelt, and then closed his eyes. "*Allons!*"

"I'm going, Dad."

He punched the Start engine button and backed out of the space. Nathan rarely spoke the Cajun French he'd learned from his grandmother, but every once in a while it slipped out unbidden. His LaSalle relatives were as fluent in French as they were with English, and there had been a time when Cameron could converse fluidly in both languages. Now he would have to search his memory for certain words.

The state capital was almost ninety miles from New Orleans. His father had fallen asleep and not having a distraction would give him time to mull over his conversation with Hannah. She'd accused him of being in love with Jasmine, and while he'd denied it, Cameron knew what he felt for Jasmine went beyond infatuation.

It was as if life had thrown him a vicious curve. Maybe karma was paying him back for all the times he stopped seeing a woman because she wanted marriage and he didn't. Hannah had warned him to give Jasmine time to come around on her own. Well, he intended to give Jasmine all the time she needed in order for him to get what he wanted.

And he wanted her! Badly!

Chapter 11

Jasmine stared numbly at her parents. They were at a restaurant celebrating her belated birthday, and she couldn't believe what she'd just heard. "You're kidding, aren't you?"

Richard Washington slowly shook his head. "No we're not. Your mother and I have been talking about selling the house and moving south for more than a year. We listed the house with a realtor and yesterday we got an offer from a couple with two small children. They've been pre-approved, so it won't take long before we'll have a closing."

Jasmine slumped in her chair as she willed the tears filling her eyes not to fall. "So, you're really moving to North Carolina?" She didn't want to appear selfish and tell them they were deserting her, but her father was right when he'd spoken of wanting to sell the house where she'd grown up.

"Yes, baby," Marta Washington crooned. "We will be moving to a retirement community where we don't have to mow lawns or shovel snow. Even though your daddy and I are still active we want a more laidback lifestyle."

Jasmine forced a smile. She had to put on a brave face for her parents because she wanted them to believe she was happy for them. "Does it have a golf course?"

"Of course," Richard and Marta chorused.

This time her smile was genuine. Her parents were avid amateur golfers. Jasmine gazed lovingly at her father, and then her mother. Her genes had compromised when she inherited her father's complexion and her mother's facial features, and hair texture. "I'm happy for you guys."

"So, you're okay with us moving away?" Richard asked.

"Of course I'm okay. You just made it easy for me to make up my mind about moving to New Orleans to become an innkeeper. And we'll be a little more than a twelve-hour car ride from each other."

Marta and Richard shared a smile. "And once the inn is open we're going to come to check out the city."

Rising from her chair, Jasmine came around the table and kissed her mother, and then her father. "I love you guys."

"Do you plan on selling your condo?" Richard asked.

"Not right now." She told them about Amelia looking to live and work downstate. "If she does find a position in the tristate area, then she can sublet it from me."

"I'm glad you've decided to hold onto it. Owning

property is the best investment one can make," her father told her.

Marta took a sip of water. "Speaking of investments, do you need money?"

"Money for what, Mom?"

"Didn't you say you have to invest in the inn?"

"Yes."

"If you don't have enough money, your father and I will give you whatever you need. We've already bought the house in North Carolina, and once we sell our place—"

"Mom, don't say it," she pleaded, interrupting Marta. "I still have money from the sale of my business along with the severance pay. So, I'm far from being a pauper." Marta and Richard relaxed in their chairs as if they'd choreographed the move in advance.

Richard slipped on a pair of half-glasses and studied the selections on the dessert menu. "I hope you'll let us know if you do need something a little extra."

"Yes, Dad. I promise."

He handed the menu to Marta. "I'm going to have the fruit assortment for dessert."

"I'm going to pass," Marta said. "What about you, Jasmine?"

"I'll share Daddy's fruit."

What had begun as a family gathering to celebrate her forty-third birthday ended with Jasmine driving back to Manhattan experiencing a mix of emotions. She was happy for her parents who'd planned for their retirement and hadn't had to pinch pennies now that they were on a fixed income, and apprehensive because she was going to leave all that was familiar to move to another state and invest in a new venture.

Activating the Bluetooth feature, she tapped on the screen for Hannah's number. Her phone rang three times before there was a break in the connection. "Hello."

"Hannah, this is Jasmine."

"I'm sorry, Jasmine, but your name and number didn't come up on my screen. How are you?"

"I'm well. I'm calling to ask if you still need someone to assist you managing the DuPont Inn."

"Honey, please. You know I do."

"Well, you're talking to your soon-to-be HR specialist." There was complete silence on the other line. "Hannah? Are you still there?"

"I'm here. I just had to do the happy dance. Jasmine, you're the answer to my most fervent prayer. I was just telling St. John the other day that I need to start looking for someone trained in hotel management to help me with the inn."

"Well, look no more because I'm in."

"I'll draft a contract and email it to you to go over. You can get your attorney to look at it. If you want, you can suggest changes."

Jasmine knew she could get Amelia to check out the contract. Once she'd decided to divorce Raymond, Jasmine had asked her cousin to represent her, but Amelia had to decline because she was involved in her own very combative divorce from a man who was requesting spousal support. "My cousin will look it over."

"That's good. Should I still expect you on the twenty-ninth?"

"Yes."

"Email me your flight information and I'll pick you up at the airport."

"You don't have to do that. I'll take a taxi."

"You don't have to, Jasmine. My cousins are on another cruise on the other side of the world, St. John is spending the next month on the West Coast for a taping of a historical documentary, and if it wasn't for Smokey I'd end up talking to myself."

"Are you telling me St. John is going to miss his cousin's wedding?" Gage Toussaint and St. John were cousins.

"No. He's flying back just for that weekend."

"You'll still have me as a houseguest after the wedding because I didn't book a return flight. But if it gets too hot like it did last year when we came down, then I'm gone."

"It's not the heat as much as it is the humidity. Hold on, Jasmine, I have another call." Seconds later, Hannah said, "That's St. John. Can I call you back?"

"You don't have to. Talk to your husband and I'll talk to you later."

"Thanks."

Jasmine ended the call, and then tapped the screen for Nydia's number. "Hey, chica."

"What's up, *mija*?"

"I'm going to invest in the DuPont Inn."

There came a pause before Nydia's voice came through the speaker. "Why did you change your mind?"

"My parents are moving to a retirement community in North Carolina."

"What about your condo?"

"My cousin's planning to move from Buffalo, and I told her she can stay at my place."

"There goes your last excuse for not relocating. I know I sound selfish, but I don't want you to leave."

"Come with me, Nydia. You're no longer involved with Danny so there's nothing to keep you in New York."

"I'm going to have to sleep on it."

"Don't sleep too long Sleeping Beauty," Jasmine teased, "or you'll miss your prince."

Nydia's distinctive high-pitched laugh echoed throughout the vehicle. "All of the princes are taken, *mija*."

"I'm certain there are a few left wandering out in the universe."

"Maybe an alternative universe, Jazz, but not the one we live in."

"They're out there even though I'm not looking for one."

"You don't have to, Jasmine, because you have one. But only if you're willing to open your eyes to acknowledge it."

"I know you're not referring to Cameron."

"Ding, ding, ring-a-ling. Right answer!"

"Cameron and I will enjoy each other for as long as it lasts. And when it's over we'll go our separate ways without malice toward each other."

"That's bullshit and you know it, Jasmine. Men don't take kindly to rejection. Remember Tonya's telling us about the man she'd been dating throwing a bitch fit when she told him she was leaving New York? They rarely saw one another, yet he accused her of cheating on him because she had been the one to end their relationship. And I don't have to tell you about Danny acting like a lost puppy looking for his master when I moved and left no forwarding address. I'm not even going there about *your* ex. Enough talk about men or the lack thereof. Have you told Hannah about your decision?"

"Yes. She admitted to doing the happy dance."

"Of course she would. You're the best when it comes to management."

"Apparently those at Wakefield Hamilton didn't think so when they gave me a pink slip."

"That's because they don't know their heads from their asses. Personally I believe they downsized their best employees."

"They did us a favor, Nydia. If they hadn't merged, we would still be there doing the same thing day after day until we retired. Hannah is now an innkeeper, Tonya will own and operate her own restaurant, and I will divide my time managing the inn and decorating interiors."

"You're serious about decorating again?"

"Yes. Cameron Singleton bought a new house and he wants me to decorate it."

"You said yes?" Nydia asked.

"I said yes. But it's not going to be for a while, because the house has to undergo extensive renovations first."

"Your condo is the best advertisement as to your talent. I'm so happy for you, *mija*."

"Thank you, chica. It looks as if I'm finally getting my life together."

"Better late than never. Are we going to get together before you leave?"

"Why not? I'll order in."

"Instead of you ordering in, I'll bring the food. How about tomorrow night?"

"Tomorrow's good."

"I'll call you to let you know when to expect me."

"*Luego,* chica."

"Later, *mija*."

Once she finalized her move, Jasmine knew she would miss Nydia's bubbly disposition and their bimonthly get-togethers. She could always count on her friend to keep it real. Her foot hit the brake as the car in front of her came to a complete stop. Smothering a curse, she shook her head. Traffic had slowed to a bumper-to-bumper crawl.

"I definitely will not miss this," she whispered to herself. After her parents relocated, she wouldn't have to drive to Long Island. Jasmine still could not believe her parents were selling their dream house to move into a cookie-cutter retirement community with all the amenities they wanted and needed for their new lifestyle.

The drive which normally took fifty minutes stretched into more than ninety when Jasmine maneuvered into her parking space in the underground garage, and walked across the street to her apartment building. The doorman on duty stopped her before she made her way to the elevator.

"Ms. Washington, there's a package for you in concierge. If you wait here, I'll get it for you."

Jasmine wondered who had sent her something, because it had been a while since she'd gone online to place an order. She didn't have long to wait when the man returned with a FedEx package. One of the many perks of living in the building was she didn't have to be home for a package delivery. Residents could also arrange for drop-off and pick-up dry cleaning services or grocery deliveries.

"Thank you." Jasmine glanced at the return address: S. Investments, New Orleans, LA. Her pulse quickened.

S. Investments had to be Singleton Investments. What, she mused, had Cameron sent her?

She managed to curb her curiosity until after she slipped off her shoes, changed out of her street clothes and into a tank top and cotton lounging pants. Sitting on the club chair in her bedroom, Jasmine opened the package, and removed pale-blue tissue paper covering a rectangular flat velvet box. Her fingers were noticeably shaking when she opened the box to see a single strand of golden South Sea pearls and matching studs resting on white satin. Jasmine knew the round baubles were at least twelve millimeters. Her fingers grazed the ruby and diamond clasp connecting the magnificent strand. Sandwiched between sheets of tissue paper was a small card: I HOPE YOU ENJOYED YOUR BIRTHDAY. HERE'S A LITTLE SOMETHING FOR YOU TO WEAR TO YOUR FRIEND'S WEDDING. C. SINGLETON.

Jasmine blinked back tears. She hadn't expected Cameron to give her anything for her birthday. Reaching for her cell, she dialed his number. Sending a text was too impersonal for what she wanted to say to him.

"Talk to me, darling."

Her smile was dazzling. "Is that how you always answer your calls?"

"Nah. Just you."

"I got the pearls and—"

"Do you like them?" he asked, cutting her off.

"Of course. They're beautiful. But you didn't have to give me anything for my birthday."

"But I wanted to. It's the least I could do to thank you for making my frat reunion the best I've ever had."

Jasmine paused, wondering if he was referring to her

sleeping with him after three encounters. "It was quite memorable for me, too."

"What's wrong, Jasmine?"

"What are you talking about?" she asked, answering his question with one of her own.

"Something in your voice changed."

Damn, she thought. Was he that insightful or was she an open book? If she hoped to have an open relationship with Cameron, then she had to be truthful. "Was it the best because we slept together?"

"Why would you ask me that?"

"Just answer the question, Cameron."

"No! It still would've been the best if we hadn't slept together. I'm no choirboy when it comes to sleeping with women, but there haven't been so many that I can't recall their names or their faces. When I came to New York to see you it wasn't my intent to sleep with you. And that's not to say I didn't want to, but if it didn't happen then so be it. You're different, Jasmine, from any other woman I've met."

"Have you ever dated a woman of color?"

"No, but that has nothing to do with you being different. You're beautiful, talented, sophisticated, and stunningly feminine. In other words, you're the total package."

She smiled. "Stop or you'll give me a swelled head."

"Wrong, darling. Every time I conjure up your naked body the head between my legs swells up."

"You're so nasty!"

"You like it, don't you?"

Jasmine covered her mouth with her free hand to smother a giggle. "Yes," she said through her fingers.

"I can't wait to see you again."

"Same here," she admitted. "Are you free June ninth?"

"What's happening on that day?"

"That's the day when my friend is marrying Gage Toussaint, and I'd like you to be my plus-one."

"Of course. What time is the wedding?"

"Seven."

"AM or PM?"

"PM, Cameron. Why?"

"Is it formal or semi-formal?"

"Semi-formal, but that's optional." Jasmine knew he'd asked because he wanted to know what to wear. "The reception will be held in St. John's garden."

"Is Eustace doing the catering?"

"I'm certain he will be. Why?"

"The man's the best cook in the whole damn state."

"I agree, but my friend Tonya is also an incredible chef. Once she opens her restaurant at the inn, she'll have to turn away folks."

"We'll see."

"Oh, you think I'm just blowing smoke when talking about Tonya's cooking."

"No, babe. I just said we'll see."

Jasmine wanted to tell Cameron that Tonya had been working with Eustace as his apprentice to perfect many of the dishes the Toussaints were known for. And her future husband was also a professional chef. Together they were certain to become more than a footnote among New Orleans's celebrity chefs.

"Do you want me to pick you up from the airport when you come in?"

"No. Hannah's going to meet me. I want to spend a few days with her before we hang out together."

"That's not a problem."

"I don't know if I told you, but I haven't booked a return flight yet."

"That's great, because that will give me time to take you around."

"What about work, Cameron?"

"What about it?"

"Are you taking a vacation?"

"No. I'll rearrange my schedule and just take off."

"It must be nice being your own boss."

"It does have its perks. Wasn't it that way when you ran your decorating firm?"

"Yes," Jasmine admitted. She'd made her own hours, and could pick and choose her clients.

"Make certain you pack lightweight clothes because it's hotter than Hades down here right now."

"Thanks for letting me know. I'm going to ring off because I have to go through my closet and pack."

"Okay, babe. I'll see you when you get here."

Jasmine set the phone on the side table and closed her eyes. She didn't want to imagine that Cameron was sending her mixed messages, but this was sounding more and more like a relationship, and for her the word was the same as a commitment. At this time in her life if she wanted to commit to anything it would be her career and not a man.

She opened her eyes and stared at the sheer fabric draping the bed. A shiver of excitement eddied through her when she thought about assisting Hannah managing the inn. Becoming Gregory's mentee helped Jasmine develop her skills as a people person. She watched him literally change a client's mind about a particular decorating scheme when he used a soft coaxing tone rather than one that was condescending. She had adopted a similar demeanor when talking with employees with complaints about their supervisors or if they were written up for some infraction.

Jasmine decided not to tell Cameron about her plan to relocate to New Orleans until after she and Hannah were in agreement with the conditions in her contract. She thought about what she had to do before leaving, and that included notifying management about her cousin coming to stay with her if or when Amelia was able to secure a position downstate.

She slipped off the chair and made her way to the walk-in closet. Winter and fall garments hung on the left side of the closet, while spring and summer garments were on the right. It was said there were four seasons in New York but for Jasmine there were only two: hot and cold.

It took more than an hour for her to select tops, slacks, skirts, and blouses suitable for the semi-tropical climate. After retrieving a Pullman from an overhead shelf, she carefully folded the garments and placed them strategically in the suitcase. She filled clear plastic storage bags with lingerie, sleepwear, and personal feminine products. Shoes went into cloth bags.

Jasmine hung the dress she planned to wear in a garment bag, along with the shoes. At the last minute she decided not to pack the dress in the event her luggage did not arrive at the same time as her flight, because she didn't have a direct flight to New Orleans. She packed the cross body bag in the Pullman, and opted to carry a tote which would allow her to board with the required two items. Cameron's birthday gift, along with her government ID, cash, and credit cards would be stored in a pouch secured inside the tote. Closing and locking the wheeled Pullman, she left it on the luggage rack.

A year ago she, Tonya, Nydia, and Hannah had toasted to happy endings, unaware how inexorably their lives would come to be entwined. Three days from now she would wake up in the Big Easy and eventually reunite with a man who'd unknowingly helped her heal and learn to trust a man again.

At forty-three she was no longer looking for her Prince Charming to come and sweep her off her feet. Now, in retrospect, Jasmine realized her relationship with Gregory was more beneficial to him than for her even though she'd willingly gave him her virginity.

Gregory had become her tutor in and out of bed when he taught her to know her body in order to give him the pleasure he wanted. It had taken a while before she experienced her first orgasm, but her attempt to take the lead in their lovemaking angered Gregory, so she acquiesced and resorted to the role as the submissive.

Making love with Raymond was satisfying enough but there were times when she wanted more foreplay, and always after he ejaculated he'd roll over and go to sleep. Raymond's passions ran hot and cold and it wasn't until after she discovered he was sleeping with another woman that she realized he desired his side chick more than his wife.

Whenever she recalled making love with Cameron her traitorous body betrayed her; she was in awe that she'd had multiple climaxes, but also that she had to wait until she was over forty to experience the full magnitude of her femininity.

A mysterious smile curved her mouth when she thought of the events of the past three years in which she'd gone through a divorce, lost her job, and bonded with three coworkers. Now she was about to start anew in a city where she could control her destiny.

Chapter 12

Jasmine followed the passengers on her flight to the baggage claim area, and saw Hannah waiting for her. The former corporate attorney had put on weight since marrying St. John. She'd cut her hair, the flaxen, chin-length strands held off her face by a narrow black headband. Hannah appeared cool in a white camp shirt she'd paired with white cropped slacks and navy, low-heeled mules.

She switched the garment bag to her opposite hand as she hugged Hannah. "Thanks for meeting me."

Hannah kissed Jasmine's cheek. "There's no need to thank me."

Jasmine held her at arm's length. "You look wonderful."

"So do you. As for myself I've put on a little weight," she said, patting her belly.

"It looks good on you because I always thought you were too thin." Jasmine hadn't lied to her friend. Hannah was five-nine in bare feet, and had been rail-thin, but it was apparent marriage agreed with her.

"That's what St. John said. He claims he likes a woman with a little meat on her bones. Enough about me. Your face looks different. Is something going on in your life you need to tell your older sister?"

Jasmine stared at Hannah, wondering if she knew about her and Cameron. "Do you know that I've been seeing Cameron?"

"I'm not going to lie and tell you I don't. When Cameron approached me at my wedding reception I knew he was interested in you, but I refused to tell him whether you were married, single, or involved with someone. He came to see me last week and told me he'd seen you in New York."

Jasmine went completely still. She prayed Cameron hadn't revealed they had been sleeping together. She wanted to be the one to make known the intimate details of their liaison. "What else did he tell you?"

"It's not so much what he told me, but what I said to him about his being in love with you."

"No, he isn't."

"That's what he said when I accused him. He admitted he likes you more than he has any other woman, but he's in denial when he says he's not in love with you. Cameron Singleton is the Big Easy quintessential swinging bachelor. He's dated a lot of women, and still manages to get out of his relationships unscathed. For some reason none of his girlfriends are willing to kiss and tell."

"Are you saying I should be careful?"

"No, Jasmine. I think it's Cameron who has to be careful, because he wants you more than you want him. He said you didn't want to get married, and for a man like Cameron that's the same as rejection. In other words, you're the one controlling the direction of your relationship and that's not easy for him to accept."

"I'm not going to lie and say I don't like him but I'm not ready for a commitment."

"Which means you'll remain friends with benefits."

She nodded. "Exactly."

Hannah smiled. "I rest my case." The sound of the luggage carousel echoed throughout the terminal as bags tumbled onto the conveyer belt. "I'm going to the lot to get the car while you wait for your bag. I'll meet you curbside."

Jasmine went over to the section with the sign indicating her flight arrival and waited for her Pullman, wondering what else Cameron had said to Hannah. It was apparent he hadn't mentioned their sleeping together and for that she was grateful. Then she remembered Hannah talking about his former girlfriends not kissing and telling. Was that something on which both agreed, or had he made it a stipulation of their relationship?

Suddenly she was annoyed with herself for bringing up his name. There was no need to know that he'd come to talk to Hannah about her. And she didn't want to know if he was or wasn't in love with her. Liking was enough for her.

She spied her bag coming down the conveyer and moved closer where she could grasp it easily. Jasmine rolled it out of the terminal and was met with a blast of heat that threatened to siphon the breath from her lungs. Cameron hadn't lied. It was hot as Hades. Moisture coated her face with a shimmering glow. Thankfully she didn't have to wait too long before Hannah's vintage Mercedes Benz came to a stop in front of her.

Hannah got out, took the Pullman, and unlocked the trunk. "Get in the car before you faint."

Jasmine slipped onto the passenger seat, and let out her breath as cool air feathered over her moist face. Seconds later, Hannah sat behind the wheel and headed for the airport exit. "This heat is a monster."

"It's hotter this year than when y'all came down last summer. And it's still spring."

"*!Coño!* That's shit in Spanish," Jasmine said, translating for Hannah.

"And *merde* in French," Hannah countered, laughing.

"That's close to *mierda,* which also means shit in Spanish."

Hannah lightly tapped the horn, and then drove around a slow-moving car. "However you say it, the weather has been brutal. It's as if Mother Nature is punishing us for not taking care of her Earth."

Jasmine made a sucking sound with her tongue and teeth. "Please don't get me started about global warming. Speaking of the Earth, where in the world are your cousins off to now?"

"Australia, New Zealand, and Hong Kong."

"Have they always been avid travelers?"

"Not really," Hannah answered. "When they were teaching they'd take short vacations, but now that they're retired they've become globetrotters. I guess they can do whatever they want because they don't have husbands or children."

"Was it their choice not to marry or have children?"

Hannah nodded. "Paige and LeAnn were always free spirits. Remember I told you about their involvement in civil rights and anti-Vietnam War demonstrations? That started what my uncle called their rebellious spirit, and while he waited for it to end, it never did. They dated whomever they wanted and lived with men without the benefit of marriage. My cousins were standard-bearers for women's liberation, which upset my mother because she thought I was going to follow in their footsteps."

"Did you?"

"Not in the beginning. My mother approved of my first husband because of his family lineage. Meanwhile I'm certain she's spinning in her grave because I married St. John."

"Are you saying she wouldn't have approved of you marrying a black man?"

"Probably not. What she forgot was there are black people on my father's family tree and probably on hers, too. All you have to do is study New Orleans' history to know there was a preponderance of race mixing."

"How's Tonya?" Jasmine asked before the conversation shifted to her and Cameron as a mixed-race couple.

"She's still working with Eustace at Chez Toussaints to perfect some of the Creole and Cajun dishes she plans to serve at her restaurant."

"Tonya can really burn some pots. I still think about the time we had our international dinner where everyone prepared their favorite dish and we ate and drank so much that we could hardly move."

Hannah gave her a quick glance. "How could I forget? That's when I realized what I'd missed not having close girlfriends growing up."

"Didn't you have girlfriends in high school or college?"

"Not really."

Jasmine listened intently as Hannah told her about transferring from a private all-girls school to a public school where most of the girls shunned her because they viewed her as a stuck-up rich girl. St. John and another black girl were the only ones to befriend her. She had a few friends in college, but none carried over to adulthood. "My first husband was a naval officer and I hated living on base. Most of the women were cliquish which reminded me of college. Again I found myself on the outside looking in. The day I invited you, Tonya, and Nydia to my apartment changed my life. It was as if I'd finally connected with women who made me feel as if I'd known them for years instead of a few hours."

"That's because we keep it real, Hannah. All of us are comfortable enough with one another to say exactly what's on our minds. It worked when we gave you business about not wanting to marry St. John. He had to have had a dammed good reason for admitting to cheating on his wife, when he just could've lied and you wouldn't have known the difference."

"He did have a very good reason," Hannah said. "I still beat up on myself for misjudging him."

"It's time you rid yourself of the self-pity, Mrs. St. John McNair."

A knowing smile spread over the blonde's delicate features. "Y'all were harder on me than we were with Nydia."

"Nydia got so tired of us preaching to her about getting rid of her deadbeat boyfriend that she finally did kick him to the curb."

"Good for her. Nydia has too much going for herself to deal with a parasite. I don't think she realizes how bright she is. Did you know she passed the CPA exam on her first attempt?"

"No, I didn't," Jasmine replied. Whenever she and Nydia got together, her friend never talked about her accomplishments. Jasmine suspected Nydia downplayed her intelligence so that she would not bruise her boyfriend's ego. Danny had barely made it out of high school. If she had known this Jasmine would've told Nydia about Raymond's disdain for anyone with a college degree.

"I'm really looking forward to Tonya's wedding so the gang can get back together again," Hannah said. There was an obvious tone of longing in her voice.

"Once Nydia gets here the gang will be complete."

"Has she said anything about joining us as innkeepers?"

"She says she's thinking about it." Jasmine repeated what Nydia had said.

"At least she didn't say no."

"I'm hoping she'll change her mind after she's here for the wedding," Jasmine said. "She's planning to spend a few days in New Orleans after the wedding before returning to New York."

Hannah headed east on Interstate 10 toward the city, accelerating into the flow of traffic. "After you rest up we'll go out for dinner. When I told Tonya you were coming today, she invited us to Sunday dinner with Gage and his son. By the way, I don't want to take up all of your time while you're here. I know Cameron wants to see you."

Jasmine recalled Cameron's promise to be her tour guide. "I'll call him later to find out what he's planned for us. He volunteered to show me the city."

Hannah gave her a sidelong glance. "If you want to go out with him tonight, I don't mind canceling dinner."

"That's not necessary. Cameron's not going anywhere and neither am I."

Jasmine didn't want to tell Hannah she didn't have the energy to do much more than shower and then take a nap. She'd gotten up early to make it to the airport ninety minutes before her departure, only to discover the terminal teeming with travelers intent on getting a head start on the long holiday weekend. There were delays boarding and even longer delays taking off. She had an hour layover in Miami before finally arriving in New Orleans.

Hannah glanced at Jasmine again when she covered her mouth to conceal a yawn. "You must be exhausted from traveling. I think we should skip going out tonight. How does salad with either grilled shrimp or chicken sound to you?"

"It sounds wonderful. I'm sorry to be a party pooper, but I was up before five to get to the airport for seven-thirty. And to top it off, the terminal was packed with folks trying to get out of town before the holiday weekend."

"Were you aware it was the Memorial Day weekend when you made your reservation?"

"Not really. When you don't work a traditional job you tend to forget the date and days of the week," Jasmine admitted. "I find myself looking at my cellphone for the date."

"I hear you," Hannah crooned. "Sit back and close your eyes. If you fall asleep I'll wake you once we get to the house."

Shifting into a more comfortable position, Jasmine closed her eyes, and soon succumbed to the lulling motion of the moving car and fell asleep.

* * *

A shower, power nap, and the green salad with chicken, apple, and maple walnuts in buttermilk dressing had revived Jasmine as she reclined on a cushioned chaise in the sunroom. She'd called Cameron to let him know she was in town and they made tentative plans to meet Saturday.

Dusk had descended on the countryside, but she still could see the expansive garden where Tonya and her new husband planned to hold their wedding reception. The year before St. John had hosted a family reunion in the garden where she got to meet the members of his family. Many of them spoke French or Haitian Creole of which she understood very few words or phrases, in addition to English.

Smokey, the McNair's cat, jumped up on the chaise and settled down next to Jasmine. The last time she saw the sooty blue-gray feline with strikingly beautiful gold eyes he had been a kitten. They had engaged in what Jasmine thought of as a stare-down before the animal flicked its tail and walked away. Hannah had explained her pet tended to intimidate strangers with a simulated death-stare, but if they didn't show fear, then Smokey would retreat.

She ran her fingers over velvety fur. "So, you do remember me. You've grown up to be a big, beautiful boy. And it looks like you eat well because your belly is nice and round."

"Everyone in this house is getting round," Hannah remarked as she entered the sunroom with tall glasses of lemonade. "I'm getting round, St. John is getting round, and our pet is also getting round." She handed a glass to Jasmine and sat on a matching chaise.

"That's because y'all are eating good in the neighborhood."

Hannah smiled at Jasmine over the rim of her glass. "Now you sound like the rest of us when you said *y'all* for you all."

Jasmine took a sip of the icy, slightly tart liquid. "Y'all keep forgetting that I have Southern roots, and that I used to spend part of my summers with my Daddy's family in North Carolina. The reason I decided to invest in the DuPont Inn is because my folks are selling their home and relocating to North Carolina."

"What about your condo?"

Jasmine smiled. Everyone knew there were two impediments to Jasmine accepting Hannah's offer to move to New Orleans: she didn't want to leave her parents and she didn't want to give up her condo. However, circumstances beyond her control made it possible for her to reverse her decision.

She told Hannah about her cousin and her offer to let Amelia live there for as long as she wanted.

"I remember you telling me about her," Hannah said. "That she couldn't handle your divorce because she was going through one herself."

"Her dirt bag of a husband was worse than Raymond. He'd been married before and had two children with his ex-wife when he married Amelia. At that time she was a junior partner in one of the most prestigious Buffalo law firms. She bought a beautiful house with enough room for her husband's children to come and stay with them during the summer months. Amelia was made full partner and her salary was high six figures. Meanwhile her husband had sued his ex for full custody of his son and daughter, and won. My cousin, who always wanted children, underwent a total hysterectomy at twenty-four after a Pap smear indicated cancer. She embraced her step-children as her own and they all lived happily. Then her husband came home one day and blindsided her by telling her that he wanted a divorce based on alienation of affection.

"Whenever she was assigned an important case she'd put in long hours and occasionally bring work home. He also asked for spousal support because as a schoolteacher he only earned a fraction of her salary. My cousin, who I've never heard a single curse word come from her mouth, let him have it. She told him there was no way she would have the stamina do her job, which allowed her to keep a roof over the heads of him and his kids and food in their greedy ass bellies if she gave into his demand to let him screw her twice a day."

With wide eyes, Hannah stared at Jasmine. "You're making this up."

"No, I'm not. The man claimed he was a sex addict and he needed to release himself at least twice a day."

"Were they going at it like rabbits before she married him?"

"No. Apparently he was taking some herbal shit that had affected his libido and gave him a perpetual erection."

"That's crazy. Why didn't he just stop taking the herb?" Hannah questioned.

"Come on, Hannah. Get real. He had to feel like a stud walking around all day with a hard-on."

"Did mister cocked-and-loaded ever get his spousal support?"

Jasmine burst out laughing, startling Smokey who jumped off the chaise and scurried away. "No. Amelia had one of the partners from the firm handle her divorce. Unbeknownst to her hubby, the partner and the judge handling the case were golfing buddies. Amelia hadn't adopted his children, and the house and the cars were all in her name. His lawyer claimed his client and kids were used to a certain lifestyle and he needed the spousal support to maintain the same standard of living. In the end he was denied spousal support and told he earned enough to take care of himself and his children. Amelia did give him one of the cars so he could get to work and take his kids to school."

Amusement shimmered in Hannah's green eyes. "So he got nothing?"

"*Nada*, zippo, zilch."

"Well damn!"

"Last Amelia heard he'd moved back with his children's mother and they're one big happy family. My cousin finally left the firm to work for a nonprofit because she was facing burnout. She sold the monstrosity of a house and rented an apartment. Unfortunately her last job was a nonprofit that has closed down and she's looking to move from Buffalo to be closer to New York City. She's a brilliant attorney and I don't think she'll have much of a problem landing another position."

"Practicing law is hard work. It doesn't matter if you're a litigator, prosecutor, or a public defender."

"Do you miss it?" Jasmine asked Hannah.

"No. I became a lawyer because Daddy made it look easy. He used to take me to his office on Saturdays where I'd do my homework while he'd search through stacks of law books to find what he needed to win a case. Years later when he was a judge I'd sneak into the back of the courtroom to watch the cases he adjudicated. He would listen intently to both sides and in the end render his judgment. He was like King Solomon because once the trial ended both parties seemed willing to accept the verdict. Everyone called him Judge, which really tickled his fancy. When I told Mama I wanted to be a lawyer she went into hysterics, claiming it was a man's profession while insisting I go into education because it was a more genteel vocation for a woman."

"Did you?" Jasmine asked, totally intrigued listening to Hannah talk about her family.

"Yes, because Mama could be quite nasty when provoked. I majored in early elementary education at Vanderbilt, but never really taught. By that time I'd married Robert and he was stationed at a naval base in California. I was a married woman, living thousands of miles away from my controlling mother and that's when I decided to apply to law school. It wasn't until my son had gone to school on the base that I'd begun studying for the LSAT, scoring high enough to be accepted to Stanford Law. I finally went to the University of San Diego School of Law because I didn't want to be away from my son. Although I was disappointed that my mother refused to attend my graduation, I was able to experience a measure of independence for the first time in my life. That day I vowed no one, not my mother or husband, would ever determine my future."

"Good for you."

Jasmine stared at the woman who'd grown up in a centuries-old mansion, no doubt with household help. She had married a midshipman from a prominent Louisiana family who'd graduated at the top of his class from the US Naval Academy. But her life was far from perfect when she'd had to deal with an overbearing, controlling mother and a husband who'd repeatedly cheated on her during their thirty-year marriage.

"What are you thinking about, Jasmine?"

"Us. Women. It's as if we have to deal with so much crap before we're able to get our lives together. You grew up privileged yet you had to deal with a controlling mother and betrayal from your duplicitous late husband. Amelia had to fight for what was hers when a man she married attempted to pimp her for all she'd worked for. Then, there's Tonya who had to escape a controlling husband who refused to support her goal to become a chef. Next up is Nydia, whose life mirrors my cousin's because her boyfriend was looking for her to take care of him. Then, there's myself. I grew up with an adoring mother and a protective father who indulged and encouraged me to become whatever I wanted to be. However, the drawback was when it came to men. I trusted them because I'd believed they'd all be like my father. I was barely legal when I slept with a man thirty years my senior."

"No!"

Jasmine laughed at Hannah's shocked expression. "Close your mouth, Hannah. He didn't take advantage of me. In fact if it hadn't been for him I never would've been able to establish my own decorating company. He also gave me the money for the down payment on my condo six months before he passed away. Gullible Jasmine believed all men were like her father and lover, and when she met a man who said he loved and adored her she fell for his sweet talk hook, line, and sinker," Jasmine continued, referring to herself in the third person.

"And despite all that we've gone through we've survived. Nydia finally got rid of her bum. You married St. John, and you're now looking forward to a new business venture. Tonya left her idiot behind, realized her dream to become a chef, and will marry her fellow chef and prince in another three weeks. Amelia is looking to start over in a new city and no doubt will land a position with a salary commensurate with her experience."

"What about you, Jasmine?"

"Yes. What about Jasmine? She'll be relocating probably before the end of the summer to invest in a new business that is certain to become the talk of the town."

"What about Jasmine's love life?"

"Her love life will do well because the man she's dating is on the same page as her."

Crossing her bare feet at the ankles, Hannah stared at the bright pink color on her toes. "We have come a long way, Jasmine, but as you say, we are survivors. I had to wait until I was fifty-nine to marry the man I'd been in love with since high school, but the wait has been worth it. If I hadn't married Robert, then I don't believe I'd cherish what I now have with St. John. Grand-mère DuPont used to say one has to taste some bitter fruit in order to appreciate the sweet ones."

"It is apparent marriage agrees with you because you look as content as Smokey when he's stretched out on the floor."

"St. John is the calm one in this marriage, and whenever I get upset about something all he has to do is look at me without saying a word so I end up talking to myself. I . . ." her words trailed off when her cellphone rang. A slight frown furrowed her smooth brow as the natural color drained from her face. "Someone's calling me from a hospital."

Jasmine heard the trepidation in Hannah's voice as her hand holding the phone began trembling. Galvanized into action, she reached for the phone and activated the speaker. "Hello."

"I'd like to know if I'm speaking to a Hannah DuPont," said a deep male voice.

"Who's calling?" Jasmine questioned, her eyes meeting Hannah's.

"I'm Dr. Bloom from Baton Rouge Memorial Hospital. I need to speak to Ms. DuPont because a patient was brought into our facility and her documents list Hannah DuPont as her next of kin."

"Hold on, Dr. Bloom, I'll see if Ms. DuPont is available to talk to you." Hannah nodded and Jasmine handed her back the phone.

"Dr. Bloom, I'm Hannah DuPont."

"Ms. DuPont, I'm going to need you to come up to Baton Rouge to sign some documents so we know how to proceed with your relative's medical treatment."

"Is it possible for you to give me the name of your patient who claims to be related to me?"

"Our records list her as Mamie DuPont Haines."

"How old is she?" Hannah asked.

"Ninety-nine. I know it's a holiday weekend, but if it is at all possible I'd like you to come as soon as you can."

Closing her eyes, Hannah sucked in a lungful of air. "I'm on my way."

"I'll be here all night, so when you get to the information desk tell them to page me and I'll meet you."

"Thank you, Dr. Bloom."

"You don't know who she is, do you?" Jasmine asked when Hannah ended the call.

"Even though I've never met her I'm familiar with the name. She's a distant cousin. Come with me. I'll tell you about the DuPonts while I pack an overnight bag. I don't know how long I'll have to be at the hospital, and I'm not going to chance driving back here late at night. I'll call St. John once I get to the hospital and let him know what's happening. I'm going to give you a set of keys to the house and the code for the security system. If you want to leave the house, there're keys to LeAnn and Paige's cars on a hook in the kitchen—"

"Calm down, Hannah, and take deep breaths. Don't worry about the house or Smokey. I'll take care of everything until you get back."

Hannah pressed her lips together. "St. John picked the wrong time to go away," she said between her teeth.

Jasmine caught Hannah's elbow and forcibly led her out of the sunroom and up the staircase to her bedroom. "Talk to me while you pack."

Hannah appeared noticeably calmer when she retrieved a floral-print quilted duffle bag. "Are you familiar with the rituals associated with quadroon balls?" she asked Jasmine.

"Yes." She'd read about the glamorous balls attended by wealthy white men looking to make beautiful mixed-race women their mistresses.

"I found a treasure trove of letters and diaries detailing there were a few *placées* and children of *plaçages* belonging to DuPont men. Some of them are descendants of distant cousins I've never met," Hannah admitted as she filled the bag with lingerie, grooming items, and several changes of clothes. "It was Grand-mère DuPont who knew most of the family's secrets. When I was a girl I'd sneak downstairs and listen outside the parlor when she'd whisper about mixed-race DuPonts who were fair enough to pass for white, and either left New Orleans for another parish or moved up North to escape Jim Crow. Some of them married into the white race, while there were a few women who gave birth to children of questionably darker hue, and that's when they had to get out of town."

"So, you're sure Mamie is related to you?"

"Very sure, because I remember seeing her name in a journal."

"How many other black relatives do you have?" Jasmine asked the older woman.

Hannah's lids slipped down over her eyes. "I have no idea."

"The DuPont men must have enjoyed dipping their *quills* into various inkwells."

Hannah smiled for the first time since the telephone call. "You're right, given the number of children they had with their mistresses." She zipped the duffle and scooped a leather tote off the window seat. She nodded to Jasmine. "I'm ready. The keys are downstairs."

Jasmine stood on the porch, watching the taillights of the Mercedes Benz sedan until they disappeared from sight. She wondered if her reaction would've been similar to Hannah if she'd gotten a call to help a relative she'd never met.

Hannah had never denied there were black people in her family. In fact, she seemed very proud of the fact her fifth generation great-grandmother was a free mulatto Haitian. It took only two generations for the main branch of the DuPont family tree to be recorded in the census as white, while their illegitimate children were recorded as Negro or colored.

Turning on her heel, she went back into the house, closing and locking the door, and then she armed the security system. She felt Smokey brush against her leg. "It's just you and me until your mama comes back." The cat meowed softly as if he understood what Jasmine was saying. She knew the cat had an automatic feeder, watering system, and self-cleaning litter box which meant she didn't have to cat-sit.

Sighing, she made her way up the staircase to the guest bedroom. Jasmine didn't know whether it was fatigue or the heat that had sapped her energy. The heat hadn't bothered her as a child when she'd slept in her grandparents' house with only a fan circulating the buildup of hot air.

Her eyelids were drooping as she brushed her teeth and washed her face. She adjusted the thermostat on the wall outside the bedrooms, climbed into bed and within minutes of closing her eyes she had fallen asleep.

Chapter 13

Cameron pulled up to the curb outside Hannah's house at the same time the front door opened and Jasmine stepped onto the porch. When she'd called to let him know she was in town he'd begun counting down the days when he would see her again.

He shifted into Park, but did not cut off the engine. He was out of the car by the time she'd come off the last stair. His eyes took in everything about her in one, sweeping glance: her hair pulled into a ponytail, bare face with only a hint of lip gloss, powder-blue slip dress ending at the knees, and blue-and-white striped espadrilles.

Cameron curved an arm around her waist, lowered his head, and brushed a light kiss over her slightly parted lips. "How are you?"

Jasmine rested a hand on his stubble. "Okay."

He pulled back, staring into a pair of eyes the color of rich dark coffee. "Just okay?"

She nodded. "It's the heat."

"I know. It's been brutal. Come, babe. I have the air on in the car." Cameron led her over to the off-white sports car. He waited until she was seated and belted-in before taking his own seat. "Is it cool enough?"

Jasmine smiled at him. "Yes. Thank you."

He rested a hand on her knee. "If it's all right with you, I'd like you to see the house before we go to brunch."

"It's fine with me."

Cameron shifted into gear, executed a U-turn and reversed direction. *She's different,* he mused. There was something about Jasmine's demeanor he found slightly unsettling. When she'd called him to let him know she was in New Orleans, she'd sounded tired and he'd attributed that to traveling and the intense heat and humidity. He'd suggested meeting on Saturday to give her a full day to rest and settle in. But, even now she appeared fatigued, lethargic.

"Were you and Hannah up until all hours talking last night?"

"No. Hannah's in Baton Rouge with a hospitalized elderly relative."

Cameron gave Jasmine a quick glance. Her eyes were closed. "When is she coming back?"

"She's not sure."

"You've been staying here alone?"

Jasmine opened her eyes. "No. Smokey keeps me company."

"He's a cat!"

"I know he's a cat."

"I can't believe Hannah went off and left you alone in the house with just a cat."

"She hadn't planned on having a family emergency."

Cameron clenched his jaw in frustration. "She could've called me and I would've had you stay with me."

"What about Smokey?"

"What about him?"

"Would you want him to come, too?"

"Yes. I love animals."

Jasmine placed her hand atop his on her knee. "You did say you'd wanted to be a vet. You don't have to worry about me because the house is wired with a high-tech security system."

Cameron reversed their hands, gently squeezing her fingers. "I worry. I don't want anything to happen to you."

"He likes me! He likes me!" Jasmine said in a spot-on imitation of Sally Fields's Academy Award speech.

Cameron laughed at her antics. He wanted to tell her he more than liked her. Yet he still wasn't ready to admit that he was falling in love with her. The emotions he felt when with Jasmine were too foreign, too unfamiliar to equate them with love because he had never loved a woman. He did not want to believe that he'd waited until he was almost fifty to become involved with someone who had him tied up in knots where he was very careful to monitor every word that came out of his mouth. He was afraid he would say the wrong thing and send her running in the opposite direction.

Perhaps karma had finally come to confront him as it had his brother. He'd chided Preston for loving and leaving a revolving door of women until he met Madison who had refused to go out with him because of his less-than-savory reputation. Now karma had come to repay another Singleton, and this time in spades. She was reminding Cameron about the women he'd dated while making it known to them they should not plan to spend the rest of their lives with him. It may have sounded cruel, unfeeling, but he had wanted them to know up front that he would not marry them.

However his way of thinking changed the instant he spied Jasmine sitting and laughing with her dining partners at the table in DuPont House. The first thing he noticed was how different she looked from the women he'd been attracted to in the past—tall, slender blondes like Hannah, and on occasion, a redhead. But when he finally asked her to dance the difference was magnetic. Everything about her for the few minutes he held her in his arms drew him in and refused to let him go. Although she hadn't outright rejected him when he'd asked to see her in New York, she didn't seem all that pleased that he'd come onto her.

Cameron was more than surprised she'd responded to his text. He was shocked. His apprehension continued when he saw her step out of the taxi and it wasn't until halfway through dinner that he was able to exhale when she invited him to accompany her to Long Island.

"You're really good. I believe you missed your calling."

"No I didn't," Jasmine said. "I never would've survived in show business. I'm not uninhibited enough."

"Didn't you tell me you performed in your school's talent show?"

"Yes. It was a lip-synch competition."

"Maybe one of these days we'll have to have a lip-synch competition, including dressing up like our favorite singers."

"Don't start something you can't finish," Jasmine teased, smiling.

"Is that a challenge, darling?"

"Yes, it is, *darling*."

"Oh, sweets," he crooned, "now it's on like Donkey Kong. You'd better start practicing if you hope to beat me."

Jasmine rested a hand at her hip. "I hate to see a grown man cry, but I suggest you hire a professional because not only do you have to lip-synch but you also have to have the dance moves to go with your song."

Cameron's laugh was low, throaty. "The song I'm going to choose doesn't need moves."

"What are you going to sing?"

He downshifted, coming to a complete stop at a traffic light in the Upper French Quarter. Resting his right hand over the back of the passenger seat, Cameron tugged Jasmine's ponytail. "I'm not telling."

"Why won't you tell me?"

"If it's a challenge, then why should I give you a hint? I don't want to know who you are going to impersonate."

"Ohhh-kay," she drawled. "Be like that."

Cameron grinned from ear to ear. "I should warn you that I'm very, very competitive."

Jasmine stared out the windshield. "So am I and you're about to meet your match." Her gaze swung back to him. "You're going down!"

He laughed loudly, the sound bouncing off the ceiling of the compact vehicle. The light changed and he shifted and took off again. Suddenly she appeared less lethargic and more animated. Cameron knew he had to be careful not to let Jasmine become overheated. It would take a while for her to become accustomed to the heat and humidity which could reach dangerous, life-threatening levels.

"We're now in the CBD," he said. Jasmine stared out the side window as Cameron drove slowly through streets in the neighborhood where he lived and worked. Some locals favored the Upper and Lower French Quarters, and others with Uptown and the Garden District, but for Cameron it was the Warehouse and Central Business District.

He drove down a street lined with Victorian warehouses built to store tons of raw cotton before the bales were loaded onto ships and transported to New England or European cotton mills. Sugar was another commodity that made those owning sugarcane plantations incredibly wealthy and afforded them a lifestyle that bordered on wretched excess.

He stopped in front of the building which would eventually become his home. "Don't move." Cameron got out and came around to assist Jasmine out of the car. "It doesn't look like much from the outside but—"

"Don't say anything, Cameron," Jasmine said in a quiet voice, stopping his words. "Let's go inside."

Jasmine waited for Cameron to unlock the massive wrought-iron door leading to a narrow cobblestone walkway that opened out into an expansive courtyard. She hadn't realized she was holding her breath until he unlocked another aged oaken door to an enormous street-level space with brick walls and stone floors. A trio of staircases led to the upper two stories.

She met Cameron's eyes. "It's perfect."

His eyebrows lifted. "There's nothing here. It was zoned for commercial use until a couple of years ago."

Jasmine touched his forearm. "It's perfect because it's a blank canvas. Once you show me the architect's rendering, I can pull up different decorating styles on my computer for you to approve."

Cameron stared at the brick floor. "You're the professional, Jasmine. I'll go along with whatever you recommend."

"This is going to become your home for many years to come, which means the furnishings have to suit your taste and lifestyle. Do you ever entertain family members, friends, or clients?"

He gave her a prolonged stare. "Yes."

"How often do you have people over?"

"It varies. Why?"

Jasmine walked over to a window facing the rear of the building. There was another open-air courtyard. "You can use the first floor for socializing." She turned and walked back to him. "You told me you have a chef, which means he or she needs a chef's kitchen to prepare dishes for your guests. And that means double sinks, ovens, dishwashers, and plenty of countertop space for prepping. I would suggest a number of seating groupings and at least one banquet table and a few others for more intimate dining. The same would go for bathrooms. You need a powder room for the ladies and a bathroom for the guys. I know I don't have to tell you about including a home theater, a.k.a. man cave."

Cameron laughed loudly. "Having a man cave is definitely a priority. What do you suggest for the second and third floors?"

"The second floor should be off-limits to everyone but you and whoever you choose to sleep over. Two thousand square feet is more than enough room for at least three to four bedrooms, each with an en suite bath. The third floor can be used as a sanctuary and home-office where you can go to relax or work undisturbed. I would create a Zen look with a bathroom resembling a personal spa."

"What about the walls? Would you cover the bricks?"

"I wouldn't because they'll add character to your home. The damaged ones can be replaced before they are sandblasted. I try and caution my clients not to make too many changes to the original design of their homes. I had a client who'd purchased a loft and wanted to cover the brick in the living room with sheetrock. Once I brought up a floor plan on the computer and dropped in leather seating groups, and natural wood tables, and an entertainment unit he claimed he loved it. He invited me to one of his launch parties to celebrate the release of a novel, and he pulled me aside to thank me for talking him out of covering the bricks."

Cameron crossed his arms over his chest. "Would you be opposed to meeting my architect?"

Jasmine's eyes grew wider. "Why?"

"He sent me the plans and rendering and even though I promised to download them to you, I decided to wait until you saw the property. I still haven't given Bram Reynard an approval of the plans."

"You're the client, Cameron, so you have the final say." He smiled, drawing Jasmine's gaze to the minute lines fanning out around his warm blue eyes. The gesture softened his features reminding her that he was an extremely attractive man. He hadn't shaved and the stubble enhanced his masculinity. Even casually dressed in a pair tan slacks, short-sleeved white shirt open at the collar, and a pair of tan loafers, he was a head-turner.

"I'll call Bram and ask when he has time to meet, but only after you let me know when you will be available."

Jasmine felt a jolt of excitement when she thought about transforming the empty space into a showcase for Cameron to live, entertain, and relax. "I want to stay close to the house until Hannah returns, then after that I'm all yours until the wedding."

"When are you leaving?"

"I don't know. When I made my reservation I didn't book a return flight."

Lowering his arms, Cameron took a step, pulled her to his chest, and rested his chin on the top of her head. "I know it's not realistic and that I sound selfish, but I don't want you to go back."

Jasmine looped her arms around his trim waist. "I have to, but I'll return around Labor Day to assist Hannah when we begin to interview staff for the inn."

Cameron froze. "What did you say?" He pulled back and met her eyes.

"I'm coming—"

"I know you said that. What I'm not getting is you working with Hannah."

Jasmine knew it was time to reveal her future plans. "I've decided to invest in the inn." She nearly laughed in Cameron's face when his jaw dropped. "My parents are definitely moving to North Carolina. They've purchased a house in a retirement community and now they're waiting for a date to close on the house in Freeport. Fortunately, I don't have to sell my condo because Danita's daughter is moving downstate and I told her she could live there for as long as she wants." Cameron picked her

up and swung her around and around until she felt the
room spinning. "Please stop before I throw up." Not only
was her head spinning but her stomach was also churn-
ing.

Cameron set her on her feet. "Sorry about that. Let's
get out of here and get something to eat. After that I'll
take you to my place and show you the plans."

Jasmine sat next to Cameron on a banquette in a
restaurant that reminded her of one she'd frequented with
her high schools friends whenever they met for a weekend brunch. The bar, with strategically placed televisions
featuring sporting events, was filled to capacity. It was
apparent Cameron had called ahead for a reservation;
when they arrived they were seated immediately.

She'd declined the complimentary unlimited mimosa
and Bellini in lieu of water, and selected eggs Benedict
with sliced melon. Jasmine nudged Cameron with her
foot when he ordered chicken and waffles. "You must
have read my mind because I was going to order that."

"Don't worry, babe. I'll let you have some."

She winked at him. "Thank you. How often do you eat
here?" she asked after the waitress set down her water
and his sweet tea.

"I come here a few times a month, but only for weekend brunch. During the week this place is filled with
wall-to-wall folks because the food is great, the drinks
are potent, and it's also a sports bar."

Jasmine glanced around the dining area. "I like it. It
has a nice vibe." Picking up the glass of water, she took a
sip at the same time she experienced a sickening feeling
in her stomach.

"What's the matter?" Cameron asked.

She took another sip. "I don't know. My stomach feels funny."

"Funny how?"

"It's like I ate something that didn't agree with me."

"What did you have this morning?" There was genuine concern in Cameron's voice.

"I had a slice of toast with a cup of coffee because I knew we'd be eating together."

"What did you eat yesterday?"

Jasmine searched her memory for what she had eaten the day before. "I bought a muffin and tea from a kiosk in the airport before my flight took off. I slept throughout the flight from New York to Miami. I had a one-hour layover, so I drank an orange juice. Hannah had offered to take me out for dinner, but I was so exhausted that she prepared a green salad with chicken, apple and maple walnuts in a buttermilk dressing."

Cameron rubbed Jasmine's back. "Maybe you picked up a bug from traveling. Being packed in a plane like sardines with recycled air isn't the healthiest environment."

She rested her head on his shoulder. "You're right about that. Maybe I'll feel better after I eat."

Her plate arrived and within seconds of taking a forkful of eggs topped with a delicious Hollandaise sauce, Jasmine grabbed her napkin, and held it to her mouth. "Excuse me," she mumbled and bolted off the seat and headed for the restroom just in time not to embarrass herself when she purged her stomach of its contents.

She rinsed her mouth and stared at her reflection in the mirror over the sink. Then she splashed water on her face and patted it dry with a paper towel. Jasmine couldn't remember the last time she'd thrown up. Once she was back in control, she left the bathroom and returned to her table.

Cameron stood up and kissed her forehead. "Are you all right?"

"I think so. I'm going to try and eat some more and hopefully I'll be able to keep it down."

Unfortunately luck wasn't with her when she found herself in the bathroom once again, regurgitating until she struggled to breathe. Tears streamed down her face and she sagged against the door to the booth to stop the room from spinning. She flushed the toilet and stumbled out to wash her face. Jasmine was rinsing her mouth when the door to the bathroom opened and Cameron walked in, carrying her cross body bag. She saw fear on his face as she stared at him with red-rimmed eyes.

"I'm still nauseous."

Cameron knew with a single glance Jasmine wasn't feeling well and if she continued to throw up she would end up dehydrated. Reaching for a paper towel, he blotted the moisture on her face. "I'm taking you to the hospital."

"No, Cameron. Just take me home and I'm sure I'll feel better after I lie down for a while."

His hand went around her upper arm, tightening slightly when she attempted to pull away. "No, Jasmine. You need to see a doctor to find out if maybe you have food poisoning."

"Okay."

He helped her out of the bathroom, signaled their waitress and pushed a large bill into her hand. "We have to leave." Bending, he scooped Jasmine up in his arms and carried her out to the parking lot.

"I can walk by myself," she slurred.

"I'll let you walk once the doctor clears you. Right now you look as if you're going to faint and wind up on the ground." He put her on the rear seats where she could lie down.

Cameron curbed the urge to speed because he didn't want to get stopped and delay getting Jasmine to the hospital. When he'd walked into the bathroom and saw her red eyes and tears streaming down her face, he felt as if someone had punched him in the gut. In that instant he knew he was in denial. Hannah had read him correctly because he was in love with Jasmine. He did not know when it'd happened or why her but that no longer mattered.

He made it to the small private hospital in record time and pulled into the lot near the entrance to Emergency. Jasmine had fallen asleep and when he attempted to gather her off the seat she woke up.

"Babe, we're here."

Jasmine sat up, blinking. "I can walk by myself."

Cameron wanted to shake her until she stopped insisting she could walk. "Okay, sweets. Let's go." He waited for her to gather her bag and put his arm around her waist and led her through the automatic doors. He seated her on a plastic chair before approaching the nurse's station.

The nurse sitting at the desk smiled at him. "May I help you?"

"My fiancée has been repeatedly throwing up. I'm afraid she may have eaten something that's making her sick." He'd said the first thing that came to his mind.

"Please take her to exam room two. Does she have her insurance information with her?"

Cameron struggled to keep his temper. The damn

woman was asking how they were going to get paid in the same breath as directing them to an exam room. "I don't know. I'll pay the bill."

"Someone will take your billing information once the doctor sees her. He may have to order a few tests."

"I said I will pay the bill." Cameron had enunciated each word.

Spots of red dotted the nurse's cheeks. "Thank you, *sir.*"

Cameron helped Jasmine to the room, she leaning weakly against him. He helped her up on the table, closed the curtain, and sat on the chair to wait for a doctor. "How are you feeling now?"

Jasmine turned her head and smiled. "Okay. I told you I'd feel all right if I lay down."

Minutes later the curtain opened a doctor who didn't look old enough to shave walked in. He extended his hand to Cameron. "I'm Dr. Benjamin."

"Cameron Singleton," he said, introducing himself.

"What seems to be the problem?" the doctor asked.

Jasmine raised her head. "I threw up. I think it's something I ate."

Cameron let go of the doctor's hand. "She threw up twice."

Dr. Benjamin walked over to Jasmine and smiled. "And who are you?"

"Jasmine Washington."

"Well, Ms. Washington, I'm going to examine you and run a few tests to find out why you're throwing up. Meanwhile someone will take your medical history." He turned to Cameron. "I'm going to ask you to step out and have a seat in the waiting room. Once we find the cause of her vomiting, I'll let you know."

Cameron nodded. He leaned over and pressed a kiss to Jasmine's forehead. "Feel better, babe."

Cameron lost track of how many times he checked the wall clock as he waited for Jasmine to be examined. Picking up a magazine devoted to golf, he thumbed through a few articles before setting it aside to get a cup of coffee from the vending machine. The minutes ticked past an hour when he saw Dr. Benjamin's approach.

He popped from the chair like a jack-in-the-box. "How is she?"

"There's nothing wrong that should concern you. You can go and see her and she'll give you the good news."

Cameron offered his hand and wasn't disappointed when the other man shook it vigorously. "Thank you." He did what he hadn't often enough—said a silent prayer of thanks. He found Jasmine sitting on the side of the bed, her hands cradled in her lap. Her eyes were slightly puffy indicating she had been crying. Reaching for her hands, he kissed her fingers. They were cold and trembling. "What's the matter, darling?"

When she looked up at him, Cameron saw fear and panic in her eyes. "I'm pregnant."

He mouthed the two words, and then shook his head in disbelief. She couldn't be pregnant. They'd made love twice and each time he used a condom. "Are you sure?"

Jasmine nodded as her face crumpled like an accordion and she cried without making a sound. He pulled her to his chest and held her. Her slender body shook like a fragile leaf in the wind. Cameron knew it wasn't the time or the place to talk about the tiny life growing inside her.

"Stay here, darling. I'll be back after I settle the bill."

Jasmine sniffled. "I have insurance."

"That's all right. I'll take care of it." Reaching into the pocket of his slacks, he took out a handkerchief and gently dabbed her face. He kissed the end of her nose. "Don't run away."

Jasmine waited for Cameron to leave to look for a restroom. The doctor had checked her heart, lungs, blood pressure, ears, nose, and throat, and then ordered the nurse to draw blood and get a urine sample from her. It was when he'd asked her for the first day of her last period she had to count backward to April. Her menses always came on time like clockwork and now it was late May and nothing. The doctor estimated that she was currently five or six weeks into her first trimester. What she couldn't understand was that Cameron had used protection each time they had made love. And the condoms were his, and not the ones she'd taken from the yacht's restroom.

She returned to the exam room to find a sheet of paper on the bed with her name written across the top. It was a listing of recommendations to avoid morning sickness. What she needed was a list of recommendations on how to avoid an unplanned pregnancy. Once she'd begun sleeping with Gregory she immediately took an oral contraceptive, and it was the same when she was married to Raymond. She'd stopped taking the pill once her marriage ended, and Jasmine knew if she was still on the pill she wouldn't find herself carrying the child of a man who didn't want children or marriage.

Jasmine detected the familiar scent of Cameron's cologne before he reentered the room. "I'm ready."

He draped an arm over her shoulders. She saw a gentleness in his eyes she'd never seen before. "You're coming home with me so we can talk."

"What is there to talk about?"

"You, me, and this baby you're carrying."

"You want it?"

"Of course I want it."

"Why, Cameron? Weren't you the one who said you didn't want children?" As their eyes met Jasmine felt like someone had dropped ice down her back when she saw his eyes change from blue to a frosty gray.

"We will not talk about it here," he said, barely moving his lips. "Let's go—please."

Jasmine picked up her bag and brushed past him. It was only when she stepped out into the smothering heat that she thought about how she was going to assist in managing an inn, decorate Cameron's house, *and* take care of a baby.

She shook off Cameron's hand when he attempted to help her into the low-slung sports car. "I told you I'm okay."

He opened his mouth to say something, and then closed it. "Suit yourself."

Chapter 14

Jasmine stared at Cameron when he parked in a re-served space in the rear of a hotel. "You live here?" He nodded. "For how long?"

Cameron shut off the engine and released his seatbelt. "Ten years. Don't move, and if you dare tell me you're all right I'll go ape-shit, Jasmine."

She stared, wordlessly, unable to form the words to come back at him. He'd shown her another side of the soft-spoken man who had managed to tear down her defenses.

Jasmine placed her hand on Cameron's outstretched palm and allowed him to pull her to her feet. He continued to hold her hand as he swiped a card on a door with a sign indicating residents and employees only.

She followed him down a hallway to an elevator. He swiped his card again, and the doors opened. This time instead of using the keycard, Cameron inserted a key into the slot for the fifth floor and the doors closed. "Why do you live in a hotel?" She had to say something, anything to break the tension between them.

"Convenience. If I had a house I would have to hire a cook and housekeeper, landscaper, and someone to make repairs. With the hotel if I want something to eat all I have to do is call room service. Or if something needs repairing, then it's maintenance. There's a laundry service on the premises, and if I have to entertain there are two lounges and several private rooms on the lobby level."

"Oh, I see."

A hint of a smile tilted the corners of Cameron's mouth. "Do you really?"

"There's no need to be condescending, Cameron."

"Was I?"

"Yes."

He angled his head, his smile in place. "I'm sorry."

She rolled her eyes. "Apology accepted."

The doors opened and Cameron stepped aside to let her exit the elevator. Instead of stepping out into a hall like in most hotels she found herself inside a living room with period pieces she recognized as a Louis XVI screen and nineteenth-century Barbedienne urns that served as lamps. Jasmine walked over and ran her fingertips over a velvet-covered Knole-style sofa. She strolled around the room, mentally cataloguing the exquisite furnishings that included a Louis XV *bergère* chair that would never go out of style.

Turning, she saw Cameron smiling at her. "Are these antiques or reproductions?"

"I've been told they are the real deal."

"Have they been appraised?"

"Yes."

"Do they belong to you or the owner of the hotel?"

"They were here when I moved in."

Jasmine caressed the silk fabric on the chair. "Everything is beautiful."

Cameron emptied his pockets and left the contents on a side table. "I'm glad you like it. I'm going to call room service because you need to eat."

She lowered her eyes. "I'm sorry I spoiled your brunch."

"Don't worry about it, darling. I'm not going to starve if I miss a meal. You, on the other hand, need food."

"What are you going to order?"

"Broiled chicken without the skin, spinach, and sweet potatoes."

"Is that for me or us?"

"It's for us."

Jasmine didn't have the energy to argue with him that she would've preferred looking at a menu to make her selections. "Do you have mouthwash?"

"Yes. The bathroom is through the dining room and on the right."

Cameron picked up the hotel phone and placed his order with the kitchen staff. When Jasmine said she was pregnant he didn't want to believe it; however, he knew for certain the baby she carried was his. He'd been with enough women to know Jasmine hadn't been sexually active for a while, and the condoms were his not hers, so he couldn't accuse her of using him to deliberately get pregnant. And judging from her reaction when the doctor told her she was going to be a mother, it was apparent the news had shocked her. But he wanted to know whether she planned to keep the baby. After all, she had a lot to consider: age, her plan to relocate, and to begin another career.

Jasmine emerged from the bathroom hair neatly brushed and pulled into a ponytail. "We need to talk before the food gets here."

That's my girl, he mused. The spunky independent woman was back in control. He pointed to the sofa. "Please sit down."

Cameron waited for Jasmine to sit when he picked up a chair to face her. "Do you plan to keep the baby?" She blinked slowly, and then the floodgates opened again and she began to cry. Reaching into his pocket, he handed her his handkerchief. She dabbed her eyes and blew her nose.

"I always wanted a baby but not like this. Not with a stranger."

Cameron caught his breath, wanting to go to Jasmine and comfort her, but willed himself not to move. Not yet. "We stopped being strangers the moment we made love, Jasmine."

She closed her eyes. "It's just so crazy."

"What is?"

Jasmine opened her eyes, moisture spiking the lashes. "We used protection yet I still end up pregnant."

"Maybe it was meant to be."

"You want this baby?"

Cameron got up and sat beside Jasmine. "I want *you* and I want *our* baby." He kissed her hair. "What if we talk about *us* after your friend's wedding? That will give us time to get to know each other better before we plan for the future. Eventually I'd like you to move in here with me, but only when you feel comfortable."

Jasmine relaxed against his side, sinking into his embrace. "I'd appreciate it if you wouldn't mention the baby until after I go through a battery of tests to determine if there are any fetal abnormalities. At my age I'm considered high-risk."

"I won't say a word." As a realist, Cameron knew he and Jasmine weren't in love with each other, but he hoped with time they would fall in love.

Jasmine lay in bed in Hannah's guest bedroom, staring up at the shadows on the ceiling. She'd spent all afternoon in Cameron's hotel apartment, eating and napping in his bed once fatigue overtook her. It wasn't only the heat which had sapped her energy, but the tiny life growing in her womb.

She placed her hand over her flat belly and closed her eyes. A part of her wanted the doctor's diagnosis to be a false positive, while the other still couldn't grasp the reality that, if she carried to term, that she would welcome a son or daughter early the following year.

She'd slept with three men over the past twenty years and during that time she never had to resort to purchasing a drugstore pregnancy test for fear she may be carrying a child. Early in their relationship, Jasmine had slept with Gregory on average of three to four times a week. But as he aged their encounters became less frequent and occasionally they would end up cuddling.

Cameron had mentioned waiting until after Tonya's wedding to talk about the baby, themselves and for that she was grateful. Two weeks would allow her time to assess what she expected from Cameron and he from her. They weren't teenagers or even twenty- or thirty-somethings who felt compelled to marry because of pressure from outside sources. Jasmine didn't need a husband; she needed a father for her child.

Her cellphone rang, and she rolled over to pick it up off the bedside table. The caller was Hannah. "Hello," she said in greeting. "How's it going?"

"She's gone, Jasmine. Mamie died in her sleep last night."

"Did you get a chance to talk to her?"

"Yes. She said her great-grandmother told her that she'd been a *placée* at fifteen to a DuPont before the Civil War. They had three sons, all who carried the DuPont surname. They married mulatto women and a few of their children were able to pass for white. Mamie had become the family historian. She married when she was a young woman, but lost her husband in the Second World War. Unfortunately, she never had any children. When her health began failing she went into a nursing home. Although her body was frail, her mind was still sharp. She'd listed me as her medical proxy, and her last wish is to be cremated. I'd arranged for a local funeral home to handle the cremation."

"When are you coming home?" Jasmine asked Hannah.

"Tomorrow morning. I'm too exhausted to get behind the wheel tonight. Tonya called to confirm for tomorrow and I told her we were coming."

"Good." Jasmine wondered how long she would be able to conceal her condition from her friends. "I'll see you tomorrow. Drive safely."

"Don't worry. I will."

* * *

Jasmine held out her arms when Tonya Martin opened the front door. The talented executive chef looked different from when she last saw her. She'd lost weight, her face appeared more sculpted, and her pixie haircut with a sprinkling of gray hugged her scalp like a neat cap. Twin dimples flashed in her flawless brown face.

"You look incredible, Tonya. You're going to be a beautiful bride."

Tonya returned the hug. "Thank you." She eased back, her eyes narrowing slightly. "Your face looks different."

"That's what I said to her," Hannah said as she joined them.

"Good gracious," Tonya said. "Where are my manners? Please come in."

Jasmine walked into the Parisian-style garret house in the Lower French Quarter that Tonya shared with her musician-turned-chef fiancé, Gage Toussaint. The courtyard, where they were scheduled to hold the wedding ceremony, resembled an emerald city with towering trees draped in Spanish moss, and flowering plants in massive clay pots. Strings of globe lights and lanterns were suspended from the beams supporting the second-story balcony.

"Your home is magnificent."

"I can't take any credit for what you see inside. Gage's mother decorated this place."

"Did I hear someone call my name?"

Jasmine turned and smiled at the man she remembered playing trumpet at a jazz club when she'd come to New Orleans last summer. It wasn't until later that Hannah told them Gage was St. John's cousin. Large gray-green eyes framed by long black lashes, a palomino-gold complexion, and delicate features, cleft chin, and cropped straight black salt-and-pepper hair made him almost too pretty to be a man.

"Yeah. It was one of your many groupies," Jasmine teased.

Gage lowered his eyes, seemingly embarrassed. "I'm too old to have groupies."

Jasmine kissed his cheek. "If Mick Jagger at seventy-something has groupies then you can definitely have groupies." Gage was at least thirty years younger than the celebrated rock and roller.

"The only groupie I want or need is the woman who's going to become my wife in two weeks." Gage winked at Hannah. "St. John has been bragging about how much he's enjoying married life so I decided it was time I turn in my bachelor card and marry his wife's friend."

Tonya swatted at Gage with the towel she'd thrown over her shoulder. "I thought you wanted to marry me because you claim you can't live without me, not because you're competing with your cousin."

Gage held up his hands. "I do, my love."

Tonya looped her arm through Gage's. "Jasmine, you won't get to meet Gage's son Wesley because he's helping Eustace cater a party tonight."

"We're going to begin with cocktails and hors d'oeuvres," Gage explained, "before we serve the main meal."

"I'm going to pass on the cocktails," Jasmine said. "It's the heat," she added quickly when Hannah stared at her. Her excuse seemed to satisfy everyone as they walked into the dining room. She'd followed the recommendation to offset morning sickness by having a slice of toast, lightly covered with peanut butter and a glass of orange juice for breakfast, and subsequently experienced only mild nausea instead of the retching episodes of the day before.

Hannah took her arm. "Come with me. I'll show you where we can wash our hands."

They stepped into the bathroom and Hannah closed the door.

"What are you doing?"

"You're pregnant." It wasn't a question but a statement.

Jasmine stared without blinking. "How did you know?"

"I didn't until you refused to drink. When I saw you the other day I noticed your face had changed but I couldn't figure out why. You're carrying Cameron's baby, aren't you?"

"Yes."

"Does he know?"

"Yes," Jasmine repeated. "And before you ask. No, we didn't plan it."

Hannah's mouth thinned until it resembled a slash in her face. "Are you getting married?"

"No."

"Why not?"

"Why the interrogation, Hannah?" She was hard-pressed to keep a tone of annoyance from creeping into her voice. "I hadn't planned to tell you about it until after my first trimester. I know I agreed to invest in the inn but having a baby may change everything."

"How so?"

"I have to take maternity leave and then look for someone to take care of the baby once I return to work."

Hannah smiled. "If you're attempting to use your pregnancy as an excuse to weasel out of becoming an innkeeper then forget it, little mama. I only asked if you were getting married because Cameron is in love with you."

"No, he's not," Jasmine countered, shaking her head.

"I've known Cameron for a long time and he's always been quite the lady's man but he's changed since meeting you. I'm willing to bet that underneath his charm and swagger, he's really a good guy in spite of his reputation as a serial dater."

Jasmine chewed the inside of her lip, not understanding why Hannah continued to bash Cameron. "I'm not going to judge him by what he did before I met him. I, too, have a skeleton in my closet. Remember, I told you that my first lover was thirty years older than me."

Hannah nodded. "I still can't imagine you sleeping with a man old enough to be your father."

Jasmine affected a smug grin. Knowing she hadn't always been the innocent young woman apparently had changed Hannah's impression of her. "Not a day goes by that I ever regretted what I had with him."

"Good for you," Hannah said. "We'd better wash our hands or Tonya and Gage will think we're in here doing something kinky," she teased.

Jasmine sat at the kitchen table in a nightgown, bare feet resting on a chair, as she watched Hannah blend a smoothie. For the next nine months she would give up coffee, tea, colas, and alcohol. She wasn't much of a milk drinker and had to devise a way in which to include dairy in her daily diet.

At lunch, Tonya and Gage had prepared sample tapas they planned to offer their patrons once they opened their supper club. Each small dish was more delicious that the one before it and Jasmine ate until she was too full to swallow another morsel. She opted for water instead of wine and the pre-dinner cocktails. And she had been forthcoming with Hannah, revealing the details leading to her relationship with Cameron, and in the process unburdening herself.

Hannah set the glass with a straw on the table. "Let me know if you like it."

Jasmine took a sip. "Wow! It's delicious. What's in it?"

"Mango, peaches, strawberries, plain yogurt, and almond milk."

She took another sip. "Giving up coffee will be worth it if I substitute smoothies."

Hannah rested her elbow on the table and cupped her chin in her hand. "And a smoothie is less fattening than ice cream. I used to crave ice cream when I was pregnant with Wyatt."

"Hopefully I won't have any cravings that will make me blow up like a balloon."

"When are you due?"

"The last week in January."

"I think you should take Cameron's suggestion and live with him."

Jasmine went completely still. "Say what?"

"If the man wants you to live with him, then do it. How else are you going to get to know him? Look at Tonya. She moved in with Gage after they were together only a few months."

"Didn't she move in with him after he asked her to marry him?"

Hannah shook her head. "No. She was staying in the guesthouse and when the gates to the property malfunctioned he suggested she stay with him. And I don't believe they were sleeping together at that time."

"Are you giving me a vacate-the-premises notice, Hannah?"

"If you say it like that, then yes I am. I'm going to call Cameron tomorrow and tell him to come and pick you up and take you home with him."

"What's going to be your excuse?"

"Don't need one."

"You invite me to stay in your house and now you're saying I have to leave. I know you want to play matchmaker but not by forcing me on Cameron. He's said he wants me and the baby and I want to believe him. Besides you're not supposed to know I'm pregnant. I made him promise not to tell anyone until I completed my first trimester."

Hannah nodded. "Okay. You win. I won't interfere again."

"You're not interfering, Hannah. I know you want for me what you have with St. John, and if it's meant to be then I'm willing to let it play out."

She lowered her arm. "Are you saying you want to marry Cameron?"

"No. But if I do marry him, it'll be because I love him and can't imagine my life without him, not because of a baby."

"Has he mentioned marriage?"

"No. And neither will I."

There came a pause before Hannah spoke again. "What do you want? Boy or girl?"

"What's the pat answer? I don't care as long as it's healthy. Aside from barfing, I don't feel pregnant," Jasmine admitted. "Once my body starts changing, then it will become more of a reality."

Hannah glanced at the clock on the microwave. "After you finish your smoothie you should head for bed. You don't realize it but your eyelids are getting heavy. I forgot to tell you that I'm going to give you the name and number of my ob-gyn."

"I'll sign a release so my doctor in New York can fax my medical records down here." Jasmine finished the smoothie, rinsed the glass, and placed it in the dishwasher. "Good night, Hannah."

"Good night. I'm going to stay up a little longer and wait for St. John's call."

Jasmine left the kitchen and climbed the staircase to her bedroom. For her, sleep had become a commodity more precious than gold.

Chapter 15

Cameron studied the numbers on the spreadsheet until they began to blur. He was daydreaming again. He'd begun the task of reviewing the portfolios of every Singleton Investments client. His father's retirement was still six months away, but Cameron felt the undertaking would help distract him from obsessing about Jasmine and the baby. He knew Jasmine wanted children while he had been ambivalent about fathering a child, but that was no longer a subject of discussion or debate because a power beyond his control deemed otherwise.

"Cameron, Mrs. Tennyson is on the phone for you." His assistant's voice coming through the intercom shattered his musings.

"Thank you, Allison. Please patch her through." He picked up the receiver and swiveled on the chair to stare out the window. "Mrs. Tennyson, how are you?" he said after hearing the elderly woman's singsong greeting.

"I'm well, Cameron. Have you given any more thought to my investing in my grandson's company?"

Cameron massaged his forehead as he recalled his client's excuse for withdrawing a million dollars from her account to invest in what he knew was a Ponzi scheme. "Yes, Mrs. Tennyson, you did tell me he's your grandson, but as your wealth manager I'm going to caution you about giving him that much money."

"What do you recommend I give him?"

"No more than five thousand." Cameron suggested the figure because he knew her lowlife grandson would reject it outright.

"But, he says he needs a million."

"Tell your grandson to call me and I'll set up a meeting with him to talk about his new venture. If I feel it's viable I'll carefully scrutinize and analyze installment transfers."

Abigail Tennyson's family had amassed a fortune in oil and natural gas and Singleton Investments had safeguarded their wealth with prudent stock ventures. Abigail's grandson had squandered his multimillion-dollar trust in less than two years and was looking for more from his indulgent grandmother. Cameron's sixth sense told him the wannabe Bernie Madoff was about to get a rude awakening if he believed Singleton Investments would randomly give him a million dollars without strict monitoring because of his grandmother's generosity.

"That sounds fair. I'll tell him to call you. Thank you, Cameron."

"You're welcome, Mrs. Tennyson."

A light knock garnered Cameron's attention. He turned on the chair and saw his brother in the doorway. "Come on in." Preston had taken a week off to take his son and daughter to the Smoky Mountains. "How was it roughing it with your kids?"

Preston walked into the office and sat on the corner of the credenza. "It was great. They'd really got the hang of fly-fishing. I came to ask you about your new lady."

Cameron's brows drew downward in a frown. "What are you talking about?"

"Madison and some of her girlfriends were having brunch at Momma's Place last week and she said she saw you with a woman who she says is definitely not your type."

A muscle flicked angrily in Cameron's jaw. He wanted to tell his brother that Madison should stay the hell out of his personal life. His sister-in-law continued to hold a grudge because he'd refused to date her best friend. "Since when does your wife determine who my type is?"

"I'm sure she didn't mean it like that," Preston said in defense of his wife.

"Please don't make excuses for her, Preston. If Madison wanted to know who the lady was with me, then she should've come over to the table and I would've introduced her."

"She was going to but you'd left. Who was she, Cam?"

Cameron leaned back in his chair and stared at his brother until Preston lowered his eyes. He wasn't about to tell his family about Jasmine and the baby until after she'd gone through the battery of tests. He knew she was concerned about fetal abnormalities because of her age, but whatever the outcome Cameron would be there for her—for them.

"She's my interior decorator." *And the mother of my unborn child,* he mused. It had taken him more than twenty-four hours to accept the reality Jasmine was carrying his child. He had stopped questioning himself about why her, and not another woman with whom he'd slept since becoming sexually active.

Jasmine had talked about destiny, and how she believed in predestination, which led Cameron to believe if Hannah hadn't invited him to her wedding, his path and Jasmine's would've never crossed.

When they'd returned from the hospital he had lost track of time when he sat on the chair next to the bed in his bedroom suite, watching Jasmine as she slept, and he didn't have to be a mind reader to know she was emotionally distraught. Her apparent shock and tears communicated she wasn't prepared for an unplanned pregnancy—and with a man with whom she hadn't known a week. She hadn't mentioned the *A* word and there was no way Cameron would have suggested she undergo an abortion. That would have to be Jasmine's call. And his passionate plea that he wanted Jasmine and the baby had come from his fear of losing her; he wanted her with or without a child.

"Have you commissioned her to decorate your home?" Preston asked.

Cameron nodded. "Yes."

"Where did you find her?"

"What's up with the inquisition, brother?"

Preston smiled. "I'm just asking, *brother,* because it's been a while since you've been seen in public with a woman."

Cameron knew Preston was right. He hadn't dated a

woman since meeting Jasmine in October. "I've taken a break."

"Good for you, Cam. And I know what you're talking about. There had been a time when I dated a lot of women before I realized they'd all begun to look and sound alike. I also took a break and when I met Madison for the first time I knew within days she was the woman I wanted to marry. I know you don't like her—"

"I never said I didn't like Madison," Cameron interrupted. "She's my sister-in-law and the mother of my niece and nephew, which means she's family. Madison is still pissed at me because I wouldn't go out with her best friend, and it's time she let that go."

Preston blinked slowly, reminding Cameron of an owl. "Maddie never said anything to me about that."

"And why should she?" Cameron asked. "It was between me, Madison, and Lindsay Worthington."

"Lindsay? You're telling me my wife tried hooking you up with Lindsay?"

Cameron bit back a smile when he saw his brother's shocked expression. "Do you know another Lindsay?"

"Well, damn, Cam. Maddie should know you'd never go out with someone like her. She talks so much that only someone who's hearing impaired would be able to spend more than ten minutes with her."

"I don't want you to say anything to Madison about this, because as far as I'm concerned it's moot."

"She has no call to act like you don't exist whenever you're around because of someone who can't get a man."

"Let it go, Preston. Your wife doesn't have to like me, but that doesn't change how I feel about her." Cameron was always polite to his sister-in-law and treated her with respect, and had forgiven her outburst when he told her he wasn't interested in her friend. What he hadn't told Madison was that he wouldn't have anything to do with Lindsay even if she was the last woman on the face of the Earth.

"No problem, Cam. I won't say anything to her."

Cameron's cellphone's ringtone indicated a call from Jasmine. "Excuse me, but I have to take this call." He picked up the phone. "Please hold on a second," he said in a quiet voice. "Preston, could you close the door on your way out? How are you?" he asked her once the door closed behind his brother.

"I'm okay."

"You're just okay?" It'd been a week since they were last together, although they managed to talk to each other at least twice a day.

"Maybe I should've said I'm good."

Cameron didn't believe her, and suspected Jasmine was still being plagued by nausea. "I'm glad to hear that."

"I just finished going over the plans and rendering of your home and I'd like to suggest a few changes, but only after discussing them with your architect and engineer."

"Let me see if I can arrange a meeting where the four of us can get together. I'll call you back as soon as I talk to them."

"Don't set it up for Thursday morning because I have an appointment with Hannah's obstetrician."

"Hannah knows?"

"Yes. She knew without my telling her. She said I looked different and when I refused a cocktail she put two and two together. I didn't want to lie to her and told her everything about us. And she knows not to say anything."

Cameron didn't know why, but he felt a measure of relief that Hannah was now aware of the significance of their relationship, that he was resolute in his commitment to Jasmine. "I'm glad she knows. Now she can stop threatening me about messing over you."

"She's just trying to protect me, Cameron."

"It can't be from me, Jasmine. I told you before I pray never to hurt you physically or emotionally."

"Hannah knows firsthand what I went through with my ex—"

"I'm not your ex, Jasmine. I'd never do to a woman what he did to you. So, there's no comparison."

There came a beat. "Can we please change the topic?"

"No problem. I'm going to call the architect and engineer and then I'll get back to you."

"I'll be here."

Cameron's mouth was tight, as a muscle quivered at his jaw. He hated when Jasmine brought up her ex-husband, and he hoped that it would not become a source of contention between them. He was willing to leave his past behind, and he expected the same from her if they were going to share a future now that they were planning to bring another human being into the world.

He tapped the intercom to his assistant's office. "Sharleen, I need you to get Bram Reynard and Lamar Pierce on the phone for a three-way." Cameron picked up a pen drawing interconnecting circles on a legal pad as he waited for the other two men to come on the line. "Gentlemen," he said in greeting when he heard their voices, "I need to set up a meeting that will include my interior decorator. This Thursday morning is out."

"I'm available later this evening," Bram said.

"Same here," the engineer confirmed.

"Let's meet at the hotel lobby at five. I'll arrange for dinner in one of the private dining rooms."

"I'll be there," Lamar said.

"Me, too," Bram said in agreement.

As promised, Cameron called Jasmine and informed her he would pick her up at Hannah's house at four o'clock for a meeting at the hotel. Her bubbly laugh came through the earpiece.

"That was fast."

"When the boss speaks, I jump."

"I'm not the boss, Cameron."

"You are when it comes to decorating our home." The instant *our home* slipped off his tongue Cameron realized he'd made a faux pas. Hannah had repeatedly warned him about moving too quickly with Jasmine, that he couldn't put any pressure on her to do what he wanted, but to allow her to take the lead on the direction of their relationship.

"I'll be ready at four."

Cameron exhaled an audible breath. Jasmine appeared to have ignored his reference to the house as their home. He knew once she relocated, she did not want to impose on Hannah and St. John by living in their house. And that meant she needed a place to stay; and that place would be an adjoining suite at the hotel and subsequently the home she would decorate, hopefully for their family.

Jasmine waved to Cameron when his car came to a stop in front of the house. The weather had cooled considerably which allowed her to sit on the porch and read for hours. She had gone online and ordered two books about pregnancy. Cameron was out of the car before she could gather her purse and come down off the porch.

Her pulse quickened when she realized just how much she'd missed him. Talking to him on the phone was one thing, but seeing him in the flesh was entirely different. Their brief time off from each other allowed her the time to reexamine her feelings about the soft-spoken, reserved man who'd come into her life and turned it upside down.

She'd slept with him after their third encounter, something she'd never done with any other man, without experiencing a modicum of guilt. After all, she was over forty, divorced, and in control of her life and her future. Being the object of a man's attention, even for a few days, had allowed her to forget her past and enjoy his company. What Jasmine hadn't planned, and neither had Cameron, was that the intimate act they'd shared would result in her becoming pregnant.

Jasmine couldn't see Cameron's eyes behind the lenses of a pair of sunglasses but his smile was enough. He was as pleased to see her as she him. Going on tiptoe, she pressed her mouth to his. "Did you go to work today?"

Cameron glanced down at his khaki walking shorts, short-sleeve white untucked shirt, and tan woven sandals. "Yes. I left the office at three. You look rather business-like."

"I thought we were having a business meeting." Jasmine had styled her hair in a twist she had pinned off the nape of her neck, and had selected a powder-blue pantsuit, a white silk blouse, and two-inch navy-blue pumps. "If you want I can go back and change."

He kissed her forehead. "Don't. You look beautiful. The meeting isn't until five. I thought I'd get you there early so you can have a snack before dinner." Cameron opened the passenger-side door and waited for her to get in.

"I find myself eating about five small meals a day instead of three full ones," Jasmine told Cameron after he'd slipped in behind the wheel.

"Are you still throwing up?"

"It comes and goes."

He started the engine and pulled smoothly away from the curb. "I'd like to go with you when you see the doctor Thursday."

Jasmine stared out the windshield. "You don't have to."

He gave her a quick glance. "But I want to. I don't ever want you to forget that we're in this together."

"Will you let me forget?"

"No way, darling. What time is your appointment?"

"Nine. Hannah has offered to go with me."

"Let Hannah know that I'm going to take you. I want you to text me the doctor's name and address."

Jasmine knew it was useless to try and talk Cameron out of accompanying her to the doctor, and she also didn't want to engage in a verbal confrontation with him. His revelation that he had grown up with two warring parents was something she did not want for their child. Yet Jasmine did not intend to become a doormat for Cameron or to genuflect or acquiesce to his every demand. She had decided to pick and choose her battles, while standing her ground for what she felt would be to her benefit.

"Okay."

"I'd also like you to let me know the time and dates for all your appointments."

Jasmine stared at him. "All of them?"

Cameron nodded. "Yes."

"Don't you have a company to run?"

"Yes, but it's not going to fall apart if I take a couple of hours off a few times a month. Don't forget my father still heads the company, and my brother Preston can always cover for me if Dad's not there."

"Tell me about the Singletons." Jasmine had Googled Singleton Investments but found scant information on the family-owned, privately held company.

"What do you want to know?"

"How did they come to settle in Louisiana?"

Jasmine listened intently as Cameron gave her an abbreviated version of his family's history. His ancestors made their fortune in shipping cotton and sugar cane to northern and European cities. During the Civil War, Union generals commandeered his great-great-great-grandfather's ships to transport armaments to supply General Grant and Sherman's troops.

"Archibald Singleton told everyone the Union general had appropriated his ships when in reality he'd willingly offered them up. No one knew he spied for the Union because he didn't own slaves, and believed in preserving the Union. Archibald was devoutly religious and believed it was a sin for one man to own another man. All of his household help and dock workers were free people of color."

"Were there that many free people of color at that time?"

Cameron smiled. "Yes. There was always a large population of free people of color in New Orleans."

"Did anyone ever uncover Archibald's double life?"

"No. He had become quite the consummate actor."

"What happened after the war?" Jasmine asked.

"Once the mode of transportation changed from shipping to railroads, Archibald's sons went into insurance. They were very conservative when it came to buying and selling stocks and bonds, and didn't believe in putting all of their money in banks. After the Crash of '29 when there was a run on the banks, the tightwad Singletons congratulated themselves because they were able to hold on to to most of their fortune. My penny-pinching great-grandfather used the Great Depression to become an accomplished hustler."

Jasmine eyes shimmered with amusement. "Please don't tell me he became a black marketeer."

Cameron chuckled. "Not quite. He set up a food pantry and gave away food to the neediest families. Meanwhile he had set up an investment company for those who believed he had kept his fortune because of prudent investments."

"So he was a Scrooge turned philanthropist."

"You could say that. Once the country recovered from the Depression, folks were standing in line begging him to take their money. He was an equal opportunity investment manager because no one was turned away whether they had one hundred dollars or a hundred thousand.

"Once my father took over he set up internal departments within the company based on a client's net worth. We treat clients who have five thousand the same as those with five hundred million."

"How many clients do you have?" Jasmine asked.

"Right now we have twenty-eight."

"That's not many."

"It's eight more than we normally handle. We're a small investment company, and unlike companies like Goldman Sachs or Merrill Lynch Wealth Management, we have a very personal relationship with our clients. I'm responsible for our wealthiest clients and they demand a greater level of service than average clients. This includes advice on estate planning, stock-option planning, and occasionally the use of hedging derivatives for large blocks of stock. Our overall services include: financial, investment, retirement, business retirement, and estate planning."

Jasmine thought about the monies she'd put away for the proverbial rainy day. She did not fall into the wealthy category, yet she had done well for herself. Hannah had given her the contract outlining the conditions of her investing in the DuPont Inn. She'd read it over before sending it to Amelia. Her cousin questioned several clauses and discussed them with Hannah. Her friend then deleted them. Jasmine signed the amended copy, and then authorized her bank to transfer the funds to Hannah's bank. She was now officially an innkeeper.

"If you have a son, would you insist he join the family company?" she asked Cameron.

"No. I would never make that a condition as to his career choice. My brothers have four boys between them to carry on the family name and they have the option of choosing to continue the tradition of running Singleton Investments. My father took me to work with him as a teenager and like an addict, investing became my drug of choice."

Jasmine understood his passion. For her it had been decorating. The first time her mother brought her a dollhouse she had become fixated on buying miniature furniture to fill up the rooms. Over the years the dollhouses became bigger and bigger until they took up half of her bedroom and she was forced to store them in the attic.

The sky had darkened quickly by the time they arrived

at the hotel. Jasmine and Cameron were able to get inside seconds before fat raindrops hit the ground. She followed him into the private elevator that took them to his suite. Jasmine continued to marvel that Cameron seemed totally unaffected by the priceless furnishings in his suite. He turned and smiled at her, as she resisted the urge to stare at his strong tanned legs in the shorts.

"I ordered a fruit plate for you, along with bottled water. Let me know if you want anything else."

Jasmine slowly shook her head. "That's fine. Thank you."

Vertical lines appeared between Cameron's eyes when he frowned. "There's no need to thank me, Jasmine. I'd take care of you even if you weren't carrying my baby."

"You really want this baby, don't you?" she asked.

His frown deepened. "Why wouldn't I? Even though I didn't plan to become a father, I'm willing to take responsible for getting you pregnant. I told you before I've never slept with a woman without using protection and, to quote you, it must be destiny that brought us together." His eyes turned a cold steel-gray. "Does that answer your question?"

Jasmine tilted her chin in a defiant gesture. "I suppose it does."

She didn't want Cameron to pledge his future to her because of the baby, but for her. Her feelings for Cameron had changed and she found herself snared in a trap of her own emotions. He was everything she wanted in a man with whom she wanted to spend the rest of her life. He wore his masculinity like a badge of honor, while at the same time exuding a gentle strength she found so endearing. When Hannah accused him of being a womanizer, Jasmine had quickly come to his defense. She hadn't realized at that time she was falling in love with the man who had changed not only her life but her destiny.

When Hannah broached the subject of turning DuPont House into DuPont Inn, Jasmine had turned down her offer to become an innkeeper. Not wanting to leave her parents and/or sell her condo, which represented her first taste of total independence, had become the deciding factors. Now she had no excuse with her mother and father relocating to North Carolina and the possibility of her cousin moving downstate from Buffalo. When she last spoke to her cousin, Amelia said she was going to move to New York City even if she hadn't secured a position with a firm; that she was willing to accept a position as an assistant DA or as a public defender as long as she could practice law.

Amelia had begun packing up her apartment, selling off what she didn't want and putting most of her personal items in storage. She had also notified building management by certified mail that she would not renew her lease, which would expire at the end of July.

"Your food should be here shortly."

A hint of a smile curved Jasmine's mouth. "Are you going to join me?"

"No. I'm going to wait until we have dinner downstairs in one of the private dining rooms."

"If that's the case, then I'm going to wash my hands."

Turning on her heel she headed for the bathroom. Jasmine stared at her reflection in the mirror over the double sink, unable to see the changes Hannah and Tonya had spoken of. Her face wasn't any fuller and her eyes looked the same. Maybe they noticed things she wasn't able to see because both had experienced their own pregnancies.

Other than the occasional nausea, fatigue, and tenderness in her breasts, Jasmine did not feel pregnant. One of the books she bought contained a journal for trimesters and a schedule for her to chart her pregnancy weight gain at each prenatal appointment in four-week intervals until her sixth month. Thereafter it would be every two weeks for the seventh and eighth months; and then every week during her ninth month.

What she didn't want to think about was being pregnant in the summer in New Orleans with the heat and humidity. Exercise was emphasized and Jasmine knew walking outdoors was not an option. St. John had an in-home gym but she didn't want to impose on him to work out in his home. She dried her hands and returned to the living room where Cameron had uncovered a plate of sliced fruit and whole grain crackers on the dining area table. The table was set with flatware and serving pieces, small plates, glasses, and bottled water.

She met Cameron's eyes. "That's more than a snack."

He smiled. "Eat what you want and I'll put away the rest in case you're hungry later."

Jasmine slipped off her jacket, draping it over the back of a dining room chair. "Do you know of a health spa I could join? I need to begin an exercise regimen of aerobics and strengthening."

"I sure do."

"Where is it?"

"It's on the lower level. There's an exercise room and Olympic-size pool. Do you swim?"

"Yes." Swimming was one of the recommended exercises for a pregnant woman. "Is it possible for me to use the pool?"

"You could if you were registered here."

Jasmine blinked slowly. "I'd have to register as a guest to use the pool?"

Cameron nodded. "Either that or you can move in with me. I'll list you as my fiancée and you'll be afforded all of the privileges I'm entitled to. I'll put you up in the adjoining suite if you have reservations about living in this one with me."

He was giving her an offer she was hard-pressed to refuse. And Jasmine knew she couldn't continue to impose on Hannah and St. John until the inn was open for business. After all they hadn't been married a year, which to Jasmine made them newlyweds.

She held out her hand. "You've got yourself a deal."

Cameron ignored her hand, took a step, and gently pulled her to his body. He lowered his head and kissed her, increasing the pressure until her lips parted under his relentless onslaught. Jolts of desire shot through Jasmine, settling in the area between her legs. The kiss reminded her of the one they'd shared on the yacht which had sparked a fire that was only quenched after Cameron joined their bodies.

Jasmine pushed against his chest, struggling to catch her breath. "Baby, no!" she moaned. Cameron pulled back. His eyes were so dark it was impossible for her to discern any blue.

"What's the matter, darling?"

She smiled. "You were holding me so tight I couldn't breathe."

"Sorry about that. I have to remember that you're in a delicate condition."

Heat stung Jasmine's cheeks. "I can assure you that I'm not going to break."

Cameron kissed her again, this time at the corner of her mouth. "If I'm going to pass you off as my fiancée, then we have to make it look good."

She went completely still. "What are you suggesting?"

"I'll buy you a ring. It's only going to be a matter of time before you're showing and folks are going to start talking. So in order not to have to explain our relationship we can tell everyone we're engaged."

Jasmine knew Cameron had concocted the ruse more for himself than for her. After all he was the scion from one of the city's prominent families and it's apparent he didn't want to tarnish the Singleton name. She pondered his suggestion realizing what did she have to lose? "Okay, we have a pretend engagement, but what do we say when folks ask when we're getting married?"

"We say we want to wait until we have the baby."

"Did you just come up with your own version of this fairytale or have you been thinking about it all along?" she said accusingly.

"I wouldn't have mentioned it if you didn't bring up the subject of joining a health club. We may not love each other, but we're going to have to get along now that we're going to share a child. At times I know I can be a little overbearing."

"I'll attest to that," Jasmine quipped.

"But I'm trying to change. If I come on too strong, then I want you to tell me."

"I'll definitely do that."

"Do you always have to have the last word, Jasmine?"

"Yes."

Shaking his head, Cameron touched the pad of his thumb to the attractive beauty mark on her right cheek.

"Now that we've determined you're the boss in this relationship, when you do plan to move into the other suite?"

"The day before Tonya's wedding." She'd said that because St. John was scheduled to return home that weekend. "If we're going to perpetuate the lie that we're engaged, then we should shop for a ring as soon as possible."

"Are you free tomorrow?"

Jasmine's eyes focused on his firm mouth. Despite his arrogance, there was something so charming about Cameron that drew her to him like a moth to a flame. "I believe I am."

Cameron glanced at his watch. "You better eat now. We have less than a half hour before we have to be downstairs." He took her hand, led her over to the table, and seated her. "Excuse me, sweets. I'm going into the bedroom to call my assistant. I need to know if she's scheduled any appointments for tomorrow, and if she has then I need her to reschedule them for later in the week."

Picking up a fork, Jasmine speared a strawberry and popped it into her mouth. It was sweet and juicy. *So this is how my life is going to unfold,* she thought. She would move into a hotel with room service and everything she'd need would be at her disposal. She would also become involved with a man who'd earned the reputation of being seen with a revolving door of different women.

What ifs came at her like pelting sleet. What if she hadn't been downsized from Wakefield Hamilton? What if she hadn't accepted Hannah's invitation to commiserate at her apartment? What if she hadn't agreed to become an attendant in Hannah's wedding to St. John McNair? And what if she hadn't given Cameron Singleton her phone number when he'd come on to her at the wedding reception. And she had to blame the final what if on Nydia, who'd urged her to accept Cameron's invitation to dinner.

If all of the past events hadn't occurred she wouldn't be sitting in a hotel suite with the man whose child was growing inside her, while she agreed to become his pretend fiancée. She had waited to reach the age of forty-three for her life to become a plot for a made-for-television movie.

Jasmine had eaten a small portion of the fruit plate and drunk a glass of water when Cameron returned. "I can't eat any more now."

Cameron covered the plate. "I'm going to put this in the fridge. You may want it later or I can have it packed up for you to take back to Hannah's."

"I'll probably take it back. I've been drinking fruit smoothies."

She picked up her jacket and slipped it on while Cameron went into the kitchen. Jasmine had to admit the luxurious suite offered amenities that exceeded her expectations. All she had to do was pick up the phone and whatever she requested would be delivered—all because of the man with whom she found herself falling in love. But that was her secret. She'd sworn never to let her heart rule her head and she had to be very careful never to let Cameron know of her love for him.

Chapter 16

Jasmine sat at a round table in the small dining room with Cameron, architect Bram Reynard, and engineer Lamar Pierce. When Cameron introduced her as his fiancée and personal interior decorator both men appeared visibly surprised by the announcement but managed to recover and congratulate her and Cameron.

She looked up through her lashes at the architect who reminded her of a younger, slimmer version of Santa Claus. Perhaps she was mistaken, but she suspected he wasn't too pleased with her suggestions when she posed them to the engineer.

Jasmine gave Lamar her full attention. She estimated he was between thirty-five and forty. His mahogany complexion seemed incongruent to a pair of shimmering hazel eyes that reminded her of Nydia's jewel-like orbs. "After closely looking at the plans, I noticed the rear of the property is large enough for a garden and an area for al fresco dining. Is it possible to extend the back hallway and erect a loggia with a cross-beamed ceiling supported by brick columns? Slate or terracotta flooring will be in keeping with the rustic appearance."

Lamar nodded. "That's doable, Ms. Washington."

"Jasmine," she corrected with a smile.

Lamar smiled, displaying a mouth filled with large white teeth, making him appear rather boyish. "How much of the rear do you want the loggia to take up?"

"What do you suggest?"

Lamar opened his laptop, and within minutes created a sample of what she'd suggested. He showed the drawing to Bram. "What do you think?"

Bram angled his head. "Make it wider and add another column. That looks good," he said when Lamar followed his instructions.

Lamar turned the laptop so Jasmine and Cameron could see his drawing. "Is this what you want?"

Jasmine met Cameron's eyes. Although she'd revealed to him that she wanted to suggest changes, she hadn't told him what they were. "What do you think?"

Cameron rested a hand on her back. "I like it." His gaze shifted to Bram. "I'd like you to add it to your plans."

Bram ran a hand over his brushy, snow-white beard. "Is there anything else your lady wants before I revise the plans?"

Cameron's expression became a mask of stone. "Why don't you ask Jasmine directly?" He ground out the query between clenched teeth.

Jasmine froze, sensing the rising tension between Cameron and Bram, and wondering if there had been enmity between the two men in the past, or if she was the result of the undercurrent of discord. She rested her hand over Cameron's fist. "Cameron and I will be doing quite a bit of entertaining and we both agreed we want a chef's kitchen with double appliances." She paused, allowing Bram to jot down her suggestion on a spiral pad. "We also don't want to cover the brick on the first floor."

"Is there anything else, Jasmine?"

She smiled. "I don't believe there is."

"How do you plan to decorate the loggia?" Lamar asked Jasmine.

"I'd like to suspend a Florentine candle-burning chandelier close to the wooden cross ceiling beams, eliminating the need to install wiring. The furnishing will resemble primitive pieces found in Mexico. I'll look for materials in wicker, teak, or wrought-iron because they weather the elements well."

Lamar angled his head. "It sounds as if the converted warehouse will become a showcase worthy of an *Architectural Digest* layout." He turned his attention to Cameron. "How soon do you want to move in?"

Cameron leaned forward. "I know it's going to take time for you to get approval for the permits."

"I have a contact who will remain nameless and he may be able to fast-track them. I'm projecting the contractor should be able to begin work by early July." Lamar paused seemingly deep in thought. "August, September, October. Maybe you'll be able to move in by Thanksgiving."

Cameron smiled. "That sounds good. Bram, you can revise the plans and send me a bill?"

Bram nodded, smiling. "Consider it done."

Cameron shifted and picked up several binders, handing one to each at the table. "We're done with business, and now we can eat."

Cameron held an umbrella over Jasmine's head when he escorted her up the path to the house in Marigny. It had been raining nonstop since the afternoon, flooding many streets and low-lying areas. He'd suggested Jasmine spend the night but she had insisted she needed to go back home. In another week she would call her suite at the Louis LaSalle home, where they would exist separated by a connecting door.

His excuse as to why he didn't want to marry vanished when Jasmine told him he was going to be a father. Nathan had drilled it into him from as long as he could remember that what made a man honorable was his ability to take care of his family. If or when he got a woman pregnant, then it was his responsibility to take care of her and the children—for Nathan that meant marriage. As a realist, Cameron knew he wasn't in love with Jasmine because he'd never been in love. Yet what he felt for Jasmine was so different that it frightened him and he could not imagine losing her.

He knew she did not want to marry again, that she was content to raise the baby as a single mother, while allowing him to be involved in their child's life. Cameron was relieved he didn't have to coerce Jasmine to move in with him or argue about going along with the pretense they were engaged. He'd asked for the engagement to spare Jasmine the embarrassment of being linked to Big Easy playboy: Cameron Averill Singleton. He was certain the news of their engagement would spread through the city like a wildfire, and shock a few people who'd believed he would spend the rest of his life as a perpetual bachelor.

He closed the umbrella, waiting as Jasmine searched her purse for the house keys. Then without warning the door opened and Hannah stared at them. "Come on in. Both of you," she urged when Cameron hesitated.

"Maybe another time, Hannah. I just came to drop Jasmine off. I need to get home before the streets become impassible." Leaning down, he brushed a kiss over Jasmine's mouth and jogged back to his car.

Jasmine slipped off her shoes, leaving them on the mat inside the door. "Why do you look like the cat that swallowed the canary?" she asked Hannah. "Not you, Smokey," she said when the cat came to see who had come into the house.

"St. John just called to tell me he finished his segment, and that he'd be coming home Wednesday night."

"Good for him, and you," Jasmine added. "I'm going to take a shower and then get into bed."

"Tired?" Hannah asked.

"Not really. I had a dinner meeting with Cameron's architect and engineer about revising some of the renovations to his house."

"How did that go?"

"Well. I made a few suggestions and fortunately they went along with them."

"What aren't you telling me, Jasmine?"

She knew it was time to tell Hannah about her future plans. "Cameron and I are getting engaged and I'll be moving in with him Friday."

Hannah clapped a hand over her mouth at the same time her eyes widened in surprise. "I don't believe it," she whispered through her fingers. "You just did what so many women have tried to do for years—get Cameron to marry them."

She didn't want to burst Hannah's happy bubble and tell her she wasn't marrying Cameron, that their engagement was a ruse. "I suppose I'll have to deflect a lot of daggers," she said jokingly.

"Child, please," Hannah drawled. "You may have to start wearing body armor." She hugged Jasmine. "Congratulations! I can't wait to host an engagement party for you."

"You can't."

Hannah dropped her arms. "Why not?"

"Because we haven't set a date for the wedding," Jasmine explained.

"When's that going to happen? Before or after the baby's born?"

"Probably after." There was no guarantee whether they would ever marry. Marriage wasn't a priority for Jasmine. Giving birth to a healthy baby was.

Hannah's smile was dazzling. "I'm warning you to be prepared when you become Mrs. Cameron Singleton. You and Cameron will become quite the sought-after couple during the fall social season when you'll be expected to attend social and political fundraisers."

"I'm not going unless you and St. John will be there."

A becoming blush suffused Hannah's fair complexion. "As a DuPont I'm still listed on the social register."

"I know the muckety-mucks will have a lot to talk about once they see my belly."

Hannah made a sucking sound with her tongue and

teeth. "Both of us will give them something to talk about when they see your belly and I show up with St. John."

Jasmine remembered the pointed looks and whispers whenever she attended parties and gallery openings and spent the entire time with Gregory despite them not arriving or leaving together. "As long as we don't flip tables like the celebrity housewives, we'll do just fine."

"You're so right."

Jasmine headed for the staircase. "I'll see you tomorrow."

She managed to shower and brush her teeth in record time. Within minutes of her head touching the pillow she fell asleep.

Jasmine sat in a chair in the jewelry shop trying on rings. "It's much too ostentatious," she whispered to Cameron. "I don't need an engagement ring totaling more than five carats."

It was apparent the salesman overheard her. "I have something in rose-gold that would be perfect for your skin tone. I have some loose emerald cut center stone diamonds that are nearly flawless."

"May we see them?" Cameron asked, speaking for the first time in more than ten minutes.

When he'd come into the shop before to buy a birthday gift for a certain woman, the elderly jeweler had suggested pearls. When he saw the single strand of magnificent South Sea pearls he knew immediately they would be perfect for Jasmine. Now he had returned. This time to select an engagement ring. He'd called ahead and told Mr. Sodano price was not an issue as to whatever Jasmine finally selected.

He and Jasmine were going to get engaged with no plans for a wedding. They would take it day-by-day and see what came of their relationship. Cameron knew it would be a challenge to convince Jasmine to make it permanent but that would have to be her choice.

The jeweler returned with a tray of loose stones. He pointed to each, identifying the carat weight. "The smallest is one carat and the largest is four."

Jasmine peered over her shoulder at Cameron. "I like the three carats. What do you think?"

He smiled. She'd read his mind. "That's the one I like, too."

Mr. Sodano called his assistant over. "Please put these back in the vault while I set this stone." He glanced up at Cameron. "I have a plain matching band if you'd like to take it today."

Cameron met Jasmine's eyes, unable to read her impassive expression. "Hold onto it. Maybe I'll have you design one as an eternity band so she can wear it alone."

"No problem, Mr. Singleton."

Fifty-five minutes after walking into the upscale jewelry shop, Jasmine and Cameron walked out with the glittering ring on her left hand. "Thank you. It's beautiful."

Lowering his head, Cameron kissed her mouth. "You're beautiful." She hadn't pinned up her hair and the heavy strands framed her face like a curtain of black satin.

Jasmine's cellphone chimed a familiar ring. "I have to answer this call." She retrieved her phone from her wristlet, and looped her free hand over Cameron's arms as they walked to where he'd parked his car. "What's up, Nydia?"

"I'm in the hospital."

"No! What happened?" Nydia was expected to arrive in New Orleans two days before Tonya's wedding.

"I'd been having abdominal pain and vomiting for about a week. The pain was so severe I'd stopped eating. I called my father and he took me to the ER. That's when I found out I had a ruptured appendix. I had surgery yesterday."

"How long are you going to be in the hospital?"

"I'm not sure. They're giving me painkillers and an antibiotic through an IV to bring down my elevated white blood cells. If you want to get high, then check into a hospital because they have the best shit."

"You're shameless, chica! I leave you alone for a couple of weeks and you fall apart on me and brag about getting high on painkillers."

"Well, it's true. Sorry, *mija,* about missing the wedding. You know I wanted to see Tonya marry her fine-ass Papi. By the way, how's your Daddy?"

"He's good."

"Just good, *mija?*"

"I'm not going to answer that."

"He's with you?"

"Yes."

"I think my painkiller is kicking in right about now. Tell Tonya and Hannah I miss them, and once I'm medically cleared to travel I'm coming down."

"I'm coming back to New York to see my parents before they sell the house, so I'll stop in and see you."

"Later, *mija.*"

"Later, chica. Feel better." She looked up at Cameron staring down at her. It was apparent he'd heard her mentioning getting high. "My friend Nydia can't come for the wedding because she's recuperating from a ruptured appendix."

He grimaced. "That's no picnic. I gather from your end of the conversation that she's quite a character."

"She's the best, Cameron. She's a tell-it-like-it-is, in-your-face kind of friend. What I love about her is she always keeps it real. What you see is what you get."

Cameron laced their fingers together. "She sounds like someone else I know."

Jasmine gave him a sidelong glance. "I know you're not talking about me. Unlike Nydia, I do have a filter. And you're a fine one to talk. The first time we had dinner at Cipriani you were up front when you told me you always used protection when you slept with a woman. At the time I thought it was too much information for a first date, so I let it slide."

"And you were also very candid when you say you never wanted to get married again."

"It's true," Jasmine said.

"Does that mean you'll never marry me?"

"Yes, because you were very candid when you said you didn't want to get married."

"That's because of what I'd witnessed seeing my parents go at each other."

"What did they fight about?" Jasmine asked. Cameron stopped at his car, and opened the door for her to get in.

"Everything," he admitted after he got in and sat beside her. "My mother went to college to become an actress. The acting bug hit her for the first time when she was in high school and got the starring role as Sandy in *Grease*. She could act, sing, and dance. She met my father in her senior year and were married three months after they graduated. Mom wanted to wait a few years before starting a family because she'd auditioned for a part in a local theater and was waiting for a call back. She didn't get the part because she later found out that Dad promised the theater director that he would finance one of his productions, but only if his wife didn't work for him. That was the beginning of a verbal war lasting thirty-five years."

"But didn't you realize when you went to your friend's homes that their parents didn't act like yours?"

"No, because I didn't have many friends. Whenever someone wanted to come to my house, I made excuses, telling them I wasn't allowed to have company because I was grounded for some fake infractions. After a while the kids stopped asking and our family secret was safe."

Jasmine reached over the gearshift and held his hand. "What about your brothers and sister?"

"It didn't seem to bother them, but as the eldest I saw them at their worse. It was like watching Martha and George go at each other in *Who's Afraid of Virginia Woolf.*"

"It really sounds like they had a love-hate relationship."

"No, babe. It was a love-resentment relationship. My mother never forgave my father for short-circuiting her career. I think he was afraid she wanted to become a movie actress and he would lose her. But my mother loved the stage and live theater."

"Did you ever see her perform?" Jasmine asked.

"Not really. Whenever she's with her grandchildren she'll sing and dance with them and they love it. I'm going to tell her about our engagement before you meet her."

Jasmine's face clouded with uneasiness. The warning voice in her head shouted fraud. She had to pretend she loved the woman's son and had accepted his marriage proposal. "Do you plan to tell her about the baby?"

"No, sweets. That's something we'll do together once you get the results of your tests."

Jasmine leaned against the leather seat in relief. She had time to gird herself once the news of her pregnancy went public. "You can drop me off at Hannah's before you go back to your office."

Cameron punched the Start engine button. "Are you trying to get rid of me?"

"No. I need to go home and take a nap."

"What about I drop you off at the hotel? You can nap there until I get back."

"No, Cameron. I need to wash my hair and put up a couple of loads of laundry. I also want to start packing so I'm ready to move in on Friday."

"Okay, babe. Then I'll see you Thursday morning."

Jasmine closed her eyes and nodded. She couldn't believe she was so fatigued she could hardly think straight. She had slept more in the past two weeks than she had in an entire month before she got pregnant. She ate and slept, and woke up to eat and then sleep again.

She slept through the ride from the Central Business District to Marigny, unaware that Cameron had carried her from the car, upstairs to the bedroom, undressed her, and covered her with a lightweight blanket.

Cameron descended the staircase to find Hannah waiting for him. "She didn't wake up."

"You love her, don't you? And please don't lie to me

again, Cameron. A man doesn't put a ring on a woman's finger like the one Jasmine's wearing because he likes her."

Cameron wanted to tell Hannah she was worse than a dog with a bone. She didn't know how to give up. "Yes, I love her, Mrs. Hannah DuPont-Lowell McNair."

"I must have really gotten to you for you to recite my entire government name," she teased.

"I could call you a few other names but I was taught to respect my elders."

Hannah's lips parted in a knowing smile. "My being older than you didn't stop you from trying to hit on me."

He winked at her. "If I remember, you didn't seem to be too insulted. Then you had to throw out that you were involved with St. John."

"Well, I was and I still am." She rested a hand on Cameron's arm. "I'm glad you met Jasmine because she deserves someone who really loves her for herself."

"She's incredible, Hannah. I never get tired of being with her. It's as if we can talk about everything, no holds barred."

"Maybe you had to date a lot of bimbos before you were able to recognize quality."

"You're right about that." Cameron hugged Hannah, pressing a kiss to her cheek. "Thank you for looking after her."

Easing back, she stared up at him. "I should be the one thanking you for giving her what has been missing in her life."

"Tell Jasmine I'll call her later."

Cameron drove back to his office a changed man. When he'd slipped the diamond ring on Jasmine's finger it signaled his promise to share their future. And when he'd admitted to Hannah that he loved Jasmine it was as if he'd been freed from an invisible prison. He no longer feared loving a woman without the angst and turmoil he'd witnessed growing up.

It wasn't as if Nathan and Belinda fought every day, but when they did they were cruel to each other. Thankfully history would not repeat itself with him and Jasmine.

Chapter 17

Jasmine felt as if she was on a treadmill and couldn't get off. She had her first appointment with the doctor and was weighed, examined, lectured with list of dos and don'ts, and finally given a prescription for prenatal vitamins. The obstetrician questioned her about nutrition, whether she exercised, and whether she and her fiancée were having sexual intercourse. Jasmine admitted they hadn't since the pregnancy was confirmed. The doctor said she could engage in sexual intimacy as long as she was feeling well. Cameron went with her to pick up her vitamins, and then drove her back to Hannah's in order for her to finish packing.

She went with Hannah to the airport to pick up St. John, and had a joyous reunion when Hannah welcomed her husband home with a special dinner. The college professor was more handsome than Jasmine had remembered.

The California sun had darkened his tawny-brown complexion. His silver hair, a neatly barbered matching goatee, and a tall, slender physique caused heads to turn whenever he walked into a room. Hannah disclosed he had been voted the best-dressed and best-looking senior in their high-school graduation, and now at fifty-nine it was still evident.

St. John congratulated her on her engagement, seemingly surprised that she was involved with Cameron Singleton. Jasmine teased St. John that now that he was back he and Hannah would have the house to themselves because she was moving out the next day.

As promised, Cameron came to get her Friday evening. He didn't get to see St. John who still hadn't recovered from jetlag. And when he parked his car in his reserved space at the hotel Jasmine felt as if she'd ended one chapter in her life and was about to begin another.

"I had housekeeping clean your suite," Cameron said when they exited the elevator. "And if you need anything there is a listing of the different departments on the table next to the house phone."

Jasmine shifted the garment bag with the dress she planned to wear for the wedding. "Are we going to eat breakfast together?" she asked as Cameron rolled her Pullman over the carpet to the door connecting his suite to hers.

He stared at her under lowered lids. "Is that what you want?"

"Yes."

Cameron opened the door and placed the Pullman on a luggage rack next to the closet. "Just open the door and come in whenever you're ready."

"I don't have to knock?"

"No, babe. My door is always open to you." He patted her bottom. "Now go to bed and get your beauty sleep. We can't have you looking like I kept you up all night."

Jasmine kissed his cheek. "Thank you, and good night."

"Good night, love."

She stood in the same spot long after Cameron had gone into his suite. He'd called her love, and she wondered if he did think of her as someone he loved. She wore his ring yet felt more distant from him than she did when they were together in New York.

They hadn't made love in weeks since that passionate day in her apartment, and it was as if he no longer found her attractive. Jasmine did not want to think he'd pursued her because he viewed her as a challenge at Hannah's wedding, and now that she was carrying his baby, he felt obligated to be in her life.

There were times when Jasmine tended to overthink a situation and make what her grandmother referred to as a mountain out of a molehill. However, the reality was she was in love with a man who through his actions demonstrated he cared for and about her, but she longed to hear him say more than an occasional term of endearment.

Jasmine decided to wait until Saturday to unpack and put her clothes away. Stripping off her street clothes, she left them on a chair and climbed into bed. She'd brushed her teeth and washed her face at Hannah's before Cameron arrived to pick her up.

The mattress in the mahogany four-poster bed felt like heaven. It was firm yet hugged her body like a glove. The sea-foam green comforter matched the floor-to-ceiling drapes. The suite was as beautifully decorated as Cameron's. Reaching over, she turned off the bedside lamp, plunging the room into darkness, and rearranged the mound of pillows under her head and shoulders.

Her last thought was to wonder whether Cameron was still awake before she floated into the comforting arms of Morpheus.

Cameron lay in bed channel surfing. He was too wound up to sleep. He couldn't stop thinking about the woman on the other side of the door. Although he had invited her to live with him, he'd mentioned the door connecting the suites would remain unlocked in the hope that Jasmine would open it and climb into bed with him. He didn't want to make love with her as much as he wanted to feel her body next to his; he wanted to listen to the soft whisper of her breathing and inhale the intoxicating fragrance of her perfume that complemented her natural scent.

Don't rush her and she will come around on her own. Hannah's words played in his head like a broken record. There was just so much he could take before he lost whatever fragile hold he had on his self-control. Cameron did not know why but he believed he was being paid back for how he had selfishly disregarded the feelings of the women who'd wanted more than he was willing to give.

He knew he was wallowing in self-pity. After all he'd gotten Jasmine to live with him and agree to an engagement which did not guarantee they would marry. And since becoming involved with her, he had begun a practice of self-examination, questioning if he was really that anti-marriage or was it that he feared he'd fail as a husband. That he wasn't willing to compromise and it had to be his way or nothing.

He'd always ended a liaison if the woman said one word that struck a nerve. Cameron would take her home and walk away without a backward glance. Then he would block her number from his cellphone as if she never existed. His mother had accused him of being too controlling like his father, possessive, moody, and irritable and that no woman would put up with him for any length of time even if he wined and dined them and gave them expensive baubles. When she told him the best thing he had done was not bring a child into the world, Cameron refused to talk to her for weeks. He didn't know if she thought he wouldn't be a good father, but one thing he knew for certain was he never would treat a woman as his father had done her.

Cameron found himself watching a movie he'd seen before and settled down to watch it again. It was a comedy and he needed something to make him smile. He managed to stay awake to see the credits, then picked up the remote and turned off the television. Sleep was slow in coming, but then exhaustion finally won out.

Cameron woke with a start when he realized he wasn't alone in the bed. Streams of sunlight came through the windows and he knew he'd slept later than usual. He turned over to find Jasmine lying next him, her unbound hair spread out on the pillow next to his.

"I was wondering when you were going to wake up," she teased.

A grin nearly split his face as he stared at her delicate features. "I was waiting for a princess to kiss me and break the magic spell the naughty witch placed on me."

Rising on her elbow, Jasmine kissed his nose, his eyebrow, eyelid, and finally his mouth. She smelled of tooth-paste and mouthwash. "Good morning, sweet prince."

In a motion too quick for the eyes to follow, Cameron had her on her back, and buried his face between her neck and shoulder. "Good morning, my love." She went com-pletely still under him. "What's the matter?"

"Am I your love, Cameron?"

He raised his head and stared into dark-brown eyes filling with tears. "Of course you are. Why would you think differently?"

Her eyelids fluttered, reminding him of the wings of a tiny delicate bird. "You've never said you love me."

"Do you think I would've put a ring on your finger if I didn't love you, Jasmine?"

She bit her lip. "I don't know. I thought you did it so as not to bring shame on your family name."

"That's crazy! I'm a grown-ass man and what I do with my life has no bearing on my family. I wanted us to get engaged now rather than later because it's usually the woman society judges because she's the one carrying the baby. Isn't it more acceptable to be known as Cameron Singleton's fiancée than his baby mama?"

"I'd be your baby mama if you were my baby daddy."

"The stigma is still on the woman, Jasmine. In some cultures women are stoned for engaging in premarital sex or bearing children out of wedlock."

"Thankfully that's not the custom in this country."

His hand searched under the cotton nightgown and covered her breast. "You're getting bigger."

Jasmine gasped. "Oh!"

"What's the matter?"

She closed her eyes. "My breasts are very tender. I

have to keep from crying out when I shower because the pressure from the water is like a thousand needles sticking me."

Cameron sat on his heels and gently lifted the top until he exposed her breasts. It was his turn to gasp when he realized how much more lush her chest was now than when he'd first made love to her. "You are more magnificent than I could have ever imagined."

Bending slightly he trailed light kisses over her chest as she writhed under him. He licked one distended nipple as if it was a sweet confectionary before lavishing the same attention on the other. Soft sounds escaped Jasmine's parted lips and he thought he was hurting her until her hand searched between his thighs to squeeze him. He hardened quickly and covering her hand with his he guided his swollen penis inside her, both sighing in pleasure.

Cameron forced himself to go slow. He didn't want to hurt her or cause harm to the baby. He growled deep in his throat with the realization she would the first and last woman he would make love to without the barrier of latex between them. She felt so good, so hot, and tight that he knew it wouldn't be long before he spilled his passion inside of her.

Throwing back his head, he breathed in deep gulps of air as her flesh closed around his penis, holding him tight before letting go over and over until the dam broke and he buried his face against her neck and ejaculated as they climaxed together. Cameron felt as if his heart would burst when he collapsed heavily on her moist body.

"Cameron, get off me!"

Reality surfaced when he realized he was crushing her. He rolled over and pulled Jasmine to lay atop him, her legs sandwiched between his. "I'm sorry, sweets. I forgot about the baby."

Jasmine kissed his ear. "It wasn't the baby. I just couldn't breathe."

He winked at her. "Are you saying I take your breath away?"

"If you're fishing for a compliment, you won't get one this morning."

"When did you get to be so hard?"

Throwing back her head, Jasmine laughed. "I remember you saying that you're the only one in this relationship that's allowed to get hard."

"I do remember saying something like that."

Jasmine scrunched up her nose. "I'm going to take a shower before breakfast. Would you like to join me?"

"My bathroom or yours?"

"Mine, because I like my body wash. But if you want you can bring yours with you."

"But we're already in my suite. Why don't you go and bring your body wash over here?"

She kissed the bridge of his straight nose. "Why are we arguing like a married couple?"

"We're not arguing."

"What are we doing, Cameron?"

"Debating an issue."

Jasmine untangled their limbs. "I'm going back to my suite. You can come if you want. If not, then I'm not going to hold it against you."

Cameron scrambled off the bed, bringing her with him. "One of these days I know I'm going to regret spoiling you."

Jasmine covered his bare buttock with her hand. "Not as much as I'm going to enjoy spoiling you."

"We'll have to see about that."

They walked into the shower stall in the adjoining suite and began a slow and sensual exploration of each other's bodies until they were forced to stop before making love again. Cameron knew it was imperative that Jasmine eat before she felt lightheaded. After breakfast he would sample her delightful body again. It was Saturday and they had all day to make love, sleep, and hopefully make love again before they had to get ready for the wedding later that evening.

Jasmine shared a smile with Cameron as he helped her out of the car, after he'd tossed the fob to a valet. Gage Toussaint had arranged for his guests' vehicles to be parked in a lot around the corner from his house.

He couldn't pull his gaze away from the swell of her breasts rising and falling above the revealing décolletage of the gold strapless gown clinging to Jasmine's midsection and flaring out around her feet. The narrow black satin ribbon accentuated her narrow waist and hem of the gown matched her black silk stilettos. Jasmine had admitted when she first tried on the dress the neckline was modest; yet that was before the increase in her bust size. The South Sea pearls resting on her chest shimmered like liquid gold on her satiny skin.

Cameron's intent to wear a white dinner jacket and black tie changed when he caught a glimpse of Jasmine's gown, opting instead for a black tuxedo, white shirt with a spread collar, and a gold silk tie. And it wasn't for the first time he applauded himself for approaching Jasmine at another wedding to let her know he was interested in her.

A slight smile tilted the corners of his mouth as he recalled the amazing morning and early afternoon in their
suite. They'd made love, ordered room service, slept, and
then made love for a second time and lay together holding hands each lost in their private thoughts. Cameron
had admitted to Jasmine that he loved her, and he would
even if she wasn't carrying his baby. He knew a new life
was growing inside her, yet it still wasn't a reality for
him, and wouldn't be until he saw her belly swell.

"Are you ready, darling?"

Jasmine nodded. "Yes."

Cameron cradled her hand in the bend of his elbow as
he led her through the narrow alleyway to the courtyard
ablaze with countless strings of tiny white lights. He stole
a glance at her profile. She'd styled her hair in a mass of
curls similar to the style she wore when meeting him at
Cipriani 55. He'd asked himself if his obsession with her
beauty was the result of masculine pride when other men
gawked at her.

A young man escorted them to a row of cushioned
chairs set up theater-style. Cameron seated Jasmine, and
then folded his body down beside her. Pre-recorded
music filled the open-air space. "This courtyard is incredible," he said in her ear. Jasmine's idea of a loggia where
they could dine al fresco had aroused his interest in different types of gardens.

"It is. We have enough property in the back of the house
to have something similar. A landscape architect can put
in trees, shrubs, flowering plants, and a waterfall with a
koi pond."

Cameron managed to conceal a smug grin. Jasmine
had said we instead of you, which translated into she

thinking of the house as theirs and not his. Reaching for her hand, he laced their fingers together.

"Fancy meeting you two here," drawled a familiar female voice.

Letting go of Jasmine's hand, Cameron came to his feet when he saw Hannah and St. John coming down their row. "Good evening, folks." Leaning over he shook St. John's hand.

Jasmine pressed her cheek to Hannah's. The former corporate attorney looked incredible in an emerald-green sheath dress ending mid-calf that was an exact match for her eyes. "How is it to get your husband back?" she whispered.

"Unbelievable. Look at you, Jasmine. You are absolutely glowing."

"It's the gold color."

"It's more than the color," Hannah argued softly. "You look very content."

"I am."

It had taken Jasmine only twenty-four hours to get a glimpse of how life would be living with Cameron. She would share his suite at the hotel, while decorating their home and once the renovations were completed, she would assist Hannah in hiring the employees for the inn when those renovations were close to completion. All the while keeping her doctor appointments and preparing for the birth of her baby early next year. She knew she had a lot on her plate and had to make certain to prioritize all of the things going on in her very busy life.

The chairs were filling quickly as guests continued to arrive to witness the wedding of one of the Big Easy's native sons. Jasmine recognized Samara, Tonya's daughter, clinging to the arm of a young man who looked at her in adoration. Jasmine smiled when she saw the diamond ring on her left hand. It was apparent the young woman had two things to celebrate: her graduation from Spelman College with a degree in economics and political science and an engagement.

"I didn't know Samara was engaged," she whispered to Hannah. Samara had come with Jasmine, Nydia and her mother when they'd driven from New York to New Orleans to spend time with Hannah last summer. Samara was not only pretty but also incredibly intelligent.

"Tonya didn't know either until Samara arrived yesterday with her young man in tow. He's a recent graduate of Morehouse School of Medicine. That's Gage's son, Wesley, in the tuxedo with the boutonniere," Hannah whispered again.

Jasmine stared at the tall, young man with sun-streaked hair fashioned into a man-bun. He looked nothing like Gage, so she assumed he resembled his mother, Gage's first wife. Jasmine knew if she wanted to know anything about people in New Orleans she just had to ask Hannah or Hannah's cousins. They were founts of knowledge about the city's history and its inhabitants.

The music changed segueing into the familiar strains of the Wedding March and everyone rose to their feet. Tonya emerged from one doorway wearing a pale pink lace wedding gown and carrying a bouquet of pink roses, while Gage walked out of another doorway in a black tuxedo with a deep rose-pink tie. He took her hand and walked over to where a black-robed judge stood waiting. Samara and Wesley stood behind their parents as witnesses.

There was an exchange of vows written by the bride and groom, followed by an exchange of rings. Twenty minutes after the ceremony began, it was over to thunderous applause when Gage dipped Tonya low and kissed her until Wesley tapped his father's back to let go of his new stepmother.

Jasmine moved closer to Cameron, wondering if they would ever marry. Despite their ability to open up about their feelings for each other, neither seemed willing to broach the subject of marriage. He smiled down at her at the same time she smiled up at him. Was he thinking what she was thinking? Would they, sometime in the future, plan to become man and wife like Tonya and Gage, Hannah and St. John?

Gage and Tonya broke protocol when they lingered, a videographer and photographer, documenting their every move, as they personally greeted and thanked their guests for coming.

Tonya pressed her cheek to Cameron's, and then reached for Jasmine's left hand, peering closely at the ring. "Dam-yum!" she said, drawing out the one word into two syllables. She smiled at Cameron. "Congratulations!"

He nodded. "Thank you. And congratulations to you and Gage."

Tonya motioned to the photographers to take a picture of her with Jasmine and Cameron. "I'm having everything taped and photographed so I can send it to Nydia." She hugged Jasmine. "I'll see you guys later at the reception."

Jasmine wanted to wait and get Tonya alone to tell her that she was carrying Cameron's child. The only one left of the quartet who wasn't aware of her condition was Nydia. She wanted to wait to tell Nydia in person.

"Wait here for me to bring the car around," Cameron said to Jasmine as the guests began filing out of the courtyard in the Lower French Quarter to head over to St. John's house in Marigny for the reception.

The sun was setting and dusk was cloaking the city by the time the McNair's garden was filled with wedding guests and the Toussaints and Baptiste extended family members. St. John had arranged for three large tents to be set up on the lawn, while dozens of candles in clay pots kept buzzing insects at bay. Gage's brother Eustace and his nieces had prepared a buffet of traditional Cajun and Creole dishes, while bartenders at two portable bars were kept busy mixing and serving cocktails. Jasmine met Tonya's retired parents for the first time, and it was apparent Tonya had told her mother and father about her innkeeper friends.

Cameron pressed his mouth to her ear. "I'm going to get you something to eat before the line gets too long." Jasmine mouthed a thank you. It had been almost five hours since her last mini-meal.

Cameron had just left to get her a plate when Tonya plopped down next to Jasmine and blew out her breath. "I told Gage that I wanted to go to the courthouse, but he said he didn't want to disappoint his family. You have to know by now that the Baptistes and Toussaints love to party."

Jasmine laughed softly. "That's because they know how to party."

Tonya looped her arm through Jasmine's. "Have you and Cameron set a date?"

"No. It's going to be a while before we even consider that."

"Why?"

She knew it was time to tell her friend about her condition. Jasmine watched Tonya's expression go from shock to puzzlement. "You're pregnant, engaged, but you don't want to marry the man?"

"It should only be that easy, Tonya. It's complicated and something I don't want to talk about here."

"Gage and I are flying to Hawaii on Monday for a two-week honeymoon. We have to get together and talk once I get back." Tonya shook her head. "I knew that man wanted you when he couldn't stop gawking at you last year. And it appears that whatever Hannah's money man wants, he gets. One thing I can say is you don't have to worry about him taking from you or not giving you a child because looking at your chest tells me you're definitely swole up."

Jasmine laughed until her side hurt. It had been a long time since she'd heard the word swole for swollen. "Your country upbringing is showing, my friend."

"Don't go and talk about country, because you're half country and Cameron is all country which makes that baby you're carrying three-quarters country."

Jasmine scrunched up her nose. "Do you think my son or daughter will talk like these folks down here?"

"Hell, yeah. Look at Hannah. She's lived in California and New York, yet she still can't get rid of her drawl. We may be Big Apple divas, but we still have Southern roots. The only one who doesn't is Nydia who's tells everyone she's a Nuyorican *princesa*. I need to go and circulate. Love you, Jazz."

"Love you, too, Mrs. Toussaint."

Cameron returned with two plates filled with red rice and beans, hush puppies, spicy garlic shrimp, and jambalaya. He set them on the tablecloth. "It's a small sampling of what they have. If you want more I'll go back again."

"Don't bother. You brought my favorite—red beans and rice."

A bartender approached their table and set down two glasses. "Here's your drinks, Mr. Singleton." Cameron thanked the man and handed Jasmine a glass of water. He touched his glass of amber liquid to her glass.

"I didn't know they were offering table service," she said.

"They're not. I gave the bartender a generous tip to bring our drinks."

Jasmine stared at the man who'd used his obvious affluence to get others to do his bidding. She wasn't even married to Cameron Singleton and she knew her connection to him would open doors closed to others not of his social class.

Chapter 18

During her tenth week Jasmine underwent CVS testing: chorionic villus sampling to detect genetic abnormalities and the results allayed her fear that she wouldn't have a healthy baby.

Once she told Cameron the news, he surprised her later that evening with the news that he was taking her to meet his parents.

They'd just finished eating dinner when her cellphone rang. When she answered the call she was shocked again when her mother informed her they were moving the next day. The buyers who'd been pre-approved had withdrawn their offer and decided to buy a house in the borough of Queens. Anxious to leave New York because they didn't want to pay two mortgages, they sold the house to the real estate company for a lower profit than they would've gotten on the open market. Jasmine told her mother she would give them time to adjust to their new community before coming to see them.

"What's the matter, Jasmine?" Cameron questioned when she set the phone on the table.

"My parents are moving tomorrow. I thought I'd go up to New York to see them before they left."

Cameron rubbed her back. "Don't look so bummed, sweets. Instead of flying up to New York, we'll just have to drive to North Carolina."

"I know, but I wanted to tell them in person that they're going to be grandparents."

Cameron kissed her ear. "We'll do that when we see them. I, too, prefer the in-person announcement. That's why I told my folks that I wanted to see them Sunday. Now that you've gotten the test results it's time our close friends and family members know about the baby."

Jasmine rested her head on his shoulder. "I need to go clothes shopping because I can't button my pants."

"You don't look as if you've put on much weight."

"So far I've gained ten pounds, and half of that is in my hips."

Cameron's hand slipped down and he cupped her bottom. "Your booty looks sexy."

She wanted to tell him she didn't feel sexy now that her waist was expanding and she had to search through her closet to find something to fit her without restricting her movements. Even her swimsuit failed to conceal her rapidly increasing breasts. She'd gone from a 34B to a 36D in less than three months and she shuddered to imagine how big she would be at full term.

Pushing back his chair, Cameron stood. "I'm going downstairs to swim. Do you want to join me?"

"Okay."

He hunkered down next to her. "What's the matter, Jasmine? You look as if you've lost your best friend."

"I don't know," she said, her voice breaking. "It has to be hormones because I feel so useless. It's too hot for me to be outside so I'm cooped up here. I read, watch television, and only leave the suite to go down to the pool. My swimsuit is too small, so I can't swim until I buy a larger size. Even when I didn't work while living in New York I always found something to do. I'd go to a museum, or hang out in the Village or Brooklyn. There were days when I'd just browse through my favorite boutiques or department stores without buying a thing. And when I'd really get restless I'd get into my truck and drive out to Long Island to see my parents or friends I'd gone to school with.

"I miss having my bimonthly dinners with Nydia and now that Tonya and Hannah are married I don't want to impose on them. The renovations to DuPont House are still ongoing, while the work on our house is in the beginning stages. I'm keeping a list of objects I want to consider to furnish each room, but it won't become a reality until I'm able to see the completed spaces. I need a blank canvas to visualize what I want to put on it."

Cameron cradled Jasmine's face in his hands. "Do you want me to take you away for a few days? We can go and see your parents and then take a side trip to the Sea Islands. We can stay in Charleston and take day trips to Jekyll and St. Simons Islands. You can buy the sweetgrass baskets to go along with the other woven baskets you plan to use to decorate the loggia."

Jasmine felt a jolt of excitement. "When are we leaving?"

"Slow down, darling. I have to check with my father

and brother and ask them to cover for me. I'll ask them when we get together tomorrow."

Her eyes grew wider. "Your entire family gathers for Sunday dinner?"

Cameron's thumb's caressed her cheekbones. "Yes. It's always the third Sunday in the month."

Jasmine tried to still her momentary panic. She was under the impression she would meet Cameron's parents, not his entire family. She knew he hadn't told his family about the baby and wondered if they knew of their engagement. The last time she was seen in public with Cameron was at Tonya and Gage's wedding, and it was apparent the word had not spread across New Orleans that he was off the market.

"Don't worry, sweets. My family is going to love you as much as I do."

Liar, liar, pants on fire! The ditty popped into Jasmine's head as she walked into the Singleton parlor and found dozens of pairs of eyes staring at her. She tried reading some of the expressions: shock, puzzlement, and indifference. Cameron had lied to her. His family had no intention of loving or even liking her, and she wondered what he'd told them about her.

The one thing he did reveal was the gatherings were always casual. No ties or jackets for the men, and no fancy dresses or heels for the women. She'd gone through her closet and managed to find a sleeveless loose-fitting, navy-blue linen dress ending mid-calf she paired with her favorite blue-and-white striped espadrilles. A light cover of makeup and her hair brushed off her face in a loose ponytail completed her casual look.

An elderly man she knew with a single glance was Cameron's father came over to meet her. He held out both hands, and Jasmine placed her palms on his. "Welcome to the family. When Cameron told his mother and me that he was bringing someone special to meet us I never would've thought it would be someone as beautiful as you." He kissed her on both cheeks. "I'm Nathan. And you are?"

Jasmine smiled. "I'm Jasmine Washington." Her initial anxiety vanishing quickly, she went on tiptoe and pressed her cheek to Nathan's. She'd taken an instant liking to the tall man with a shock of silver hair and laughing blue eyes. He was as charming as he was elegant.

Nathan held her left hand firmly, his eyes going to the ring on her finger. "Is this what I think it is?"

"Yes, Dad," Cameron said, speaking for the first time. "Jasmine and I are engaged."

Gasps and murmurs filled the room as those in attendance turned to one another, shaking their heads and lifting shoulders as if to confirm they had no inkling Cameron was bringing his fiancée to Sunday dinner.

A slender woman with gray eyes and coiffed snow-white hair walked into the parlor. Cameron may have resembled his father, but Jasmine knew the woman was his mother. A minute network of lines fanned out around her eyes when she saw Jasmine.

"Aren't you lovely," she crooned.

Jasmine lowered her eyes. "Thank you."

"Don't thank me, honey. Thank your parents for creating such a beautiful child. By the way, I'm Belinda."

Jasmine extended her hand to the older woman. "I'm Jasmine Washington."

Belinda brushed aside her hand and hugged Jasmine. "You were named for a flower. It really fits you."

"Belinda, Cameron and Jasmine are engaged," Nathan announced loudly.

Belinda dropped her arms as if she'd been told Jasmine was carrying a communicable disease. Reacting, seemingly in slow motion, she raised Jasmine's left hand and stared numbly at the diamond ring. "Why didn't you tell us, Cameron?"

He approached Jasmine and wrapped his arm around her waist. "I wanted to surprise you."

Belinda frowned at him. "You did more than surprise us."

"Cam, you're being rude," said a woman whom Jasmine knew was his sister. She was a younger version of Belinda. "Isn't it time you introduce us to our future sister-in-law?"

The men rose to their feet as Cameron led Jasmine over to the adults who'd gathered in the parlor for pre-dinner cocktails. "Jasmine, I'd like you to meet my illustrious family, beginning with my brother Preston. The lovely woman clinging to his arm as if he's going to run away is his wife, Madison. Preston and Maddie are the parents of a son and daughter who're probably either playing games or texting friends on their electronic devices. Next up is my brother Leighton and his also-lovely wife, Melanie, who are blessed with three rather active boys. And last, but definitely not least, is my adorable and perfect sister, Evangeline, and my brother-in-law, Daniel. Evie and Daniel have twin daughters who are unquestionably the bosses of the entire Singleton clan. Everyone, I'd like you to meet Jasmine Washington."

One by one the men and women approached Jasmine and politely welcomed her into the family. Straightening her shoulders, she knew they expected her to say something. What they didn't know was she wanted to give Cameron a good cussing out for not alerting his family of their engagement.

"I know all of you are stunned because Cameron neglected to tell you that he was bringing his fiancée to meet you, which makes me just as taken aback as you are. However, he and I will definitely have a heart-to-heart talk later tonight."

"It sounds like your ass is toast, brother," Leighton said under his breath.

Madison took Jasmine's left hand and stared at the ring. "It's really beautiful. I wish you and Cameron all the best life has to offer you."

Jasmine hugged Madison with her free arm. "Thank you so much." Besides Nathan, the petite brunette was the first one to actually make her feel welcomed.

"The Singletons aren't the friendliest folks when you first meet them," she whispered in Jasmine's ear, "but once you push out a baby you'll become a part of their pseudo royal family."

"Thanks for letting me know," Jasmine whispered back.

"What are you two whispering about?" Preston asked.

"Madison and I are talking about getting together to do a little shopping." It was the first thing to pop into Jasmine's head. Perhaps it was because she'd complained to Cameron that she needed to buy clothes to accommodate her changing body.

Preston groaned and tossed back his drink. "The only time Maddie gives up shopping is during Lent."

Leighton handed Cameron a double old-fashioned glass. "Preston, you knew Maddie was a shopaholic before you married her, so don't act so put out because she's found a new accomplice."

"That's not nice, Lee," Madison countered.

Leighton waved a hand in dismissal. "Jasmine, can I get you something from the bar?"

"Just water please."

Leighton's laser-blue eyes seemed to go through Jasmine when he stared at her. "Are you certain you don't want anything stronger?"

Jasmine met his direct stare. "I am very certain."

"Water it is." Leighton opened a bottle of water, emptied it into a glass, and handed it to Jasmine.

"Thank you."

He executed a mock-bow. "You're welcome."

"Cameron, I hope you don't mind if I steal your fiancée for a few minutes before we go in and sit down for dinner," Belinda said.

Jasmine met Cameron's eyes. "It's not up to me, Mom. You'll have to ask Jasmine."

Belinda lifted her eyebrows questioningly. "Jasmine?"

"Of course." She followed Cameron's mother out of the parlor and down a hallway to a room off the formal dining room.

When Cameron drove along the road leading to his parents' home, Jasmine did not know what to expect but when the Regency-style house came into view it literally had taken her breath away. Her practiced eye took in the first-story tall windows, the columns holding up the second-story portico over the front door, and the many shuttered upstairs windows. Cameron hadn't exhibited the spoiled rich-boy attitude but there were occasions when he'd shown signs of a sense of entitlement.

There was no doubt he'd grown up without having to concern himself with securing student loans to pay for college, or working days and attending classes at night because there was no money for him to attend full time. He'd left New Orleans, enrolled in an Ivy League university, shared an apartment with another student, and had enough money on which to live and socialize with friends. Madison had referred to the Singletons as pseudo royalty and suddenly Jasmine knew why. Like the DuPonts, the Singletons were on the Crescent City's social register.

Belinda pointed to a brocade loveseat. "Please sit down, Jasmine."

"You first, Mrs. Singleton."

A slight smile parted Belinda's lips. "Thank you, dear. If you're going to become my daughter-in-law, then I insist you call me Belinda. Right now there are too many Mrs. Singletons to differentiate who's who."

"What do you want to know, Belinda?" Jasmine had decided to take the lead in the conversation to make the older woman aware that she had no intention of being intimidated.

Belinda's smile vanished. "My, aren't you direct."

"I meant no disrespect. I find being direct is necessary to avoid misunderstandings."

There was a barely perceptible nod from Belinda as she smoothed down her white linen blouse over the waistband of a pair of matching slacks. "I believe you and I are going to get along very well. How long have you known my son?"

Jasmine was more than prepared for the interrogation. "We met last October when I came here for Hannah DuPont's wedding."

"How well do you know Hannah?"

"Very well. I was in Hannah's wedding party."

"Nathan and I had received invitations to her wedding to that brilliant, handsome college professor, but we were unable to attend because I was still recovering from a bout of pneumonia. Back to you and Cameron. So, you've been dating?"

"We have."

"I'm surprised none of us heard that he was seeing someone new. The last time someone told me they'd seen him with a woman was around maybe Halloween. Then nothing after that." Belinda paused. "I know you must think I'm a nosey old lady, but I'd like to know a little bit about the woman who's managed to do what so many others weren't able to do—and that is to get Cameron to marry her."

"We're engaged, not married."

"Have you set a date?"

Jasmine shook her head. "Not yet."

"Why are you waiting?"

"You'll have to ask your son, Belinda."

A beat passed. "How old are you, Jasmine?"

"Forty-three."

Belinda recoiled and placed a hand over her heart. "Good grief! I didn't think you were that old."

Jasmine sat straight. "Forty-three isn't old."

"I . . . I know, but I thought you were in your early to maybe mid-thirties. How do you expect to give my son children at your age?"

A sly smile softened Jasmine's mouth. Now she knew it was time to let the cat out of the bag. "I expect to give Cameron a son or daughter early next year."

Belinda's eyes were as big as silver dollars. "You are pregnant . . . now?"

"Yes."

"Oh mercy! I . . . I . . ." Belinda stuttered, unable to get the words out. Tears were streaming down her face.

Jasmine moved closer to Cameron's mother. "Are you all right?"

With trembling hands, Belinda managed to get a tissue from the pocket of her slacks and dabbed her cheeks, and then blew her nose. "Yes. I'm sorry I got emotional. You don't know how long I've waited for Cameron to find someone to love and have a family of his own with. The one time I'd asked him why he wasn't married and a father he told me he never wanted to marry because he didn't want his children to go through what he had because his parents hated each other." Dots of color appeared on Belinda's pale cheeks. "My husband and I spent our first thirty-five years together in a tumultuous marriage that scarred our children. And as the eldest, Cameron was the most affected. I'll never forget his face when he told me that, because there was no way I could undo the past. I know nothing about you, Jasmine, but you have to be very special for my son to plan for a future with you and my unborn grandchild." She sniffled. "I have three sons and I always wanted more daughters, and now with you, Melanie, and Maddie, in addition to Evie, I finally get my wish."

Jasmine hugged Belinda and she wasn't disappointed when the woman hugged her back. "Cameron wanted to wait before we said anything about the baby."

"Are you okay?"

"All of the tests indicate the baby's healthy."

"Do you know what you're having?"

"No. I want to be surprised."

"Good for you." Belinda dabbed her eyes again. "Now

that I've gotten into your business I think it's time we head back to the others."

All conversations ended when they walked back into the parlor. Jasmine stared at Cameron. She smiled and nodded. He crossed the room and took her hand. "Well folks I think this is as good a time as any to let everyone know Jasmine and I are expecting a baby next year."

"Shiiit!" Leighton drawled. "This calls for a round of drinks. It looks as if big brother isn't shooting blanks after all."

Evangeline slapped the back of her brother's head. "I told you about all that profanity."

"Evie's right," Daniel said, backing up his wife's reprimand. "Our girls are at the age where they repeat everything they hear and I don't want you to curse around them."

Leighton nodded to his brother-in-law. "I'm sorry."

"Don't be sorry, Lee. Just don't do it," Cameron said.

The uncomfortable moment ended when Nathan unlocked the doors to a built-in bar and took out a fully leaded decanter with an amber liquid. "You guys know I only break out this thirty-year-old boy for special occasions, and this is a really, really special one." Glasses were filled with a small amount of the aged bourbon and everyone touched glasses.

"To Cameron and Jasmine," the assembly chorused, and then tossed back the liquor in one swallow.

"It's too late to back out even if you want to," Cameron said in her ear. "Now that everyone knows you're carrying a Singleton you're stuck with us."

Jasmine's smile did not quite reach her eyes. She didn't want to spoil the mood and tell Cameron she wasn't stuck with the Singletons and they weren't stuck with her. The only thing that connected her with this boisterous extended family was the child growing under her heart.

A man dressed in chef whites entered the parlor and nodded to Belinda. "Evie and Maddie, could you please go and get the children. It's time to eat."

Cameron and Jasmine lay in bed like spoons, his groin molded to her hips. He rested an arm over her waist and cradled her rounded belly. Since she had moved in with him, Cameron found himself watching for the subtle changes in Jasmine's lush, feminine body. He'd likened her to a tightly closed rosebud which gradually opened over time to exhibit its splendid, fragile beauty.

She'd charmed the pants off his family, while Madison invited Jasmine to join her and her friends for brunch at Momma's Place. His sister-in-law had pulled him aside and apologized for holding a grudge because he wouldn't date her college sorority sister. She felt Jasmine was perfect for him.

Once Jasmine revealed she was from New York she was bombarded with questions about what it was like to grow up in a city with millions of people jostling for their own personal space. They appeared disappointed when she admitted not growing up in the city, but in the suburbs. Their interest was sparked again as she modestly name-dropped the celebrities she'd met as a protégée for a much sought-after celebrated interior decorator.

Cameron was transfixed when she'd cradled one of his sister's fretful toddlers to her chest, singing to the child until she fell asleep. The realization that she was going to give birth to his child rocked him to the core. That and informing his family that they would welcome another Singleton at the end of January made her condition all the more real.

"I'm all yours for the next two weeks," he said quietly.

"Your dad really let you off?"

"Yes. I never take more than a few days off at a time except when I go to New York in May. Now that Dad's semi-retired I'm responsible for covering the office."

"What about Preston?" Jasmine asked.

"He's committed to spend as much time with his kids as he can. He'll take a couple of weeks off in the summer to go camping or fishing with them, and the entire family will go away when classes are in recess. He just got back from the Smoky Mountains."

Jasmine pushed her hips to his groin. "I'd love to go to New York to see my friend Nydia because she's still not medically cleared to travel but I don't want to spend hours in an airport waiting for a flight."

"I have a client who owns a private jet. I can ask him to bring her down."

"I can't ask you to impose on your client like that."

"It wouldn't be an imposition." The man had arranged for his travel to and from New York for his frat reunion.

"Maybe another time." She sighed. "I really want to see my parents so I can tell them about the baby."

"I thought you'd told them."

"I was going to the last time I spoke to Mom, and then changed my mind. Telling her on the phone is just too impersonal."

Cameron caressed her belly over the nightgown. "Do you want to go to North Carolina?"

"Yes. I like your suggestion about driving to the Sea Islands. We can stop along the way in small towns where I can look for furnishings to decorate the house."

"Have you decided on the style?" he asked.

"Yes. The kitchen will be high-tech ultramodern, while the rest of the first story open floor plan will be furnished with natural wood, fabrics, and rustic artifacts that complement the brickwork. I'm still vacillating between European classics and American formal for the bedrooms. You'll have to tell me what you want for your home office retreat."

"I know nothing about doodads or doohickeys, so I'm going to leave that up to you. Buy whatever you want."

"You may come to regret that, my love."

Cameron's hand went still as he closed his eyes. "Am I your love, Jasmine?"

Her hand covered his on her belly. "Yes. I love you very much."

Overcome with emotion, a lump forming in his throat and denying him the ability to speak, the seconds ticked until he registered the soft snores coming from Jasmine. She had fallen asleep.

He loved her, she loved him, and now Cameron knew the day of reckoning could not be postponed forever. They had to decide when and where to marry.

Chapter 19

Jasmine stared out the passenger-side window, looking at house numbers along the street in her parents' retirement community. She'd called her parents to let them know she was coming to North Carolina with a friend. However, she did not reveal that friend was her fiancé and the father of her unborn child.

Cameron had rented an SUV for the drive after she told him there wasn't enough space in the Porsche to store the items she hoped to pick up during their travels. He had also loaded his golf clubs in the cargo area along with their luggage. His eyes had lit up like a child on Christmas morning when she revealed there was a golf course and driving range at the retirement community.

"Please slow down. Daddy said he would be on the porch." She pointed. "There he is. Pull into the driveway behind his Infiniti."

"I'll help you down," Cameron said, as Jasmine undid her seatbelt before he turned off the engine.

Richard Washington came down off the porch and opened the passenger-side door for Jasmine. She had to admit he looked well. He'd been shaving his head since he started losing his hair and his shaved head always reminded her of a smooth chocolate Milk Dud. His dark complexion radiated good health even though he had to monitor his blood pressure.

"Welcome to North Carolina, baby girl."

Jasmine rested her hands on his shoulders as he tightened his hands at her waist. She knew by his expression that he knew her waistline had expanded. Her feet touched the ground, and she leaned closer to him. "Don't say anything, Daddy."

When she extended her hand to Cameron, the sun reflected off the diamond on her finger, drawing Richard's gaze to linger there. "This is your call, Jasmine."

She looped her arm through Cameron's. "Daddy, I'd like you to meet my fiancé, Cameron Singleton. Cameron, this is my father, Richard Washington."

Cameron shook the proffered hand, smiling. "It's a pleasure to meet you, sir. Jasmine told me there's a golf course nearby."

Richard vigorously pumped his daughter's intended's hand. "The pleasure is mine, son. This comes as a complete surprise to me, because my daughter hadn't mentioned she was planning to get married."

"It surprised me, too, when I proposed to her. But once the words were out I had to go through with it."

Richard smiled. "I like a man who doesn't go back on his word. Do you golf, Cameron?"

"My clubs are in the back of the truck."

"Say no more. Y'all come in the house and relax. Your mama's busy getting the guest room ready."

Jasmine hesitated. "I forgot to tell you we won't be staying here. Cameron and I checked into the Doubletree a couple of miles back."

Richard gave her pointed look. "You're going to have to take that up with your mother."

Cameron rested a hand at the small of Jasmine's back as they climbed the porch steps and into the newly built home that was an exact replica of the others along the street in the gated retirement community. Once the guard in the gatehouse raised the barrier to allow them to drive through, the first thing he'd noticed was the absence of noise, which reminded him the age requirement for someone living there was fifty-five and older. Vehicles were parked in driveways, and he noticed several bicycles on porches as he drove past.

A petite woman with a salt-and-pepper bob walked into the living room, her eyes filling with tears when she saw Jasmine. Cameron averted his gaze as mother and daughter had their tearful reunion.

"Why didn't you tell us?" Marta said accusingly.

Jasmine kissed her mother's cheek. "You didn't wait for me to tell you."

Marta held her at arms' length. "You forget I'm a nurse. All I had to do was look at your face and I know you're pregnant."

"Aren't you happy you're going to be a grandmother?"

"Of course I'm happy. I'm just upset you didn't tell me

sooner." She stared at Jasmine's engagement ring. She narrowed her eyes at Cameron. "Aren't you going to introduce me to your young man?"

Taking long strides, Cameron leaned over and kissed Jasmine's mother's cheek. "I'm Cameron Singleton. I see where Jasmine gets her incredible beauty," he said without a hint of guile. The woman's natural beauty hadn't faded with age.

Marta lowered her eyes, blushing. "Thank you. I'm Marta."

He kissed her again on the other cheek. "I'm honored."

"I fixed up the guestroom for you. I wasn't certain what time you would get here, so dinner's not quite ready. Meanwhile you can bring in your bags."

"They've already checked into a hotel," Richard told his wife. "Cameron brought his clubs, and we're scheduled to golf tomorrow morning, so he'll be joining us."

"And I'm going to chill out here while you guys golf," Jasmine announced.

"Are you feeling all right?" Marta asked Jasmine.

"Other than fatigue and an occasional bout of nausea, I'm real good."

Marta took Jasmine's hand. "Come and sit down. You two must be exhausted from all that driving."

"I'll bring you something cool to drink," Richard offered. "I don't keep hard liquor in the house because I have to monitor my blood pressure and Marta is a borderline diabetic. We're trying to live and eat clean." He beckoned to Cameron. "Come and help me carry the glasses so I don't have to make two trips."

Cameron knew the older man wanted to say things to him he didn't want the women to hear. "Sure. What do you want to talk about?" he asked in a quiet voice after they'd entered the kitchen.

Richard gave him an incredulous look before he recovered. "What is it you do?"

"I'm in wealth management."

Opening the refrigerator, Richard took out four lemons and three limes. "How's your net worth?"

Cameron struggled not to smile. "It's good. If you're asking whether I have enough money to take care of your daughter and our child, our grandchildren, *and* great-grandchildren then the answer is yes. I've made provisions to take care of Jasmine in the event something happens to me before we're married."

"I'm only asking because her first husband—"

"I know about the slug," he interrupted, angrily.

"If that's the case I'll never bring him up again."

"Agreed, Richard," Cameron said, addressing Jasmine's father by his name.

"We'll come back before the baby comes," Cameron promised Jasmine as he headed south.

They'd spent six days with her parents, and he had enjoyed every moment. She'd said her parents were amateur golfers, but he'd discovered they were good enough to join the semi-pro circuit. One day they'd rented bikes and rode into the countryside, stopping for several hours to enjoy a picnic lunch, and when they returned everyone retired to their bedrooms to rest before going out later that evening. Richard had insisted they check out of the hotel and stay at the house. When Marta recognized Cameron's hesitation she said they had to be sharing a bed in order for Jasmine to get pregnant. That said he drove back to the hotel, packed up their belongings, checked out, and moved into the guestroom.

Jasmine stretched out her legs. "I know. Mama told me she can't wait until the baby comes. She said as soon as the inn is open for business she and Daddy are coming to New Orleans to stay."

Cameron squeezed her knee. "My mother has seven grandbabies, and for her it's still not enough."

"Well she'll soon have eight. I doubt if she'll get another one out of us, which means it's up to Evie to try again after having twins."

"Evie's done. She had a hard time carrying two babies at the same time. She was on bed rest for the last two months." He took his eyes off the road for a second. "Are you sure you're not carrying more than one baby?"

"Bite your tongue, Cameron. There's only one baby inside of me."

"It's only wishful thinking."

"Wishful nothing," she drawled. "We lucked out with this one and I'm not willing to toss the dice again and come up craps. This will be my first and last baby."

Cameron knew she was referring to sterilization and again he refused to discuss what she wanted to do with her body. He saw the signs for Route 17 and headed in that direction. Jasmine wanted to spend three days in Charleston and another three in Savannah before heading back to New Orleans.

It was nightfall when they checked in the hotel in downtown Charleston. They showered, ordered room service and fell asleep, not waking until the next morning when the sun was high in the sky. Cameron suggested eating in one of the more popular restaurants before embarking on the Gullah Tour.

Cameron noticed Jasmine was much more animated and she didn't sleep as much as before. Her eating schedule had also changed when she had three full meals with two light snacks rather than five small meals. She stopped in a shop along King Street and purchased a number of tops, leggings, and slacks with stretchable waistbands. It was as if she'd grown comfortable with her body.

She was like a kid in a candy store when she couldn't decide among the many vendors selling sweetgrass baskets and planters. In the end she purchased several from each, and arranged to have them shipped to New Orleans. Her eyes shimmered in excitement when viewing an elderly woman with a collection of handmade quilts. She bought six and when the woman tallied the total Cameron stepped in and handed her one of his credit cards, whispering in Jasmine's ear that he didn't want her to max out her card when his had no spending limit.

She pouted when they left Charleston for Savannah because she'd fallen in love with the city, and Cameron promised they would return next year, but she reminded him she wouldn't have much spare time with taking care of the baby and working at the inn.

When she told him she would take maternity leave and then make arrangements for someone to look after the baby while she helped Hannah manage the inn, he was filled with rage. He'd expected her to take at least a year off before going back into the workforce.

Cameron stood with his back to the window in their Savannah hotel suite, hands clenched behind his back as he watched Jasmine slather lotion over her belly. She claimed she wanted to prevent stretch marks.

"When you told me you'd be working with Hannah I

thought you were only going to be responsible for hiring."

She glanced up, her unbound hair falling over her shoulders. Her hair was longer now than it had been when she lived in New York. "I'm going to be doing more than hiring, Cameron. I'll have to conduct training and development sessions, and oversee employee benefits."

"Why can't Hannah do that? After all, it's her inn."

Jasmine looked at him as if he was speaking a language he didn't understand. "Hannah is the owner and I'm H.R."

"But—"

"I'm not going to argue with you, Cameron. I have enough on my plate trying to carry this baby to term, decorate our home, and staff the inn once it's up and running, and not in that order. So please don't try and pressure me about something I've invested my hard-earned money into and have no intention of backing out of."

"I'll give you the money—"

"Enough!" She closed her eyes, breathing deeply. She opened her eyes. "I don't want to talk about it." Jasmine had enunciated each word.

Cameron glared at her as he struggled to control his temper. "Okay." He'd only conceded because he saw the vein throbbing in her neck.

She set the tube on the table, stood up, closed the distance between them, and held his hands. "I don't want to fight with you, Cameron. But I want you to understand I'm committed to working with Hannah at least until the inn is fully operational. My agreeing to become an innkeeper isn't something that just came up. We talked about this more than a year ago and even though I wanted to go in with her, there were other circumstances that would not permit me to do it. Now that my parents are settled and my cousin has agreed to move into my condo everything has worked out for the good.

"I sent building management a certified letter a couple of weeks ago to inform them I'm traveling and my cousin will be staying in my unit until I either return or sell it. I made a copy of the keys to the apartment and my vehicle and sent them to her by an overnight carrier. She sent me a text yesterday to let me know she's moved in and loving it." She rested her forehead on his chest. "I left one life behind to start over as an innkeeper, not knowing you'd become a part of that new life. I know you don't hear me say it enough but I love you, Cameron. And if I didn't I wouldn't be carrying this baby, although I've always wanted to be a mother. I knew I had feelings for you from the time I picked you up to introduce you to my aunt and uncle. You're the first man I'd ever slept with after a third date. I think about what would've happened if I'd sent you back to your hotel that morning."

Cameron cupped her belly. "You never would've looked like this."

"No, I wouldn't have. Neither of us even knew I'd been moving down here."

He stared at Jasmine, unable to believe he'd been blessed to have found someone like her. He loved her and she loved him. They were engaged, expecting a baby, and planning to move in together, yet hadn't talked about marriage.

"How much do you love me, Jasmine?"

Her eyelids fluttered. "More than words can express."

"Do you love me enough to become my wife?"

An emotion he interpreted as fear flittered over her features. "Are you asking me to marry you?"

"Isn't it the same as asking you to become my wife? Yes. I want you to marry me."

"Why?"

"What the f—!" Cameron swallowed the expletive before it came out. "Because I love you, Jasmine," he said as if speaking to a child. "I love you, I want to go to bed with you and wake up with you beside me for the rest of my life. I want to protect you and our child for the rest of my life. I want . . ."

Jasmine placed her fingers over his mouth, stopping his entreaty. "Yes, Cameron. I will marry you and spend the rest of my life with you."

Cameron picked her up and carried her over to the bed. He took off her bra and panties, tossing them on the floor. Rising, his eyes held her captive as he undressed, watching her eyes move lower when blood pooled in his penis.

Moving over her and mindful of her belly, he supported his weight on his forearms. "I love you," he murmured as his mouth barely touched hers. He said it over and over until it became a litany. His hand searched her inner thigh, moving up. His thumb grazed her clitoris and her hips moved sensuously as he continued to massage the swollen nub of flesh.

Jasmine's breathing deepened, coming faster and when he knew she was close to climaxing, he lay behind her, raised her leg to rest on his, angled his body, and entered her slowly until their bodies became one.

His groan of satisfaction echoed in the room as he savored the feel of her hot warmth sending chills throughout his body. Her soft moans were his undoing as he quickened his thrusting until the dam burst and he pressed his mouth to her shoulder and surrendered to the passion taking him beyond himself. He'd just returned from his free-fall when he felt Jasmine's vaginal walls grip, and then release, his still semi-hard penis over and over until both were mewling in the lingering ecstasy that shattered them into tiny pieces.

They lay joined with his arm over her waist, and as if they'd rehearsed it in advance, they burst into laughter. They were still laughing when his flaccid penis slipped out and Jasmine turned to face him. "When?" she asked once they recovered.

He knew she was asking when he wanted to marry. "August eighteenth."

"What day of the week is it? And why that day?"

"It's a Saturday. We're throwing a fiftieth anniversary celebration for my parents on the seventeenth. That's a Friday night. I figure if folks are coming in for my parents, they will just have to delay their departure for one day while they get two events for the price of one."

"But that's less than three weeks away. How am I going to put together a wedding in that time?"

"You don't, darling. The planner who's handling my parents' party will take care of everything."

"Where will we hold it?"

"It can be at the hotel in one of the ballrooms."

Jasmine sat up, supporting her shoulders on a mound of pillows. "Are you certain you'll be able to get a room? Party rooms are usually booked up in the summer months."

"I'll let you know in a minute." Reaching over, he picked up his cellphone and tapped the number for the banquet manager. "Hi, Rachel. This is Cameron."

"Hi, Cameron. What's up, boss?"

"I need to reserve a ballroom for August eighteenth. Do you have anything available?"

"The Lafayette is open. How many people?"

"Book it for one twenty-five."

"Got it. Will you be using the hotel kitchen for the banquet?"

Cameron did not want to use the same caterer for his wedding and his parents' celebration. If the guests were going to attend back-to-back soirées then he wanted variety. "I'll call you right back."

He placed a call to the event planner and shocked her when he said he wanted her to coordinate his wedding the day after the anniversary party. He apologized for the short notice and promised to make it up to her. "I'll get you the names of the guests as soon as I can." He hung up and dialed the number to Chez Toussaints.

"Chez Toussaints. This is Tonya. How may I help you?"

"Good morning, Mrs. Toussaint. This Cameron Singleton."

"Hey, Cameron. Are you calling to place an order for a pick up?"

"No. I'm calling to ask you Toussaints whether you can cater my wedding on August eighteenth at the Louis LaSalle hotel. Tonya, are you there?" he asked when he encountered silence on the other end of the line.

"I'm here. Are you trying to say you're marrying Jasmine?"

He smiled, winking at Jasmine. "I'm not trying to say. We're getting married next month and I'd like to know if you and your family can provide the food."

"Hold on, Cameron. Let me check with Eustace."

Cameron covered the mouthpiece with his hand. "She's checking."

"She checking and screaming," Jasmine said. "I have to find a gown to fit this body. After you confirm everything, I'll call my parents, Nydia, and Hannah." She paused. "Now that I think of it, we need to go back to New Orleans today."

He nodded. "You're right. Start packing, sweets."

"Eustace said he'll do it. How many people?"

"At least one twenty-five."

"I'll let him know. Cameron?"

"Yes?"

"Thanks for marrying my friend before you made her a baby mama."

"I would've married her a long time ago," he whispered, "but she was the one with cold feet."

"I heard that," Jasmine called out from the bathroom.

"Damn! She must have ears like a bat."

Tonya laughed. "Do you always get what you want, Cameron?"

He went completely still. "Why would you say that?"

"Everyone saw you drooling over Jasmine at Hannah's wedding, and that's when we warned her about you."

"She didn't make it easy for me."

"I'm glad. Because you're just a little too cocky for your own good."

He smiled. "Being cocky got me the woman I wanted as a wife, and with the added bonus of a baby."

"I'm going to hang up now before I say something that ain't too ladylike. Congratulations and tell Jasmine I'm going to call her."

"We're in Savannah right now and we should be back home around midnight. Jasmine will call you once we're on the road."

"Drive carefully. You're carrying precious cargo."

"I will. Bye, Tonya." He set the phone on the table and headed for the bathroom to shower. Cameron pulled back the curtain and stepped into the tub with Jasmine. He kissed her passionately, and then reached for a bottle of shampoo to wash his hair.

Events in his life were moving at warp speed and he didn't want it to slow down until he exchanged vows with Jasmine, and then held their baby in his arms. Only then did he want to sit back and enjoy his new family.

Chapter 20

"**T**his has to be some crazy shit!" Nydia spat out as she helped Jasmine into her wedding gown. "You call and give me less than three weeks' notice that you want me to be your maid of honor. You showed up last night as Daddy's fiancée at his parents' anniversary and now twenty-four hours later, you're about to be Mrs. Daddy."

Jasmine pulled the dress up over her belly and breasts, and slipped the straps over her shoulders. The Empire waist on the gown of beaded silk crepe and silk georgette artfully disguised her slightly rounded belly. She was four months into her term and hoping that what she wore could conceal her condition.

When the news that Cameron was getting married swept through New Orleans, he'd become somewhat of a local celebrity and everyone wanted to catch a glimpse of the woman who'd captured the bachelor's eye and heart. Jasmine had attended the Singletons' anniversary dinner without wearing her ring and didn't sit with Cameron or any of his family members. She had stayed for an hour before retreating to their suite to get some rest for her big day.

His family had all agreed to the subterfuge to keep everyone in suspense as to who he would marry the following day. Many of the guests, as close friends of the Singletons, were also invited to attend the nuptials.

Nydia fastened the tiny covered buttons on the back of the golden beaded bodice. "I was talking to Hannah yesterday and the woman's worse than Rasputin. She like a Svengali weaving her spell to get me to move down here and handle the inn's finances."

"You have until January to make a decision, Nydia. The grand opening has been pushed back again to February. When they were installing the electrical cables in the elevator something shorted out and caused a smoky fire that damaged all of the walls throughout the mansion. Hannah was so upset that St. John threatened to have her sedated. Once she recovered she sued the company and hired the same company who maintains the elevators in the hotel."

"Good for her," Nydia said. "At least she didn't have to hire anyone to handle the suit."

"You're right about that," Jasmine said. "Thankfully she has insurance but it's going to take several months to clean up the mess."

"Tonya and Gage didn't seem that upset that they won't be able to open their restaurants."

"That's because they're working at Chez Toussaints and catering a lot of parties."

Nydia smacked her lips. "Yum, yum. I'm glad they're catering your wedding because I need my food to have *un poco de sabor.*"

"Well, you definitely get some flavor from the food Eustace and his family prepare."

There came a knock on the door. "Ten minutes."

"Okay, Daddy," Jasmine called out. She just needed to put on her shoes and engagement ring. Cameron had elected to wear a wedding band and when they returned to the jeweler he had ordered a rose-gold band with a brushed finish. Her wedding set included a rose-gold diamond eternity band.

She checked her reflection in the full-length mirror. Her hair was a mass of tiny black curls that reminded her of the pictures of Grecian goddesses. The stylist had threaded a narrow silk ribbon through the curls, tied it in a bow with streamers flowing down her back and ending at the hem of the gown. Her only jewelry besides her ring was a pair of diamond studs.

She turned to stare at Nydia. Her friend looked stunning in a sunny-yellow, one-shoulder chiffon gown, nipped at the waist, and flowing around her feet like frothy meringue. The color brought out the green and gold in her large hazel eyes. Her curly hair, brushed off her round face, was secured on top of her head with jeweled hairpins that added height to her diminutive frame.

There was another knock on the door. "We're ready out here."

"Coming," Jasmine and Nydia chorused.

Jasmine slipped her ring on her right hand, pushed her feet into a pair of silk pumps, and then picked up her bouquet of yellow and white roses with matching streamers, as Nydia picked her own bouquet of yellow roses, mums, and daisies. Cameron's band was on her left thumb.

She opened the door to find her father dressed in wedding finery. Jasmine took his hand as they walked to the private elevator, Nydia following. Cameron had selected Philip Baxter, his former college roommate and frat brother, as his best man. A hotel employee waited for them to enter the elevator car and swiped his keycard. When it reached the lobby level, he escorted them to the ballroom where Philip waited for Nydia. His eyes widened when he saw her, but Nydia was prepared for the overly flirtatious man. Jasmine had told her about the number of times he'd been married so to ignore his not-so-subtle advances.

The doors to the ballroom opened and a string quartet continued to play as Philip processed in with Nydia on his arm. Necks craned to see who the bride could possibly be, but Jasmine remained concealed behind her father's back.

"Ready, baby girl?" Richard whispered.

"Let's kick it, Daddy," she said, grinning from ear to ear.

The music changed as the familiar strains of the Wedding March filled the ballroom. Jasmine stared straight ahead as she walked over the white rug, her smile still in place when Cameron looked at her for the first time in twenty-four hours. He was grinning like a Cheshire cat as a loud gasp went up from the assembly amid the applause from the Singletons.

Everyone had finally settled down when Richard relinquished his hold on Jasmine's hand to Cameron's elbow. Everything occurred in a blur as she repeated her vows, without taking her eyes from Cameron's. She hadn't realized just how much she loved him until now. His voice rang clearly throughout the ballroom as he confessed to falling in love with her at another wedding. She prayed for the tears filling her eyes not to fall and ruin her makeup. There was an exchange of rings and a prolonged kiss that elicited a smattering of laughter. When the minister introduced them as Mr. and Mrs. Cameron Averill Singleton, Cameron's frat brothers broke into their fraternity hymn.

She shook her head, knowing she had been accepted into the raucous bunch who she'd met in May in New York . . .

Five months later . . .

Jasmine moved slowly, holding her back as she tried to ignore sharp pains which cut through her like a knife. It was early January and she still had another four weeks until her due date.

She had gained twenty-eight pounds but it could've been eighty-eight because she felt as if she was carrying a baby calf. The renovations on the house were nearing completion and she and Cameron were hoping to move in before she gave birth. She had ordered furniture for most of the rooms, but had to wait several more months for special orders.

Bending from her knees, she picked up the package, and carried it closer to the chair so she could open it and see what had been delivered. The suites were quickly looking like a warehouse from the number of deliveries to the hotel.

"What the hell do you think you're doing? How can

you even think of picking up something that heavy in your condition?"

Her head popped up, and she dropped the box on her foot, when she saw Cameron looming over her like an avenging angel. Her temper flared. "Don't you dare talk to me like that."

Cameron's face was dark with rage. "I'll talk to you anyway I want when I see you do something stupid. Who do you think you are? Superwoman?"

Her back hurt and her foot was on fire. She hoped she hadn't broken it. Limping on one foot she managed to make it to the chair without collapsing. "Get away from me," she ordered when he came closer.

"Let me look at your foot."

She made a fist. "If you take one more step it will be your nose you'll need someone to look at."

He glared at her, his eyes an icy gray. "You wouldn't hit me."

Jasmine narrowed her eyes. "You don't want to find out." The last word wasn't off her tongue when Cameron caught her wrist and swept her off the chair. She struggled to free herself but he was too strong. "Let me go."

"No. Not until I check your foot. And I don't know why you walk around without your shoes."

"Because walking around barefoot is more comfortable for me."

Cameron carried her to the bedroom and set her on the bed and held her ankle. "Damn!" he spat out.

Jasmine looked at her foot for the first time. Her instep was beginning to swell and she couldn't move her toes. "Ouch! You're squeezing my ankle."

"That's because your whole foot is swelling. You

probably broke it. Why in hell didn't you wait for me to get home to move the damn box?"

"Stop cursing at me, Cameron. You're not your father and I am definitely not your mother."

"I'm calling 911."

"No! Just put some ice on it and it will take down the swelling."

Cameron ignored her when he picked up the house phone and told the front desk he needed an ambulance. He slammed the phone in the cradle. "I'm going to get a coat for you because it's cold outside."

Two hours after she was wheeled into the same ER where she'd discovered she was pregnant, Jasmine sat in a bed with a light cast on her foot. She was seen immediately because of her advanced stage.

She lay back on the pillows in the private room staring at the rain sluicing down the windows. The doctor had recommended she stay in the hospital for several days so he could monitor her since she'd complained about pain in her back. She had also been spotting but hadn't told Cameron because it wasn't every day.

She closed her eyes, willing the pain in her back and foot to go away and leave her alone. Jasmine had read up on back pain and she'd attributed it to stress rather than weight gain.

"Why didn't you tell me you were bleeding?"

Jasmine opened her eyes to find Cameron standing at the foot of the bed. "I'm not bleeding."

"That's not what the doctor told me."

"I'm spotting, not bleeding."

"You shouldn't be spotting, Jasmine. You still have another four weeks before the baby's due. The problem is you've been doing too much. You're running between the hotel and the house. You've been stressing yourself doing things that don't have to be done. Maybe it's a blessing that the inn isn't open now, because you'd never be able to work there while trying to decorate the house."

She glared at him. "Are you finished?"

"For now. Yes."

"If that's the case then I'd like you to leave so I can rest. My foot and my back are throbbing like a freaking toothache and they can't give me anything for pain."

"I'm leaving, but I'll be back later."

Jasmine closed her eyes, hearing but not seeing him leave. She was pissed at him for taking her to task. He'd talked about how his father treated his mother and he was no different. If she'd seen this side of him before she'd agreed to marry him, she would've remained a baby mama.

Cameron knew he'd messed up when he raised his voice to Jasmine, but seeing her pick up and drop the heavy box had unhinged him. He'd watched her hold her back when she thought he was looking elsewhere. The one time he offered to give her a massage she came at him like an angry cat. Over the past few months she appeared to move more slowly and when he tried to make love with her she complained she was too tired. If she was tired, then that meant she was doing too much.

He couldn't watch her around the clock when he had to cover the office. His father had finally retired and it had become his responsibility to take over as the head of Singleton Investments. Cameron knew Jasmine had grown tired of living in the hotel. She wanted her own house where she could prepare her own meals and have a lot more independence. She'd ordered furniture for the nursery but did not want to set it up until the end of the month.

He ran a hand over his chin, unable to get the image of her face out of his head when she'd accused him of turning into his father. For more than half his life he'd resented the man who'd made his and his mother's life a living hell because of his need to control everyone around him. Cameron sat in the waiting room instead of going to the lot to get his car. He would wait around until Jasmine had napped before he went back to her room.

Jasmine realized she must have dozed off when no daylight came through the window. A small scream escaped her lips when she saw someone move from the shadows. She reached up and turned on the light attached to the bed.

"Cameron. What are you doing here?"

"I was waiting for you to wake up."

"What time is it?" she asked him.

"It's a couple minutes after midnight."

Jasmine pushed into a sitting position. "You need to go home. I'll be here when you come back tomorrow."

He came closer to the bed, and held her hand. "How are you feeling?"

"The pain isn't as bad as it was earlier."

"Are you sure you're going to be all right?"

"Yes." Jasmine ran a finger over the lines of fatigue bracketing his mouth. "Go home and get some sleep. Hopefully, they'll let me out of this prison tomorrow."

"I'm not going to sign you out until you promise me you'll stay home and take it easy."

"Where am I going with a cast on my foot? I can't

even drive because if I get in an accident I'll be charged with causing it."

Cameron smiled. "Thank goodness for small favors." He leaned over and kissed her. "I'm going home, but I'll be back in the morning."

"Go to work, Cameron. I'm not going anywhere. Maybe I'll lie here for a couple of days and let folks wait on me. Then when I come home I promise to take it easy and wait for the birth of our baby. Now kiss me again and go."

"What if I sleep here with you tonight?" he teased.

Her fingers grazed his stubble. "Go home, darling." She kissed his mouth. "I love you."

He increased the pressure of his mouth on hers. "I love you more. And I promise never to raise my voice at you again."

"I promise never to punch you in the nose."

Jasmine waited for her husband to leave, and turned off the light. It had taken her breaking her foot to slow down and prepare for the birth of her baby and not concern herself with decorating a house. After all, she did have a luxurious hotel suite with room service to live in until they moved into their dream home.

It was a cold and raining early February morning when Sabrina Maya Singleton, red-faced and crying at the top of her lungs, came into the world. She weighed in at six pounds, two ounces and measured twenty inches. Jasmine had been in labor for less than three hours when her water broke.

Cameron had panicked while she had remained calm throughout the ordeal. And when he held his daughter in his arms Jasmine saw him cry for the first time. It took the birth of his daughter to crack his stoic, cocky, over-confident exterior.

The cast had been removed after three weeks and during that time she and Cameron had grown even closer. It had been a time of revelation when he told her he owned the hotel and had sold it to a group of foreign businessmen. They'd allowed him to stay in the suite until his home was ready.

Jasmine was shocked when he said he'd put the proceeds of the sale in a trust for their daughter's future.

Cameron sat on the chair next to the hospital bed. Sabrina lay in a bassinet on the other side of the bed. "There was a time when I only had myself to think of. Things are different now," he said, smiling, "because I now have a wife and child, so nothing else matters except you two." Rising slightly, he brushed a kiss over Jasmine's mouth. "Thank you for making me the happiest man in the world."

Jasmine smiled. She never thought when she answered Cameron's text to go out with him that it would result in her becoming a wife, mother, and a soon-to-be innkeeper.

Her heart was full.

Connect with

Visit us online at
KensingtonBooks.com
to read more from your favorite authors, see books
by series, view reading group guides, and more.

for sneak peeks, chances to win books and prize packs,
and to share your thoughts with other readers.

facebook.com/kensingtonpublishing
twitter.com/kensingtonbooks

Tell us what you think!

To share your thoughts, submit a review,
or sign up for our eNewsletters, please visit:
KensingtonBooks.com/TellUs.